A FAIRER PARADISE

Text Copyright

© 2013 By Randall Marcus Gutierrez
        Gray Iguana Publishing Company

Copyrights of watercolors and oils depicted
on the cover and in the chapters:

Big River – artwork, "Paradise Point;
Steamboat Slough – artwork, "Steamboat Slough";
Saturday Night – artwork, "Welcome To Locke";
Puy – artwork, "Mt. Diablo Sunset"; and the cover layout in
the section at the end of this book, described in "A Fairer
Paradise II" – artwork, "A View From Ryde".

© 1997 By Marty Stanley

Gray Iguana Publishing Company
Randall Marcus Gutierrez

First Edition

ISBN-13: 978-0615636146 (Custom Universal)
ISBN-10: 0615636144

DEDICATION

A Fairer Paradise is dedicated to my daughter, Leslie and
son Ryan;
to my sisters Tanya, Olivia and brother, Gunther;
and to my mother Lucie and father Richard, for bringing
me into this world and to my extended family and friends.

And to my goddaughter, Miranda Ripoli and her family, for
what families should strive to be.

I have talked about this book for years and
well,
here it is.

ACKNOWLEDGEMENTS

The permission granted by Sherry Stanley for the use of the cover art, "Georgiana Slough", created by her husband Marty Stanley, is greatly appreciated. This work and other Stanley works of the California Delta are a delightful influence on the written descriptions in, "A Fairer Paradise", visual expressions in paint, shared by those who live in, have lived in, or had the pleasure of visiting and experiencing the California Delta, a river delta molded by mankind with the reluctant passiveness of nature. Information regarding Marty Stanley's works can be viewed at **www.martystanley.com**.

Few cross over the river.
Most are stranded on this side.

On the riverbank they run up and down.
But the wise man, following the way,
Crosses over, beyond the reach of death.

He leaves the dark way
For the way of light.

He leaves his home, seeking
Happiness on the hard road.

Free from desire,
Free from possessions,
Free from the dark places of the heart.
Free from attachment and appetite,
Following the seven lights of awakening,
And rejoicing greatly in his freedom,
In this world the wise man
Becomes himself a light,
Pure, shining, free.

- Dhammapada Buddhist quote

A Fairer Paradise

Tales of the California Delta during the period of the Great Depression and Prohibition; of those people who've experienced the beauty, bliss and maladies of their existence, emanating from the natural and man-made creations of California's waterways.

BIG RIVER

9

Snodgrass Slough

STEAMBOAT SLOUGH

18

Opium Den

RIVER OASIS

28

The Dream

SATURDAY NIGHT

106

Steamboat Explosion

DELTA MOON

153

Mountain Idol

PUY

191

BIG RIVER

Dreaming the dream of big river, the old man slept, his frail body molded to the wooden chair on the splintered porch, overlooking the bend of the river. His chest rose slowly, absorbing the thick, moist, river air with each laborious breath. Slumbering weakness turned to strength as the old man soared with condor's wings through time to the river's adolescence, in a cloudless, pastel-blue sky, above brown and green valleys and gray jagged mountains. Clear streams and small, rushing rivers fell from the range of snow tipped peaks, through green hills and small canyons. The streams and small rivers emptied into two great rivers, one flowing north to south, the other south to north, meeting in the center of a wide flat valley, edged by tall mountains to the east and north, and hills and small mountains to the south and west.

Above the great Delta where the two rivers met, the condor viewed tired waters among small islands, green marshes and inland seas, resting in the middle of a spring blanket of crimson, lavender and gold. The river's journey continued between rows of hills paralleling its shores, flowing through a narrow, natural gate and into a large beautiful bay abundant with marine life; continuing onward to the pacific kingdom of calming and pounding waves, covering the sea life of red and purple and green.

On the river's banks, native men and women lunged after fish in shallows with long pointed spears made from cottonwood branches; other natives aboard tule reed boats throwing fishing nets made from river grass and weed. The condor became native, his dark, muscular arm thrusting the water; his sharp, spear piercing the soft, flesh of silvery salmon.

Browning in the warmth of the sun, the native turned slowly gazing at the surrounding splendor; armies of salmon battling the current to spawn in their birthplace; flocks of birds darkening the sky with fluid ballets of aerial dance; herds of elk, deer and bear, basking in the sun. Music floated with the light breeze, orchestrated from the alto of birds singing, the tenor of animals talking and the bass of the river's flow.

From an undulating haze of red, white and brown, men with swords appeared on horseback, hoisting banners emblazoned with red crosses and walking behind, more men clothed in robes and sandals of leather, carrying rosaries and bibles. With silver helmet and sword, a gray haired, Spanish soldier dismounted his white horse and stood fronting the kneeling native. Unsheathing his sword, the Spaniard gently laid the blade to the head of the native *and upon the touch of flesh and metal, the Spaniard's dreams flowed through the warm, hard steel to the dream of the native. The native felt the power of the Spaniard's dreams; dreams of discovery, dreams of promotion, dreams of immortality in the eyes of his God. And the Spaniard spoke, claiming the land for his queen. Viewing the snowy mountain range to the east he spoke, "Sierra Nevada". Turning to the river of the north and the abundant lands honoring the holy sacrament he spoke, "Sacramento". Knowing the river of the south in honor of the father of the Virgin Mary he spoke, "San Joaquin". Turning west from the straits of the bay from whence he came and of the natives who settled there he spoke, "Carquinez". Looking through the dark, brown, eyes of the kneeling native, he whispered, "California", encompassing all of the land and the mythical name painted the romance of the dream.*

The native changed back to condor, soaring to the peak of a lone mountain and through crystal skies, the Isles of Farallon appeared in the center of the sea kingdom to the West. To the East, below the mountains and peaks of the Sierra Nevada, golden stars glistened, revealing themselves for brief moments, then, disappeared into the hills of brown and green. A low hum, then a violent rumble resonated from the bay as fleets of ships carrying men from many different lands and of many different languages, came in search of the elusive golden stars. The swarm of men moved through the straits of Carquinez, through the marshes, rivers and hills and to the Sierra Nevada Mountains. The swarm bore deep into the hills and when the frenzy calmed, most left; empty of their dreams. The condor soared above the Delta viewing the destruction. Where groves of oak and cottonwood once stood, emptiness reigned. Where bear, deer and elk once grazed, few remained.

Flying above the Delta, the condor viewed farms and levees created by the fleeing swarm, machinery below crossed the fields, smoke bellowing from each one. Bridges crossed the myriad of levees; trucks and tractors slowly passed through. Loud gunshots sprayed the air; thousands of ducks, geese and gulls fell to the river and lands below. The farmers' weapons cleansed the sky, securing crops from hungry flocks.

From a spray of gunshots, the condor felt a sudden pain in his chest, searing hot fire spread through his body and he began tumbling down, his wings, limp and uncontrollable. Falling rapidly, the browns and blues of the land and river flowed through the blues and whites of the clouds and sky; the condor landing upon a soft, green pile of river grass with one wing flapping. The condor gazed across the river and through a haze of gray, viewed his old man body slumping on the river chair, lines in his weathered face writhing in pain. The condor watched his old man arm flapping, toppling the opium pipe the old man held. Breathing heavily, the condor wing and the old man arm stopped flapping and his condor chest and old man chest moved slowly, then; under the bright, orange afternoon sun, the condor and the old man stopped moving, each laying to rest, on opposite sides of Big River.

*   *   *   *

The steamboat Delta King quietly rounds the bend in the river. In the distance Mount Diablo pierces the sky, a lone monument towering above the western edge of the valley. As the steamboat churns up river through the heart of the Sacramento Delta, towns slowly appear and disappear along the tree-lined river's edge. Majestic willow trees and river oaks extend from the shallows; branches and leaves spread wildly across the river's glassy shell, casting cool, dark-shadows along the banks. In the pools and along the shaded brim, children swim, fish, laugh and scream, interrupting the peaceful, rhythmic flow of the river current.

Tips of white Victorian farmhouses shaded by great oaks, rise above River Road, concealing flat lands greeting the bottom of the levees on both sides of the river. Lands with fields of asparagus, pears and grain, lay colorfully painted on a checkerboard canvas. Women and children fill the porches and lawns of the farmhouses; the women keep a watchful eye while cleaning, sweeping and dusting their homes. The farm owners survey the workers picking and boxing in wooden crates, with colored labels, the fruit and vegetables born in the rich, peat soil of the Delta. The workers' skin, leathered and brown, reveal lines and bends, like the bark of the pear trees in the lands they farm.

Along river's edge, wooden, weathered buildings stand over the river as small ripples lap gently against their algae covered stilts; their stilts vanishing beneath the surface. Chinese men sit on crates on decks smoking cigarettes from knotted fingers, while Chinese women scrub clothing with soapy, river water in large, tin tubs. Chinese children run and jump into the cool, green water, over and over again like a recurring carnival ride where tickets are endlessly given. Wooden buildings surrounded by alleys, walkways and stairs, lead from River Road to the streets below where shops, bars and diners serve their patrons. The alleys; clouded with the scent of garlic and chili oils, sneak through the windows and cracks of buildings along the narrow streets. When the sun sets, yelling and laughter in musical tone float from Bing Lee's gambling den, where lotteries and Fan Tan are played on green, wooden tables obscured in a gray-haze of tobacco smoke.

Next to Bing Lee's, Al the Wop's bursts with laughter where Joe the bartender reigns king behind the bar stocked with bottles and drums of bootleg liquor. On Saturday nights, crackling gravel under hot rubber tires, of Fords, Buicks and Packards, announce the arrival of men from the cities of Sacramento, Stockton and San Francisco, from Modesto, Merced and Fresno, from Pittsburg, Martinez and Benicia; the Italian, Greek and Portuguese fishing towns lining the river, west to San Francisco bay. In polished black, leather shoes, crisp-white shirts, freshly shaven and smothered with splashes of Barbasol and Pinaud; they arrive in anticipation of a visit to Miss Janey's place, after drinking, smoking and telling lies on the stools and wooden bar of Al the Wop's.

Across the river and past the gray-steel drawbridge, the Ryde Hotel bordered by tall, tropical palms, towers majestically and with dignity, above River Road. The hotel gracefully introduces itself in the evenings, announcing its name with a sparkling red, green and blue neon sign; visible a great distance along the winding, levee road. The Ryde Hotel; an oasis, sparkles in the midst of the Delta like a diamond in the setting of a coveted brooch, surrounded by inferior gems. On Saturday evenings, varnished yachts nestle along the wooden pier fronting the hotel; dark automobiles line the levee road with sparkling chrome. Brass trumpets, trombones, clarinets and drums fill the air with the sound of thumping melodies. Men in black tuxedos and women in colorful, flapper dresses; dance wildly to the pulsating beat. Throughout the Ryde night, men and women wander through the floors of the hotel, through doors and rooms of friends, old and new. They sit on chairs and beds; some with crystal glasses filled with wine; some with Champagne and pastel-colored drinks; some with engraved lockets filled with cocaine; some with pipes of opium. As the evening ferments, laughter and inhibitions are slowly swept away by the warm river breeze through open windows, evidenced only by the gentle dance of white-lace curtains.

The Delta King slows and nestles along the splintered dock at Walnut Grove. From the passenger decks come those searching for the playful decadence of the Ryde Hotel; others search for various jobs among the settlements lining River Road. The steamboat will carry to and from, "Big River", or, "Tai Han", as known by the Chinese laborers upon whose backs the levees were built; the river people; whose dreams have grown beyond and within the boundaries of the Delta.

And their stories ebb and flow, with the timeless tides and free flowing currents, of Big River.

Snodgrass Slough

They walked side by side, holding hands along the brown, dusty path, their feet hot and bare, the waters of Snodgrass Slough strewn with hyacinths blooming in lavender, lay still in the heat of the afternoon. "This will be your last visit before you head to college in Fresno, down highway 99," he said with a tone of optimism hiding sadness. "I'm going to miss the visits to your uncle's farm every summer. Since we met years ago, I've looked forward to the few weeks in July when we rode your uncle's horses and swam in this slough."

She looked to the boy, now a young man, a foot taller than when they met at Chauncey Chew's store in Courtland ten years before, his dark hair, deep-green eyes, light-brown skin, slender build and pleasant demeanor enhanced his appeal to her, year after year. "I've looked forward to our visits too, although we've never spent as much time together as I would've liked. I've thought of you often, sitting on the porch of mother's Lockeford home, rocking in the rocker, gazing at the moon and the stars."

They stopped where the water moved from the slough to the ditches leading through the dormant asparagus fields. Simon turned and looked into her eyes. "When will I see you again?" he asked.

Shelly removed her shorts and shirt, her body nude, full in the sunlight. "You can see me now." She winked, smiled and dove under the hyacinths and into the cool, green water of Snodgrass Slough.

STEAMBOAT SLOUGH

The sun shone bright in the early morning revealing river grass and tules bent with dew, the musty scent of river algae floated in the stillness above Steamboat Slough. They stood on the shore near the remnant of a small fishing boat, submerged with broken hull piercing the surface, its name, *Sorroca*, worn and faded.

"Dad, you have to do something. You have to save him," said the boy, dropping his fishing pole on the grassy bank, running to the water's edge.

The man looked to the middle of the slough. Among the decayed and cragged debris of old branches and fallen trees, the duckling flailed in the placid water. Earlier, the man and his son watched the mother and brothers and sisters waddle downstream, unaware of the straggler behind.

"But it's just a damned duck," and knew before he finished the sentence, it was the wrong thing to say to a seven year old boy. He glanced at the boy and recognized shock and fear and possibly revulsion in his son's face; the boy's eyes began filling with tears. "Crap son. I didn't mean it that way. Look, I know it may seem cruel but sometimes nature is cruel. Ya' know; things tend to take care of themselves in nature. I believe it best we let that little 'yella fella' fend for itself," said the man snickering somewhat proudly at the rhyme in his profound statement.

They both looked towards the duckling wildly flapping its little wings attempting to traverse the thicket of branches, the receding tide making the duckling's escape impossible.

"But he is stuck. Maybe he will die or maybe some bigger thing will find and eat him."

"Such is nature and bigger things tend to eat littler things like we do. When you're a little older we're gonna' get you hunting with your own gun and hunting getup and we'll shoot duck and pheasant and quail like I learned to do with your grandfather. We can shoot bigger animals like deer and elk and bear and you'll learn to clean 'em and cook 'em and eat 'em."

"But I don't want to kill those things."

"Sometimes you have to, to eat and survive. It's the law of nature."

"It's mean."

"Catching, killing and eating catfish doesn't bother you."

"That's different. Catfish are ugly with big eyes and whiskers and antennas and slimy skin like giant bugs that live in the water and they don't really have mommies and daddies and brothers and sisters, like furry and feathery animals."

The man looked deeply into the eyes of his son and began to worry. Obviously the boy was spending too much time with his mother. The man recalled his fishing trips with the old man and his first hunting trip in the marshes of Brown's Island and he was carrying on the tradition with his son in the same manner. It was Sunday and in his family Sunday was 'man day'. Men in the family fished and hunted. Manly things. And now his son seemed a bit squeamish. The man recalled the pride of his first shotgun at nine years old and of his first kill, a Mallard shot clean through the breast. After the hunt the old man boasted the accomplishment to friends and patrons at Foster's bar and bought a round of beer and a soda for him, the nine year old duck hunter, to celebrate. And now, his own son was acting more like the boy's mother, a bit fairy-like and not so manly.

"Buck up boy. You gotta learn these things. It's what real men do."

The conversation lulled for a brief moment, the silence broken by the frantic peeps of the duckling.

"No dad. I don't want to kill things," whimpered the boy.

"But it's what we do," said the man, emphasizing the word 'we' strongly. It's what man does to survive and it's the law of nature. Animals kill each other to eat and are eaten when stuck in predicaments like that little fella over there," the man said nodding towards the duckling.

"Would you let something kill and eat me?"

"Well. No. That's different," countered the man.

"But we are in nature."

"But you are my son. I will always protect and defend you," said the man, puffing his chest, recognizing the nobility of his statement.

"Then you have to save him," begged the boy, pointing towards the little duckling peeping softly. "He is the mommy duck's son."

"But it's just a Goddamned duck," the man said, exasperated his well reasoned argument wasn't getting through. He wondered why this was so damn hard. He never questioned his own father. Wouldn't think of it. He did everything his father told him, listened to every piece of advice and learned to like the things he didn't like, or tolerate them, such as fishing, which he found a little boring and bear hunting, since you don't really eat bear and it seemed such a waste, to kill a strong and majestic creature just for the honor of having killed it and the award of its stuffed head hanging on some wall. But he played his part, the son of the prosperous farmer, a farmer himself now, the father of a son and daughter, a fisherman and a hunter, the hunting being his proudest skill and achievement. He favored hunting duck and pheasant and quail and deer and used every bit of the kill for dining with family and friends, even the non-meaty parts, turning them to sausage, using the intestines for the skin, grinding the organs and refuse all by hand, in the makeshift butcher's shop attached to the barn. The man's sausage made famous in these parts, since he gave generously to neighbors and to friends.

"The best shot in Solano, Yolo and Sacramento Counties, possibly the whole damn state of California," boasted his friends and begrudgingly, even his few enemies. "Like the old man, must be something passed down through the family. Junior will probably be a great sportsman too."

The man's thoughts were interrupted by his son who repeated, "Dad, you have to save him."

The man grabbed a twig from the riverbank snapping it in two and felt a growing anger, a reaction his short tempered father would have expressed in this situation. The old man would've handled it firmly and the man would have backed down. The man knew he needed to be stern. It is how men handled things. He quelled his anger, tossed both ends of the broken twig into the brown water, turned to his son and said, "No son. I am not going into the slough to save that duck. Nature will tend to it. Besides, I would get wet and the water is still pretty damn cold in early spring and we wouldn't know how to care for the duck, like feeding it and...," the man didn't finish the sentence realizing he was reasoning with the boy, like his attempts to reason with the boy's mother, and the man's father wouldn't have reasoned at all, so the man turned to his son firmly stating in a loud, even tone, "I am not going to save the duck."

"Okay dad," and the boy began taking off his shoes, "then I will."

This would have been the point when the old man would've smacked him hard against the back of the head, packed the fishing gear and pushed him home along the river trail. The man studied the boy closely, his dark bushy dishevelled hair, big, round, dark eyes, button nose, pink lips, stick arms and stick legs, skin the color of cow's milk and the man laughed out loud at the sight of this 'man' in front of him.

"Why are you laughing?"

"No reason," chuckled the man. The man began removing his shoes and the boy ceased removing his.

The boy smiled and asked, "You gonna do it dad? Are ya?" while the man murmured, *"headstrong boy...like his mother...if the old man saw me now...Yes,* I'm gonna save the duck."

The man unbuttoned his shirt and thought of pear farmer Jesse from Courtland and of Jesse Jr, farmer Jesse's son, now grown and Jesse Jr's odd nature, never exactly right as a man. Jesse Jr grew up favoring things folks from this part of the state didn't approve of, unmanly things, like Jesse Jr's love of the moving pictures, of moving picture stars and his dislike of farming, hunting and fishing and the man recalled Jesse Jr's role in a Courtland High play, some Shakespeare thing wearing green tights and talking funny, moving in a flowing way, pretending to be something he wasn't, kind of childish like and how all of farmer Jesse's friends spoke of Jesse Jr's odd nature, his inability to fit in, of farmer Jesse's embarrassment of Jesse Jr's behavior. Jesse Jr moved to Los Angeles to get into the moving picture business, to keep pretending to be someone other than himself, to get paid for it and the man wasn't sure how he felt about Jesser Jr, since pretending to be someone else wasn't work for a real man, wasn't work at all, although the man did like watching the moving pictures at the theater in Walnut

Grove, especially the ones with Errol Flynn. The man glanced at his son who sat at the edge of the slough, peering with concern at the baby duck and wondered if he was teaching the right lesson after all. "You sure you want me to do this?" hoping his son would say, "Hell with the duck dad."

The boy looked over at the man and said, "Yes. He is small and needs our help."

The man sighed and began removing his pants and thought once again of his father, the old man, the picture of manhood, big and burly, always with a strong opinion, able to make decisions with certainty. The old man taught the man his motto, spoken to him often when the man was young.

"Son, to make your way as a man in this world, you need to prove your manhood every day, to your family, to your friends, to your enemies and more importantly to yourself."

"Was he mistaken by saving the duck and diluting the teachings of manhood from his own father? Would his action mean he was 'less of a man' and therefore his son 'even less of', 'less of a man', because of it?" he thought, somewhat confused. "Nah. My son is just a boy," and thought again, "but a boy is the beginning of a little man." The man thought of his wife's opinion of his father, how she tolerated the old man for the sake of family harmony, but thoroughly disliked him. "Your father is an overbearing arrogant ogre," she had said to him once, "and frankly, a pig." She disliked the man's father's demeanor, the loud voice, needing to be heard over all others, demanding to be the center of attention at all gatherings, public and private, the irritating habit of pointing his thick index finger when making a point, as if firing a bullet from a pistol, his self made image as the big hunter, killing and stuffing the bodies and heads and mounting them with his name, place and date of the kill, given to the owner of Foster's Bar for public display, a monument to himself, the ultimate in self promotion and self proclamation. She really did not like the old man and she wasn't the only one. The man removed all but his briefs, stepped to the edge of the slough, put his right foot into the water, quickly removing it after feeling the chill. "Damn it's cold. This isn't gonna be much fun," he thought. He turned to his son who stood with a look of hope and anticipation and the man knew he had to go through with the rescue. The man turned towards the water and stepped, right leg first into the cold, his foot reaching bottom as silt and river mud oozed between his toes. The man slowly waded towards the center of the slough and when the water reached the level of his chest, he began breast stroking, navigating around the broken branches and fallen trees littering the waterway. One, large, broken, oak trunk protruded from the depths and the man pulled himself onto the smooth, water worn surface, then fell backwards with a loud splash. When he surfaced, he looked towards his son doubled over with laughter and the man smiled. He swam slowly to the duckling snared in the tangled branches, gently engulfing the duckling in his right hand. The duckling peeped softly, offering no resistance as the man began swimming back to shore, using one arm to stroke while holding the duckling high above the water with his other arm. The man stepped onto shore, nuzzling the duckling against his cheek, feeling its warmth and breathing the aroma of the dander, an aroma familiar to him, an aroma not unlike that of his son's dander, invoking the memory of napping with the boy on the living room couch and wrestling on the fresh, cut grass of their Victorian home. The man gently handed the duckling to his son and dressed, cold and shivering.

Snuggling the duckling against his face, the boy smiled at the man. "Thanks dad. You did it. You saved him."

"No problem. I suppose it was the right thing to do."

"Dad, Let's go home. I really don't like fishing anyway. I do it 'cause you like it."

The man lifted his son, hugging him tightly. "Hell son," said the man, grabbing the poles in his right hand, holding the boy; the boy still holding the duckling. "I never liked fishing either. Just thought it was always something a man had to like." The man kissed the boy on the forehead and both walked down the worn trail between the tules. "You're never going to be a hunter either; are you son?"

"I don't think so. But I like the sausages you make after you hunt. They taste really good."

The man smiled. "That they do son. That they do."

Opium Den

The man opened the door of the dark, dank lower floor of the two story wooden building. The sun struck his eyes painfully like a dagger, the scent of algae hung heavy in the air, the winds blowing wildly across the river surface, rushing downriver towards the Isleton Bridge; choppy waves violently lapping the trestles. The man walked through the alley and up the stairs slowly towards the edge of the river, his clothes rumpled and disheveled, the taste in his mouth dry and harsh, his lips chafed, bodily revulsions repulsed with the ragged memory of his long stay in the den of smokers, lost in the fog of opium.

RIVER OASIS

The steamboat Delta Queen moved slowly past the bright orange and white neon sign defining the sugar mill, the name *C&H Pure Cane Sugar* shined its colorful ornament through the light fog hovering above the water's surface. The journey continued through the straits of Carquinez, past the industrial air escaping from the Martinez refineries, under the Southern Pacific railroad bridge crossing the strait and onward through the Sacramento River, each mile revealed shadows on the shoreline, each hour more peaceful as the Delta Queen ventured into the Delta. The steamboat glided along the levee, the sparse stars high above cut through the dusk as the fog lifted, the river air evolved into a scent of freshness, green trees and tall, brown grasses lined the shore. The climate slowly revealed a zone of temperate heat as the steamboat traveled into the Delta through the dark, placid night, arriving under the morning sun. Ronny and Michela awakened and disembarked on the dock of the Ryde Hotel. Feeling rested after a peaceful sleep on the Delta Queen, they checked into their room, walked briskly to the small boat coveted by *Cleopatra* and hurriedly rowed to the brown and green plot across the river.

*   *   *   *

One last gasp simultaneously trumpeted from their lips, a crescendo of pleasure like the blast of the final notes of a brass jazz band, their bodies quivering with relief. Michela cried out with pleasure, the remnants of her loud passions soared across the water's surface where it met and dissolved in the light laughter coming from the few guests on the patio and through the open windows of the three story hotel. Ronny rolled over onto the thick patch bordered by willow trees and tules. Lying on the grass, their hearts pumped and their breaths grasped the air. After a few blissful minutes kneeling nude, covered in beads of sweat, they peeked across the river through the gaps between the stalks of the tall, dry tules, glancing back and forth at one another with feigned embarrassment.

"I hope no one saw us," said Ronny, smiling.

Michela winked at Ronny, whispering sensually, "It wouldn't have mattered if they had." Lifting her crumpled dress from the grass, she slid it over her shoulders. Ronny grabbed his pants hanging loosely in the tules.

"We got busy pretty quickly. We weren't too careful where our clothes landed." Ronny paused and pointed across the river. "Jim, the hotel owner, when checking in, described this area a quintessential *Vortex of love*. He sure wasn't fooling," he said, stepping lightly into his white linen pants.

Ronny placed the still corked bottle of red, bootleg wine into the boat, both he and Michela having declined the temptation of drink, artificial seductive influences often distracting from their natural sensual pleasures. Upon entering the boat, they rowed the short distance across the river to the hotel dock, walking rapidly under the black front awning through the multi-paned, glass doorway; ceiling fans spun rapidly under the foyer sending a steady, warm breeze through the lobby. Running to the top floor, laughing and touching playfully, they slowed and walked to the end of the hall, into the room where luxury shone smooth, the spacious, third floor, corner room enjoyed an aerial scene of serenity; the calm river laid still; the hazy peak of Mount Diablo rested in the distance. The brass bed shined a golden sheen, fluffed comfortable with beige, silk coverings and large, sky-blue soft, pillows inviting the two to revel in its midst.

Ronny Kottaras and Michela Borrus eased onto their bed, talking excitedly of the evening's promise in the basement speakeasy, of exotic cocktails, wine and jazz music, the pounding of the drum, the melodies of the trumpet, clarinet and saxophone and rhythms of the tangos, waltzes, Charleston and foxtrots; dances of the age. Ronny looked to the ceiling. The fan droned a low hum, spinning slowly. White blades cut the view of the pink ceiling in colored layers of pink and white.

"You know Michela, we don't really belong here."

"Why not?"

"The people in the hotel, they're not our kind. Prancing

around in fancy clothes, sailing yachts and driving upscale cars make them appear smug and uppity. I feel like a duck in a pond surrounded by swans."

"You'd think after our pleasurable tryst by the river your mind would be cleansed of those insecurities, at least temporarily. Enjoy the moment. You have no reason to feel insecure or intimidated, you do belong here. You don't need to drive a fancy car, captain a yacht or wear fancy clothes. I like your Dodge pickup, that cute little boat you borrowed works for me and well...I prefer you without clothes. Besides, there's nothing wrong with feeling like a duck. Ducks are friendlier. They're not as haughty as some swans. So let's not worry about these swans hovering around us. It'd benefit you to mingle with a swan or two, you might learn something," reasoned Michela.

Gaining confidence from Michela's words, Ronny leaned on his elbow, smiled and said, "You're right, I'll try to be more positive but you know my attitude in crowds is not always pleasant, especially around those with luxuries or who pretend they are more important than they are," and he wrapped his arm around Michela, pulled her head to his shoulder, settled on the fluffed pillows and in the September heat of mid morning, both quietly lapsed into a restful sleep.

*   *   *   *

The voices of the hotel guests floated through the windows from the patio below waking Ronny and Michela. She gently lifted her head, yawned and stretched her arms.

"Wake up," she said shaking Ronny lightly. "We need to get moving. We need to bathe, unpack and join the pre-party festivities."

Ronny, drowsy from being awakened from the short nap sat up and grunted, "Yeah, I guess we should. I'm relaxed, but I'm hot and sweaty, even with that fan spinning overhead. A cool, fresh bath and tall, cold, glass of water would sure be refreshing about now."

Michela rose from the bed, opening the leather suitcase lying on the wooden chair where Ronny placed it. She rummaged through the clothes lying folded, layered and packed neatly. "I don't see it Ronny."

"What don't you see babe?"

"My dress, my new dress isn't here. It was left hanging on the door in our bedroom. I remember setting it apart from my other clothes so I'd notice and pack it carefully before we left. But the dress was too isolated. In the end it was forgotten. How could I be so ditzy?"

"Wasn't the dress a new dress?"

"Yes, I chose the dress at the clothing store downtown on Sutter Street, just for this occasion. What am I going to do now?" questioned Michela.

"Don't worry. We'll find you another dress, prettier than the one you had before. We have plenty of time before the party to shop for one somewhere around here. We'll find something special," said Ronny, with confidence.

"But there is no here, here. We're in the middle of nowhere." Michela's shoulders slumped in frustration, fearing the forgotten dress would ruin their evening.

Needing to bolster her confidence, Ronny said, "Michela, being in the middle of nowhere is somewhere. We're somewhere. And we're in the middle of where we are. You can't have middle and be nowhere. We're here and therefore we're somewhere and when we find the clothing store that has your dress, we'll be there and when we're there, it'll be a here to us at that point of time and we'll be in the middle." Ronny ended his explanation staring at Michela, waiting for a response, but received nothing other than a blank look and confused expression. Ronny stared back in silence, turned away slowly and stammered, "I...I...I'll just go down to the lobby and ask one of the hotel employees to help find a place." Ronny rose from the bed thinking, "Where the hell did that come from?" fearing his explanation caused Michela to believe him a little loopy. He walked down the stairs, approached the concierge desk where a pretty, young woman with bobbed, brunette hair and hazel eyes greeted him.

"Good morning sir. May I help you," she asked.

"I sure hope so Miss. My name's Ronny and my lady friend and I checked in earlier in preparation for tonight's party and, well, she seems to have forgotten her pretty dress and requires another for the evening. I told her we'd get a dress even prettier than the dress she forgot. Is there a clothing store somewhere in the area where we could buy a new dress?"

"You are in quite a predicament Ronny, but maybe I can help. By the way, my name's Lydia. Since you'll be in the hotel for the weekend, it's best we greet each other in a more personal, informal manner. It's a Saturday and late in the morning, almost noon in fact and we're far from the nearest store where an appropriate dress would be available. I don't believe you'll have the time or can guarantee you'd find a new dress, but let's think this through."

"How much time would it take to get to Sacramento?" asked Ronny.

"By car it would take about an hour. Do you have a car?"

"Unfortunately no. We arrived on the Delta Queen this morning and have no options."

"We could ask some of the guests if they'd loan you a car though it'd be a bit intrusive and the time spent searching for an appropriate dress would certainly cut into your enjoyment of the day. Let's consider the time requirements for finding a dress in Sacramento. It may take an hour to prepare for your trip and find someone to loan you a car or drive you, assuming they'd be willing. It will take another hour to travel to Sacramento, then another hour or two to find a dress. Let's be conservative and assume two hours to locate a dress, then another hour for your return trip. So all in, you're looking at five hours end-to-end, best case. Since it's...," Lydia looked to the dainty, gold watch on her wrist, "...noon now, you'd be back by five o'clock, so you'd have a couple of hours to get ready and mingle before the party begins at seven o'clock, if the trip and events occur as planned."

"That might work."

"There are potential problems however. You might encounter situations that slow you down, such as a flat tire, an accident on the road to or from Sacramento, difficulty finding a dress to your liking or other reasons causing delay, so you'd end up spending time with your search, rather than spending time relaxing and enjoying the scenery, enjoying the cocktails and wine, enjoying other guests attending the party or just enjoying each other. The roads from here to Sacramento aren't in the best of shape due to a major storm hitting the area hard last March. The main road between here and Sacramento washed out and still hasn't been repaired to an appropriate level of safety. Since March the number of disruptive traffic incidents has been much higher. There may be an alternative however. I have a dress I wore only once to a wedding a few months ago in Modesto, a town in the lower Central Valley, one I could loan you for the evening."

Acknowledging the risk of the search and conversely, the promise of the opportunity Lydia posed, Ronny said, "We'd be cutting it close searching for a dress and if some of the incidents you've mentioned did happen; we wouldn't want to spend the whole day looking for a dress. I did promise Michela we'd find her a dress. What color is the dress?"

"An indigo silk that would fit snugly around her hips to emphasize her shape and would certainly please you both."

"Indigo is blue isn't it?"

"Yes it is Ronny, a deep, dark and very sexy blue."

"But what if it doesn't fit?"

Lydia winked. "It should fit. I must admit I saw you and your lady friend sneak across the river earlier when you borrowed the small boat from *Cleopatra*, the seductive yacht out front. You rowed across neatly dressed and on the return trip a short while later, you weren't so neat, your clothes were disheveled and you…," Lydia paused, "…you looked flush and happy, smiling and laughing, apparently enjoying yourselves after visiting the area behind the dock across the river. Whatever happened behind the tules seems to have brightened your day. Your lady friend is a very pretty woman with curves similar to mine, the same height, weight and her Auburn hair contrasting with the indigo dress would definitely fit and compliment her appearance."

Embarrassed, Ronny lowered his head and whispered, "Let's keep what you assumed occurred across the river a secret, we don't want to foul our reputation."

"You shouldn't be worried about your reputation. Those who patronize the Ryde Hotel would be very proud and supportive of your visit to the *Vortex* of love, you should be as well."

"So you know of the area behind the dock, the *Vortex*?"

"Jim's not one to hold back on explaining the magic of the *Vortex* and recommends the area to those who visit Ryde and believe would find the *Vortex* appealing. Jim says it's a perk that ensures the right minded customers return to Ryde to receive the benefits of the *Vortex*," explained Lydia.

His embarrassment pushed aside, Ronny focused on his dilemma. "Maybe borrowing your dress is the answer. How long will it take for you to get your dress? Michela and I would love to spend the time here at Ryde mingling before the big event and maybe visit the *Vortex* once more. We do find the *Vortex* unusually erotic. The energy from the land, the sun, the breeze, the scent of the river and the gentle drone of the slow moving current integrated with our carnal fervor erupt in a cornucopia of senses and hypnotic release of pleasurable emotions while there." Feeling he'd shared too much, he said, "Lydia, I'm sorry for divulging our most intimate experiences and explaining my feelings but being there was very special. Now, concerning the dress, I hope Michela wouldn't mind wearing another woman's clothes, you know how you women can be."

"Yes Ronny," laughed Lydia. I know how we women can be, but I believe she'll be fine and don't worry about divulging your feelings of the *Vortex*. I'm happy you and Michela have enjoyed the *Vortex,* but for me, I'm not yet ready for intimacy with any man, let alone cross over to the zone and through the *Vortex*. I'll take your word it's all you've said it is and cross into the *Vortex* when the time is right for me. The dress; it's a beautiful dress and with the situation Michela's in, wearing a once worn dress isn't a bad compromise, especially the dress as pretty as the one I'm going to show you. I live in the house down the alley at the back of the hotel, a house I share with a few other people who work here occasionally, but rarely during the foggy season when the hotel isn't always open. The roads prove hazardous for drivers that prefer to not take the chance of driving off the edge of the levees into the river and the steamboats don't come often, because of the lack of visibility. It's pretty dangerous on the levees and in the river during the season of the valley of the fog. Give me a couple of minutes and I'll get the dress from my closet for you and Michela to take a look." Lydia turned to the doorman, "Frank. Please keep watch for a few minutes. I need to get a dress for Ronny."

"Sure thing, Miss Lydia."

Lydia turned and walked to the back of the hotel, out the door leading to the alley and down the gravel slope to the house bordered behind by the array of corn stalks rising from the flat lands of Grand Island.

With his arms crossed behind his back, Frank looked at Ronny from head to toe, cocked his head and joked, "I don't believe you're going to look so good in a dress Mister Ronny, but if it makes you happy, have at it."

Ronny laughed, "I know you're kidding Frank, at least I hope you're kidding. I'm not that kind of guy. Maybe you didn't hear correctly. The dress is for my lady friend Michela, who left hers at home, so we need to find a dress that works for her. Lydia says she has just the dress." Ronny turned, crossed his arms behind his back mocking Frank playfully, looked past the open, glass, entry doors to the small, red, yellow, blue and white flags waving on the masts of the yachts docked against the levee across River Road fronting the hotel. Ronny admired the yachts sitting on the calm, motionless river, absorbing the relaxation the isolation provided, away from the hubbub of the busy towns and cities. Rocking lightly back and forth on his toes and heels, he inhaled the fresh, river air deeply into his lungs, enjoying the serenity the moment offered.

"Here it is," said Lydia, rushing noisily from the back of the hotel through the hall and to the lobby, interrupting Ronny's momentary trance. "Take a look and let me know if you like it." She lifted the covering from the dress and a dark, bluish-violet fabric glowed on the hanger."

Startled by Lydia's abrupt entrance, Ronny turned from the glass doors and looked at the dress. "Wow, that's a beautiful color. I thought indigo was blue. This dress isn't entirely blue. It's sort of blue but the color in front of me I've never seen before. There are shades of dark blue and intermittent shades of violet and maybe even light gray blended into one color at times, but at times doesn't blend, behaving like a slowly changing sunset. Looking at the dress from different angles, the color appears to change shades slightly, like a Chameleon changes color in the woods. Although the color of the dress doesn't entirely change like a Chameleon changes to match the rocks and plants it's close to, this dress just shifts its shade. It's beautiful, may I touch?"

"Of course you may touch Ronny."

Ronny stepped towards Lydia, brushing his fingers across the fabric. "The dress is silk, but the texture of the fabric feels slightly different. Like the impression I receive from the changing visual shades of indigo, I've never experienced a fabric that feels so...so fine. Does the sight of the color indigo create a change in thinking that makes one feel what is being touched is something it isn't?"

"I don't know Ronny. Your comments are a little deep for me right now. All I know is I like the color, the feel, the look and fit of the dress," said Lydia.

"I do too, except the fit part since I'll never wear it. I'll never know how the fit feels, but that's okay, Michela will let me know and I'll enjoy the look of the fit on her. Let me take this...this...work of art to Michela and see if she likes the dress. Thank you Lydia, you're a genius. A regular Renoir of dresses and although you didn't create this masterpiece, you certainly have the talent to choose artful dresses," said Ronny, amazed by the look and feel as he gently folded the dress over his arm.

*   *   *   *

Michela watched Ronny walk out the door thinking of his last statement, worried not of the meaning, but of the verbal, labyrinthine delivery. "He was just trying to make me feel comfortable, to make me believe he'd find a dress no matter how far we are from where a dress could be found, especially the kind of dress I'd want," thought Michela. "But he did express himself rather oddly and that worries me." Michela rose from the bed, walked to the tub, turned the handles of the faucet, adjusting the water, letting it seep through her fingers until the temperature cooled from the flowing, hot water trapped in the hotel pipes. Sitting on the edge of the tub, she waited until it filled, then stepped into the clear, warm water and lay comfortably in its midst. Unable to shake her concerns, her thoughts stayed with Ronny. "He's been acting flittingly lately, his increased sensitivity and insecurity, the incessant need to cater to my every desire, his comments sometimes confusing, yet endearing. I wonder what's bothering him. I know the past year has been difficult, he's sacrificed so much and obviously adores me. I love him and I'm going to help him through this life changing event for his and my benefit." She closed her eyes and focused her attention to the music from the Victrola radio wafting from the room next door, Rudy Valle singing through the walls, Michela humming softly with the words, *"...and when two lovers woo...they still say I love you...on that you can rely...no matter what the future brings...as time goes by..."*

Ronny hopped excitedly up the three flights of stairs, down the hall and to the corner room where Michela lay humming and soaking in the lion claw tub, her head above the soapy water, her slender legs dangling comfortably across the rounded porcelain edge. Michela moved her head slowly to the side and smiled when the door opened, his faced beamed with satisfaction, her face with anticipation; the alluring, indigo dress hung gracefully over his arm.

"What do you think? Will this work for you?"

"It's a pretty color," said Michela, raising her head above the tub. "Let me try it on. Where did you get it? Do you think it'll fit?"

"Lydia said she thought it might. She noticed you and me rowing back from the *Vortex,* when we stepped from the boat onto the dock. She thought you had a similar body to hers."

"Who's Lydia?"

"Lydia's the young lady I met at the concierge desk who offered to loan us her dress for the evening. We discussed the logistics of obtaining an appropriate dress in Sacramento, the closest possible place we'd be able to get one and the risk of problems with the transportation and potential mishaps, causing us to be late to the party."

"But the dress has been previously worn. It'd be strange wearing the dress of another woman."

"That's what I told Lydia, but she said she only wore it once and it's been cleaned and I believe she's a virgin, so the chance of it being lousy with a man's odor and all is small. Come here, get out of the tub and try it on."

Michela stood, and stepped from the tub, grabbed the towel hanging on the edge, her nude body glistening wet in the sun's rays beaming through the window. Ronny gazed at Michela gracefully towelling up and down her legs, across her breasts and around her waist, dropping the towel on the crimson carpet, reaching for the dress.

"Alright, let me have it."

Ronny extended the dress from his outstretched arm. Michela took it, spreading the shoulders of the dress, holding it high for a full view.

"It's a nicely tailored dress. The color is amazing. The shades shift when moved slightly. It's collarless, the thin straps wrap tightly over the shoulders. The top of the dress appears to cover much of the breasts and with the plunging neckline, allows the visibility of some cleavage and there are no sleeves, a good thing." Michela pulled the dress against her chest, smoothing it along her knees. Satisfied with her initial assessment, she draped the dress over her head and shoulders, wriggled until fitting snugly around her waist and hips, the lower part of the dress loosely flowing along her thighs. "The fit is a little tight around my waist and my butt is really snug, but it feels really good." Michela with her back facing Ronny, turned her head sideways, looked over her shoulder and asked, "How do I look?"

Amazed by the enhanced beauty the dress provided, Ronny waxed poetic, "Your appearance is that of the goddess Aphrodite; your reddish blonde hair flows gently over your shoulders; the glow of indigo and its shifting shades contrast nicely with the ivory hue of your skin; the fit wraps you tightly like a beautiful butterfly, freed from its cocoon. We couldn't have found a better dress."

Pleased with Ronny's complimentary comments, Michela stepped to the standing walnut framed mirror in the corner of the room, turning, viewing her appearance posing in different stances. "You're right Ronny. It is a beautiful dress and the fit is flattering. Perfect. I suppose I could get over the fact the dress was worn by another woman. By the way, how did you know Lydia is a virgin?" questioned Michela, suspiciously.

"Don't worry," said Ronny laughing, sensing jealousy from Michela. "When Lydia and I were discussing finding you a dress, she mentioned noticing us rowing from the *Vortex* and suspected the reason for our being there. She knows of the *Vortex* and apparently many of the guests and hotel workers know of the *Vortex's* magic and she explained never having the pleasure experiencing the *Vortex* and never would experience the *Vortex,* until finding the right man, so, I figured, she's never ventured down the path to the *Vortex,* or any other path leading to, you know...the thing we did in the *Vortex.* Having just met her and given our differences in age and me being a man and her being a woman, we probably shouldn't have ventured down that path of discussion, but we did. Lydia's a pretty young lady, but you're much more beautiful in body and soul and the woman I'm in love with, so let's not fret over these petty jealousies."

Michela, reassured, smiled and stepped towards Ronny, pressed her hands gently against his cheeks, framed his face and kissed him passionately. "I love the dress Ronny, it'll be just fine and it's a good thing we can spend our time on the patio and the grounds of Ryde, enjoying the ambience of the river, the people and the amenities this place has to offer. Let's finish getting cleaned up, venture downstairs and mingle with some of these swans."

Ronny undressed, stepped into the tub and quickly bathed in the now tepid, soapy water. Michela removed the indigo dress, carefully placing it on the hanger and into the walnut armoire, unpacked the remainder of her clothes and shoes, placing them into the drawers and shelves of the armoire. Dressed in her yellow, cotton, summer dress and white sandals, she sat on the chair and began brushing her long, wavy hair while looking into the mirror. Ronny hurriedly towelled and dressed in his tan, linen pants, white, cotton shirt and brown, leather sandals.

"I'm ready. Let's head downstairs and do some mingling," said Ronny, eagerly.

Michela rose from her chair, placed her brush on the table, joined hands with Ronny and walked through the hall and down the stairs leading to the hotel lobby. Upon entering the lobby, the face on the wall clock in the entryway showed one o'clock, an hour from the time Ronny met Lydia, presented the dress to Michela, bathed, dressed and walked the stairs and within that hour, many hotel guests had filled the dining and bar area of the Ryde Hotel, spilling through the doors and onto the front patio. Standing at the foot of the stairs to the right, the entrance to the dining area featured a wide, double glass door with both doors opening inward. The wall at the top of the doors displayed arched glass with frosted figures of shapely women, etched on each side of the words, *"Ryde Hotel,"* the doors forming a seamless entry to the manic activity within. On the dining room floor stood tables with crisp, white, table cloths hanging over the table tops and young waiters and waitresses placed crystal platters, plates, silver serving utensils and tall, cobalt blue, glasses in a rhythmic dance of movement. Potted palms and potted banana trees with giant leaves, stood on the floor in the gaps between the long windows facing the hotel grounds. On the inside wall of the hotel, large, gold framed, colorful paintings hung in the open spaces between the windows. A large, ebony grand piano, waiting to be played sat in the corner under a tall, potted palm tree. Ronny and Michela walked through the doorway and to the right of the double doors stood a long, black, lacquer bar with mahogany bar stools, topped with white, leather cushions, where hotel guests sat drinking colorful drinks.

"A lot has happened while we were in our room," said Michela, impressed with the rapid pace of activity. "I've never paid much attention to the decor until now, such a beautiful design and style they've incorporated on this floor."

"The fervor of the staff provides a high level of energy.

They're getting ready to serve the drinks and hors d'oeuvres mentioned in the steamboat's flyer. Let's get something to drink and step outside, enjoy the sun and view of the river and free ourselves from this pandemonium for now," suggested Ronny. Ronny gently nudged Michela forward to the side of the bar and stepped in front, raised his hand and spoke to the young bartender. "We'd like a couple of...," and before he finished the order, turned to Michela and asked, "what do you want by the way?"

Michela, enamored with the elegance of the bar and dining area scanned the room and said, "Let's just have a tall glass of water with ice. We need to pace ourselves. We don't want to get tipsy too early."

"Good point. A tall glass of water would be just fine for now. Bartender, we'd like two tall glasses of ice water, one for the pretty lady, one for me and then we'll slowly ease into the evening with the good stuff later."

"Right away sir, that's a smart move. Many of the guests are starting much too early this afternoon with the cocktails, thirsty, like Bedouin lost in search of an oasis in the Sahara desert," said the bartender, smiling with casual levity. The bartender scooped the cracked ice from the metal tray, filled two tall glasses and poured sparkling water from the spouts under the bar. Before handing them to Ronny the bartender asked, "Lemon or Lime?"

"Lime," stated Ronny and Michela, chuckling at their simultaneous response.

The bartender reached for the bowl of piled, cut limes, grabbed two, plopped one in each of the glasses, handing them to Ronny. "Enjoy the refreshments and come back for more when you're ready. We can blend many different cocktails for you, made of liquor from many exotic countries and regions, smuggled on riverboats from the ports in San Francisco." Ronny nodded to the bartender, handing Michela the glass, motioning her towards the door leading to the patio. The door opened and an attractive, tall mustached man stepped aside, providing a path for Michela to exit, his arm gestured her to pass; the man and Michela's eyes met, their lips began to turn upwards towards a smile, hesitating to a half smile, uncertain of whether to complete the smile, each with the apprehension of greeting a stranger and the desire to acknowledge the gesture of friendliness and the unintended fleeting attraction to one another. Ronny noticed the unspoken exchange, feeling a discomfort from jealousy, but said nothing. Michela passed over the threshold and Ronny followed, graciously thanking mustache man with a smile, preceded with a frown and walked to the patio where four, round tables on each side of the entryway sat under the umbrellas, in the shade.

Michela, feeling some guilt from the awkward greeting with the mustache man turned to Ronny, asking sheepishly, "Would you like to walk to the edge of the river and look at the yachts? *Cleopatra* seems to be courting a yacht in front and one behind, and although they're smaller, they appear to be worth admiring."

"Sure," said Ronny, fighting to quell the negative response fuelled by his jealousy. "We can do that. I hope *Cleopatra* won't recognize us as the two who snuck away with her little friend and rowed across the river."

"We rowed her friend back, so we'll be forgiven."

They stepped along the walk splitting the patio and crossed River Road to the stairs leading to the dock where the yachts berthed. The heat of the day was intense, their water glasses sweated, tiny beads formed on their surface. The small yacht, *Windstream* in front and *Wavejumper* behind, floated proudly, yet were diminished by *Cleopatra's* noble position perched high, at the center of the dock.

"Both *Windstream* and *Wavejumper* are fine boats, but *Cleopatra* has a name befitting her style. The names of the other two boats work for them, but that *Cleopatra*, she's a real, regal, river craft, one I'd be proud riding," said Ronny, with admiration.

"We've become boat experts haven't we Ronny? Rowing *Cleopatra's* little companion to the *Vortex* has shown us the benefits of water recreation."

"I don't know Michela. *Cleopatra's* companion was helpful, but *Windstream* and *Wavejumper,* or any other boat would've given us the same opportunity. We don't need to be boat experts to experience the benefits of recreation at the *Vortex*. We could've swum to the *Vortex* and achieved the same thing. Let's walk along the road and view the river and surroundings away from the hotel." Ronny took Michela by the hand and walked along the river bank in the direction of Isleton. Walking silently with the water glasses in hand, the river flat and calm, the upper floors of a Victorian home peaked above the road on the other side of the river, reflecting the home upside down in the river's glassy mirror.

"Such a beautiful house, it must be peaceful living out

here. Could you imagine waking up every day with a view of the river and the warm climate, the space, the quiet, the serenity?" wondered Michela.

"I suppose I could. People here lead a different way of life than our lives in the city. Slow living, but like us, hard working. The further we walk from the hotel, the quieter it becomes, making me feel a part of this natural environment, rather than a gear in the machine of city civilization trying to keep the machine running. And look, there, across the road, are acres and acres of trees with small, green pears hanging from the branches. Let's walk over and pick a couple."

Michela and Ronny crossed and walked along the road for about a mile, then carefully slid down the dirt embankment to a row of pear trees.

"Do you think they're ripe? They may be sour. The pears are small and I believe it may be little early for harvest, since they're all still hanging on the trees."

"We won't know until we try them," said Ronny, picking two pears from the lower branches, handing one to Michela. She grabbed the pear, wiping it against Ronny's trousers.

"Sorry, but we have to make sure the pears are clean before we take a bite." Bringing the pear to her mouth, the crunch of the pear forced Michela's face into a distorted expression, giving Ronny the answer to her question of ripeness.

Ronny laughed, dropping his pear to the ground. "I won't need to test my pear, you've already determined whether it's ripe and clearly it isn't."

Michela spat the chunks of pear on the dusty ground, flinging the bitten, bitter fruit across River Road where it plopped into the river. They sat on the ground under the shade of the pear tree, drinking the last of the water from their glasses.

"Do you think your children like me?" asked Michela.

"That's an odd question," responded Ronny, bewildered.

"I'm worried Lori and Ricky will never adjust to your new life with me. It's already been a year and whenever we're together, they don't respond to my questions eagerly, and never initiate conversation on their own. I see them laughing with you from a distance and it's clear they love you and love being with you. I thought by now they would warm to me and treat me like their mother."

"You'll never be like their mother. They have a mother, a good mother. I hope they treat you more as a friend or maybe even a big sister. They're both still young Michela, Ricky is only five and Lori is eight, not much older. It's been hard for them to adjust to you and they're going to need more time. The children don't dislike you. Obviously, they're experiencing some discomfort because of my decision."

Feeling hurt by Ronny's surprisingly harsh comments of his children having a mother and not needing another, cut deep, so Michela decided to abandon those thoughts and acquiesce to Ronny's position. "After all," she thought, "I have Ronny and know Lori and Ricky will come around eventually. They're good kids and will understand our situation as they grow older." Michela lightly touched Ronny's hand. "Okay. I'll be patient and let our lives evolve.

They're your children and you're their father. I know I'm odd woman out in this family. The issues will eventually resolve themselves."

Ronny smiled at Michela, feeling sympathy for her, knowing the frustration she felt with his reticence pushing the relationship forward. They were both having fun, enjoying the parts of life they envisioned in their late thirties, an age Ronny felt was appropriate to evaluate his situation in life, where both he and Michela needed to be. He knew after many years of living with his wife and children and although loved them, felt trapped and stuck in a life of tedium, from the stress of building his metal strapping business, his endless chores on the weekends at their Sunset district home, at Ricky's and Lori's school and sporting events, participating in the family's awe inspiring yet hypocritical church events and the most significant issue, the lack of intimacy with his wife, after many years of sexual frustration after the birth of Ricky, all time spent impeding the adventures he longed for. He felt guilt from having these feelings, guilt he felt was warranted, guilt he accepted after losing the battle with the negative feelings countering the positive feelings of the experiences with his family. A warm feeling of happiness and some relief was felt after the decision he made to leave his family, for Michela, a woman fulfilling his sexual and emotional needs and the vibrancy and flare his mind and body yearned for at this point in his life. But he just couldn't shed the guilt and loneliness felt not being with Lori and Ricky and yes, even his wife and wasn't yet sure if his decision had been the right one. "From the frying pan into the fire," he thought, remembering the standard cliché of the belief of solving one problem and creating yet another. Frustrated, he pushed the strong feelings of guilt from his mind.

"Let's head back and walk through the pear orchard," suggested Ronny, rising and helping Michela from under the pear tree. "We should reach the parking area below the hotel through this row of trees. It'd be nice to enjoy the beauty of the trees and the not so ripe fruit waiting for harvest," continued Ronny with feigned cheer.

Stepping forward holding hands, they carried their empty glasses, engaged in light conversation and walked between the rows of pear trees with small, green pears nestled in the myriad of leaves and branches, growing from the slim gray trunks. Halfway to the hotel, muffled sounds of sharp tongued voices came from within a row of trees, where Chinese men sat on crates smoking, drinking and yelling at one another, enjoying the camaraderie of each other's company.

"I feel like I'm in Chinatown;. They're sure having a good time," said Ronny, as he waved and passed the row where the men sat. The men, noticing the couple walking through the trees, stopped their chattering, waved back, then continued to carry on their early afternoon party in the orchard. "Everyone in and around this remote oasis are certainly enjoying themselves," said Michela, feeling warmth in her surroundings. They continued walking slowly through the row of trees, butterflies fluttered, small sparrows darted from tree to tree then branch to branch, the musical chirping lent an aura of serenity, contrasting to the memory of the noise of streetcars, sirens and the bustle of their city by the bay, noises of their urban culture they were accustomed to. The Ryde Hotel water tower loomed in the distance, its metal reservoir topped with the cone shaped cap, sat on the tall, four legged trestle, high above the trees. Crossing the lot, their steps grating the gravel, voices and laughter filled the air as they approached the side of the hotel. Cement steps led to the front patio where guests laughed and talked with drinks in hand, music from the ebony piano played classical melodies of *Bach,* gracefully floating through the patio doors. Michela and Ronny entered, making their way across the floor and to the bar, Ronny raising his arm to get the attention of the bartender.

"Did you enjoy the outdoors and the walk along the river?" asked the bartender, recognizing Ronny.

"We sure did," answered Michela quickly. "We've some dust covering our sandals and the grains of dirt are irritating the spaces between our toes from our walk through the orchard and needless to say, we're parched and would sure like a couple more glasses of the lime, laced ice water you served us earlier."

"No cocktails yet?" asked the bartender.

"No cocktails yet," mirrored Ronny. "We're still pacing."

The bartender performed the same water and lime routine as before, handing the glasses to Ronny and Michela. Michela plucked the lime from the glass; bit the moist, sour insides torn from the green rind, and expressed the same contorted face when chomping the unripe pear earlier in the day.

"You like that sour taste, don't you lady?" asked Ronny,

laughing at her distorted, facial expression.

"I'm beginning to," said Michela, frowning, her lips puckering from the bite.

Stepping away from the crowded bar, they walked to the front patio towards a table, surrounded by a man and a woman sitting under a white umbrella, where two chairs sat empty. Michela motioned to the chair addressing the gray haired man and olive skinned woman sitting, asking, "Excuse me. Are these seats taken?"

The man responded, "They're not taken. You both may sit if you wish, we could use the company and those lonely, little chairs are waiting just for you." Pointing to the glass of water and ice in Michela's hand, the man continued, "I see you and your friend aren't drinking the fermented fruits of this humble hotel this hot afternoon."

"No sir, not yet, we're drinking the crisp, clear water with only a little piece of lime carousing among the cubes. The stronger drink in the form of fermented, fruit laden cocktails will come later. We're just pacing ourselves," winked Michela, as she and Ronny sat in the empty seats.

"Well, when you're done pacing yourselves and ready to un-pace, try the fruits of the grape in the form of this fine, red wine," the man bragged, swirling the wine in his glass. "I guarantee this beverage is a step above any cocktail you'll receive in this fancy hotel, a good earthy wine they say, more than worthy of the Valley of Sonoma, where the grapes were grown and the wine fermented in two hundred year old, charred casks, made from the finest oak from the finest foothills in this here California."

"And how do you know of this so called fine wine you're

promoting so strongly," questioned Ronny.

"I made it," answered the man, with a cocky inflection. "My family has been making wine since we acquired an old winery in the late 1800's, a winery with acres of old, gnarled, mission vines and a dust filled, abandoned, wine cellar infiltrated with masses of spiders, covered with their webs. My family migrated from the northern part of Virginia, originally from the northern part of Italy; then ventured here to the northern part of California. The family Sebastiani appear to enjoy the northern parts of territories; came out west in search of land and prosperity, finding it on the cheap after purchasing the abandoned mission vineyards and winery. The old California lost it all to Mexico in the Mexican American war and the land eventually grabbed by the good and new, Ol' *U S of A*. My dad worked the dirt in the fields turning the vines and winery into a profitable business, but unfortunately died of a black widow spider bite in the year of the San Francisco quake, leaving me at the age of twenty to carry his work forward. Being the only son, my mother and I worked hard to continue the legacy of our family's wine business, which remained profitable until the government passed that damned Volstead act, almost making us bankrupt."

"So how are you surviving?" asked Ronny, with genuine interest, knowing the difficulties the act of Prohibition had on businessmen participating in the liquor production and distribution industries.

"There's a little loophole in the law, put there by some savvy lawmakers influenced by bishops, cardinals and maybe even the Pope himself, needing a way to bypass the

self proclaimed moralists who lobbied for Prohibition. Those in the high levels of the Christian church needed a way to serve the parishioners of Christianity, who believe in weekly communion in the form of the eating of bread, representing the body of Christ and the drinking of wine, representing the blood of Christ, a contradiction because the moralists, some Christians, deny wine as a basis for what is called the Eucharist, yet other Christians, who are also driven by a moral code, need the wine for their communion based on a long, standing tradition."

"But why don't all Christians, all who believe in God and the Bible, accept the tradition of drinking wine as a symbol of the blood of Christ?" asked Ronny.

"That's a damn good question. Each form of Christianity interprets the Bible differently. I'm speculating, but our winery and vineyards survive by selling large numbers of barrels and bottles to the churches in support of those Christians whose belief in God support the tradition of drinking the blood of Jesus, in the form of wine during communion and appear to require substantial amounts."

"But why don't the other Christian moralists, who support Prohibition, drink the blood of Jesus in the form of wine, since they both believe in God and believe Jesus is the son of God?" questioned Ronny, still not understanding the differences of the interpretation of the Bible, by those of the same faith.

"I could imagine drinking the blood of another man is abhorrent to some Christians, who still claim a belief in God. I could see their point of view, I can't believe it is very healthy drinking the blood of any man in the form of wine, but being self serving, I see the benefit."

"I'm still confused, why do those who believe in God don't follow the same rules?"

"I can't tell you. I don't understand why there are differences between Catholics or Baptists or Protestants or Lutherans or Mormons or Muslims, or any other religions who believe in one God. But I do know the form and symbol of wine as the blood of Christ has provided a means for normal "religious" ones to imbibe in a bottle or barrel full of the nectar of the son of God, on occasion to honor his memory and the memory of Jesus dying for our sins. That poor young man, Jesus, died centuries ago and people still sin, so I don't see the point. Not understanding the explanation of Jesus dying for our sins and not knowing what the hell it means, has allowed me to distribute the wine by justifying conversion through honoring Jesus, under rules allowing the consumption defined by our lord God and apparently hoards of other citizens in our state have converted as well. They say there's a run on religion in these parts."

"But we don't need to convert, we can find the wine and other alcoholic beverages in many towns and cities, without being Christians," said Ronny bewildered.

"You have a point but the lawmakers needed a loophole in the law to allow the sale and distribution of wine to not disrupt their political base that consists of some religions, Catholic Christianity is a good example. We see the effects of the loophole, because we ship many more barrels and bottles of wine, to churches due to the increase in church attendance and the increased number of communions. We also find our barrels and bottles in places other than churches throughout our fine state. What the priests and church administrators do with the barrels and bottles, I don't know and don't want to know, but that channel of religious worship is what keeps us afloat. God I love Christianity."

Chuckling at the man's sarcastic comment, Ronny said, "I can see how Catholic Christianity benefits you, but does your seemingly feigned belief in God and support of Catholic Christianity truly make you believe you're protected from the law and don't you think the law will eventually clamp down on the churches and close your business?"

"I don't think so. The law and government aren't going to step on the toes of God, that wouldn't be too good for their business of governing. In time, people will tire of the ridiculous unenforccable law of Prohibition, since those like you and I and most in our country will ignore the law anyway, like we're doing now. We just need time for it to run its course, for non-drinking Christian moralists and for new law makers to come to their senses and repeal the act. Until then; *bottoms up*," said the man, tipping his glass and drinking the last of the wine, as did the pleasantly plump, black haired, olive skinned woman, silently listening, all the while maintaining a smile.

Ronny extended his hand to the interesting man. "I'm Ronny, my lady friend is Michela," gesturing towards Michela, who sat silently, also with a smile, happily absorbing Ronny's and the man's conversation.

"I'm sorry I hadn't introduced myself before beginning my mantra on my political and somewhat selfish views. My name's Jackson, Jackson Sebastiani, but you can call me Jack. As you can see, my first name is southern United States, my birth country. My last name is northern Italy, my ancestor's birth country. Next to me is my lovely wife Angelina, but you can call her Angela, I call her Angel however, but that's a name I use privately on amorous occasions," said Jack, extending a wink and a smile towards Angelina.

"And you can call me any one of those names, Angelina, Angel or even, Lina," said the wife of Jackson, escaping her opaque shell of silence.

"It's nice to meet you both. Michela and I are certainly enjoying learning of your lives and interesting, albeit controversial opinions. We'd like to meet with you this evening in the speakeasy, to learn more while enjoying a glass or two of your fine, red wine if you'd be willing," asked Ronny.

"Would love to Ronny, but we're heading out real soon, in fact we have to leave about now, back to Sonoma to get an early start prepping for early harvest. We took the long drive down, two days ago, to beat the crowds and for some short lived privacy, but are ready to pack it up and get back to work. It was nice meeting you both. Enjoy yourselves in this wonderful enclave of Ryde and ask the bartender for the Sebastiani Red and he'll certainly oblige."

Jack and Angelina rose from their chairs, as did Ronny and Michela, shaking hands all around, Jack and Angelina walked through the hotel lobby and up the stairs.

Ronny and Michela returned to their chairs, Michela commenting, "He was an interesting man and carried on an interesting conversation. I would've liked to have heard more of his winery and more of the Sonoma Valley. We should take a ride there sometime and explore."

"We'll definitely explore Sonoma and the Napa Valley as well. I hear both valleys are beautiful with woods, creeks and old vineyards strewn throughout the hills. We'll add it to our growing list of future adventures you're always suggesting. You know, Michela, I learned a few things from Jackson. He is certainly no haughty swan. He's a dark, swan with a sharp edge. I prefer the name Jackson instead of the name Jack, by the way, it fits his personality. He's a bit arrogant and hypocritical with his religious views, but you know; I like him. He certainly has strong opinions about God and religion, being a religious man it appears, only for convenience, benefitting his wine business, but he's a hard working man, whose family has built something with their own hands, winning the battle with the adversity caused by his father's death, a very interesting life with challenges like mine," stressed Ronny, clenching his hands into a fist for emphasis. "It's a shame he won't be around this evening to talk, but hopefully, we'll find some other swans to engage with."

"Are we done pacing ourselves?" asked Michela, in an obvious hurry to move the afternoon forward, influenced by the prospect of obtaining the enjoyable feeling from the allure of Ronny's excited and passionate state.

"I'm not yet ready to un-pace if that's what you mean. I'd like to hang on to my wits for a little while longer. Let's wander around the grounds of Ryde, before we prep for the evening."

They rose from the chairs, walked around the corner of the building and down the gravel path heading to the area behind the hotel. Michela's thoughts turned to her observations of Ronny's conversation with Jackson and intense concentration of Jackson Sebastiani's wine business. Michela was proud of Ronny and his sincere interest in Jackson's story, an interest Ronny rarely had for the stories of the lives of others. Ronny's interests had always been rightly self centered, of Ronny's focus on family and his metal strapping business, a business Ronny built when his father was killed in the big quake of '06, their father's deaths a common tragedy shared with Jackson, both fathers dying in the same year, but under different circumstances. Tumultuous shaking of the city sent their modest home in the Mission District sliding from its foundation, destroyed in the ensuing fire. The Kottaras family had lost it all, his father buried in the rubble along with the immediate loss of their modest livelihood. Ronny and his mother, rendered homeless, survived in the Presidio tent city, with few possessions and little hope. Promising to "figure things out," Ronny worked hard during the reconstruction of San Francisco, performing odd jobs in construction, meeting contacts for future business on the docks of San Francisco, founding and growing his niche, metal strapping business serving the shipping industry, a business now grown to over twenty employees. Michela thought Ronny, a social hermit of sorts, a loner, a boy turned man, in an instant, with the goal in life, to focus his energies caring for his mother and eventually his wife Tina, daughter Lori and son Ricky. Michela wasn't surprised Ronny didn't volunteer his story to Jackson Sebastiani, he wasn't geared that way. Ronny kept his passions and successes close to heart. She respected Ronny due to his focus, his passion for life and recently unlocked, adventurous spirit. She knew he was the right man for her.

Interrupting her thoughts, Ronny's voice came to her. "No one is enjoying the pool, you'd think on such a hot day people would be cooling in the water."

Michela looked to the pool, the lounge chairs empty, the pool water devoid of swimmers. "We aren't there either, most are preoccupied like us, enjoying the surroundings, the early cocktails and just mingling, getting to know the other guests, preparing for this evening's party. Tomorrow you'll see people lounging around the pool, lazing and suffering with their hangovers."

"You're probably right. Hopefully we won't be a couple of those poor, suffering souls."

Michela abruptly walked towards Ronny, grabbed his hand, pulling him towards the tight, rows of cornstalks bordering the hotel grounds.

"Where are we going?" asked Ronny.

"We're going to appreciate the wildness of nature once more, this time in the stalks of corn; we're going to create our own *Vortex of love*," said Michela, struggling to control her growing desire for Ronny.

"But, we're too close to the hotel, people may see us, we can't lay in the grove of corn and the stalks are thick and bushy and..."

"Shhh," said Michela, pressing her fingers gently to Ronny's lips. "Follow me." Michela led him through a row of corn, swiping the stalks, the dry leaves and husks crackling and swiping back, angrily slapping their cheeks. After tramping into the grove twenty yards deep, she stopped and ordered, "You push those stalks near you to the ground until they're laying flat. I'll push the stalks near me to the ground and we'll make a comfortable spot to lie in." They pushed and stomped the corn stalks creating an uneven area hidden from the hotel, the bright, orange, late afternoon sun guarding their movements.

Once again, their clothes went flying, landing among the stalks of corn decorating the new *Vortex,* like a poor man's Christmas tree. They kissed and groped and pushed and pulled, like two animals in a kingdom of lust. Once again, Ronny rolled on his back, tiny beads of sweat clung to their skin, their passions released without noise.

"You got me again," said Ronny, the words spoken quietly, hesitantly with his heavy breathing.

Michela, breathless, turned her head to Ronny, nodded, agreeing with a slow blink and satisfied gaze. Remaining silent for minutes, Ronny sat up, brushed Michela's leg and said, "You're a little white tiger in the jungle, insatiable."

"You're a big maned lion, lying on a cleft in a mountain cliff, easily satiated," responded Michela, recovering from her pleasure induced stupor. They raised and slowly stood, retrieved their clothing from the stalks, picked the corn husk, fibers clinging to their fabric, dressed and walked back to the pool area behind the hotel.

Ronny stopped, viewing the vacant pool and remarked, "Well, what do you think?"

Michela looked to the pool, knowing and answering with a nod and a smile in agreement. They rushed to the pool's edge, jumped in, fully clothed, the warm water flowed upward as they slowly drifted downward, suspending them briefly, then slowly floating back to the surface, where their faces met. Wrapping their arms around one another, they kissed, while their legs slowly treaded. Stroking gently to the steps, they raised themselves to the deck, laughing heartily, their soaked clothing sagged streams of water dripping on the concrete surface.

"How will we get through the lobby and to our room, soaking wet, with no one seeing us?" asked Ronny.

Michela, with a solution for every challenge, looked to the roof of the hotel, paused, raised her arm, pointed to the black, iron fire escape ladder running along the pink, side wall, leading to the top floor.

"There's how."

*   *   *   *

Opening the door to their room, the water dripped from their clothing, darkening the carpet leading from the end of the hall.

"Great idea, Michela, we made it up the ladder and managed to enter through the window."

"Yes, thank goodness the window was open and the guests were out front mingling. We missed the afternoon's event. The hors d'oeuvres and cocktails seem to have eluded us."

"It's more like we eluded them. Pacing ourselves has outrun its usefulness, Michela. We need to ramp it up. We've had a great time, but we've more people to meet, cocktails to drink..."

"...and much dancing to the brass, jazz beat," interrupted Michela.

"Yeah, that too. Go ahead and bathe first, I'll wait and jump in when you're finished."

"Michela turned the faucet filling the tub. Ronny grabbed the wooden chair, placing it next to the window, threw off his sopping, wet clothing, wrapped a towel around his waist, sat with his arm resting on the window sill, looking to the river below. Shiny black, brown and green cars with sparkling, chrome grills and bumpers, lined the road extending along the river. *Gypsy* and *Moon Dancer*, two newly arrived yachts, crowded *Cleopatra*, *Wavejumper* and *Windstream*. People stood, with drinks in hand, talking and laughing. Hearing Michela enter the tub with a soft splash, he turned and smiled. Being with Michela was a dream come true, his desires fulfilled after many years of family focus and tiring responsibilities he still maintained and felt obligated to perform. He felt free after meeting Michela, free to explore with a companion of like mind, a companion with the time and intellect to appreciate what life had to offer, but he also felt selfish, knew he had that damn chip on his shoulder, knew he didn't always appreciate the swans of this world and their often condescending demeanor.

"What are you thinking about?" asked Michela.

"Nothing Babe, just fondly reminiscing of the day and the fun we've had. I'm having a great time."

"I'm having a great time too and looking forward to the evening."

Ronny's thoughts turned to the novel, *Tolstoy's, Anna Karenina*, the most recent of many books he'd read over the years in his never ending quest of self education, feeling both fear and happiness, of the plight of the main characters. Of *Anna*, the aristocratic, philandering, woman whose fate began with sin and bliss, but ended tragically due to her husband's stubborn refusal to accept her request for a divorce. Of *Vronsky*, the once promising military officer, *Anna's* partner in infidelity, a man whose initial infatuation with *Anna,* slowly faded into unhappiness. Of *Levin*, the hardworking, sensible farmer, who achieved his goal of a simple, happy, life after the initial rejection from *Kitty*, the innocent jilted lover of *Vronsky*. Ronny identified with these characters, unsure of which of their fates, if any, would befall him.

"I'm almost finished Ronny, you can bathe after me," Michela's barely audible voice, sifting through Ronny's thoughts.

Ronny nodded, his gaze focused on the sunset hovering over the horizon, behind the peak of Mount Diablo. The sunset with layers of pink, blue, gray, lavender and red, an exotic and beautiful array of color, mesmerized Ronny. The scenery suspending him in thought, briefly, until feeling the light touch of Michela's hand on his shoulder.

"It's all yours."

Ronny rose. Dropping his towel, he stepped across the floor, entered the tub, quickly bathed and towelled dry. After drying her hair, Michela sat in front of the mirror brushing with long, slow strokes, the indigo dress hung hauntingly, elegant in the open armoire. Ronny walked to the armoire, pulled his black tuxedo from the hanger, dressed and stood behind Michela, adjusting his shirt collar in the mirror.

"What do you think?" asked Ronny, uncomfortable with the formality of his appearance.

"You look like a D.C. senator, waiting to give a speech."

"I'll take that as a compliment," said Ronny, smiling, then turned, stepped to the bed and sat on the bed's edge. "I want to see you in the indigo dress. I've been waiting all day for this moment."

"Well then, let's not make you wait any longer."

Ronny watched Michela lift the dress from the armoire, raising it over her head, sliding it over her shoulders. She shifted her feet back and forth, snugly fitting the dress around her hips with the lower portion of the dress hanging, loosely covering her knees. "My you're a beautiful butterfly," thought Ronny, continuing to watch Michela flip her long, wavy hair over her shoulder. Her sky blue eyes, ivory skin, hair of Auburn hue, covered with the shade changing indigo blue dress created an image of a blue swallowtail butterfly, perched on the petal of a bright, white rose. "Why don't you bob your hair, like all the other young women?"

"I'm not like other young women, I'm not so young. Being thirty eight makes me uncomfortable with the new hair style. Wearing bobbed hair will be a passing fad, worn temporarily in that manner for women to rebel against the status quo, against the prior generation of stuffy, Victorian women."

"But those young women are of your generation, you're just on the outer edge. Don't get me wrong, I love your hair the way it is and I'm not sure I like the bobbed style either. It's certainly different, but the length of your hair and the manner in which you carry it, so beautifully, not all bound up, like a tightly woven hive of the pre-bobbed generation. Your hair naturally flows, which can be considered somewhat *avant garde*."

"That's nice of you to say," said Michela, twirling, admiring her look in the tall, standing, walnut grained mirror. She pulled the shoes with the short heels and straps from the armoire shelf, slipped her feet in slowly, stood and curtsied. "Take me to the oasis, *mon ami and* let's revel in sinful celebration."

"I am at your command and mercy," said Ronny, pulling a small, silver box from his coat pocket, "but first we need the finishing touches on you, your natural beauty enhanced by the indigo dress, is a masterful work of art." Opening the box, he pulled the thin gold chain with the large, dark, teal, glowing pearl, stood and walked behind Michela, looping the chain around her neck. "A South Sea pearl, purchased from Shreve on Post and Grant, a pearl of natural beauty, like the beauty granted you, by nature."

Michela looked into the mirror, watching the pearl drop

gently to the peak of her cleavage, positioned, like a coveting sentinel. "Oh Ronny, It is so beautiful."

Ronny grabbed her hand and said with pride, "Onward to the oasis *mon amour* and the open gates of the sinful parts of heaven."

*   *   *   *

The steps down the stairwell trembled from the vibration within the speakeasy. The scent of the hot, early evening permeated the stairway with a mix of perfumes, colognes, tobacco, and river breeze. Men and women filled the room with the chattering of talk and singing of laughter, sitting on tables, standing at the bar, in the corners, smoking cigars and cigarettes, moving to the soft beat of the drum and the temperate melody of the clarinet. Walking through the crowd towards the black, lacquer bar, Michela stepped in rhythm to the beat of the drum, her smile spread wide. Ronny felt the vibrating beat as he crossed the floor, his steps faltering, attempting to synchronize with Michela's movements. Frustrated from his failed attempts, he abandoned his offbeat walk, never having adjusted to the beats of the music of the times. Approaching the bar, he held Michela's hand protectively. Nestling between the couples at the crowded bar, Ronny stepped forward, raising his arm to get the attention of the bartender with the red, bow tie standing in the corner, tending to a middle aged couple, while smiling and laughing cheerily. The bartender in black pants, white shirt, slim suspenders and light brown, slicked hair walked towards Ronny, twirling a long, tall glass in his hand and with one acrobatic movement, placed it firmly and loudly on the bar top in front of Michela.

"What can I get for you and the lovely lady enjoying the beat of the jazz floating its rhythm among the souls of us river rovers?" questioned the bartender, smiling, crow's feet forming at the corners of his light, blue eyes.

Michela reached into her small purse, leaned forward, presenting a small card with the names, Ronny Kottaras and Michela Borrus, written on the card's front." I made this card and others, to ease the beginning of our conversations with people we meet, our names may be difficult to pronounce."

The bartender picked the card from Michela's fingers. "Interesting names, So Michela..."

"That's pronounced "Me-kay-la", Mister Bartender, the letters 'C' and 'H' should be pronounced like the letter 'K', not pronounced like the letters 'C' and 'H', as in the word *chair*, like you're saying," said Michela coyly, with a grin.

Ronny gently wrapped his arm around Michela's shoulder, jealous, from the immediate flirtation between the two.

"Apparently the card didn't work for me, so I stand corrected Mee-kayy-laaa," said the bartender, pronouncing her name slowly and deliberately. "Both of your names seem foreign, where are you from?"

"We're from here. We're both American. Born and bred," said Ronny, proudly. "My parents are from Missouri, Michela's from Jersey. We met at a ball game, Seals stadium in San Francisco."

"Good to know. Your names are a bit odd and not common in these parts, or not regal like those that visit from the more ritzy parts of the state. People may think you foreign and may not be as friendly as you'd like them to be. How about we use your initials this evening for ease and informality, say RG for you Mister Ronny and MB for you, Miss Mee-kayy-laaa?" suggested the bartender.

"So you don't believe our names are good enough?" responded Ronny, defensively. "Our names are our names. We're plain folk, real folk. We don't need to put on airs, or be *hoity toity* to be accepted by those here in this speakeasy."

Michela stood silently watching the imaginary chip weighing down Ronny's shoulder, yet was entertained by the testosterone laden conversation occurring between the two men.

"Now Ronny, hang on there now," said the bartender, shocked with Ronny's reaction. "I didn't mean to rub you the wrong way. I just want to help you fit in, in a neighborly sort of way. You see, my name's Chuck Harris, named by my dad who didn't have the sense to know the name Chuck is short for Charles. Right there on my birth certificate, I tell you, the name Chuck. So, I make myself known as Charles Harrison III, to those that visit this establishment. I added the 'O' and 'N' to the end of the name Harris, to appear more regal. It helps me feel like I fit in. So people call me Charles. You know, most in this speakeasy aren't locals, not from around here. Those from around here don't normally visit swanky places like this. So, yeah, I do put on airs. I wouldn't exactly call myself *hoity toity,* but I don't want to be looked down upon. I'm a simple guy, somewhat plain like you appear to be. No offense. I mean that in a complimentary way. I work the railroad, the Southern Pacific and maintain the tracks from here to Sacramento, my day job. That's my explanation Ronny, so let me know what you want me to call you and I'll oblige."

Ronny, his temper diffused, calmly stated, "We've already met a few people in the hotel and they all have been very nice if you interact with them without judgment, but go ahead, address me as RG and the pretty lady, MB, if Michela agrees."

"I do agree," said Michela, perkily. "It makes me appear secretive and I like that."

"But I don't know how changing your name to sound more regal makes you appear more regal, you're a bartender and railroad worker for goodness sake. It's good to have a job that keeps your feet to the earth, where the feet of men should be. Your desire to have a more aristocratic name is pretentious. But, to accommodate your foibles, how about I call you CH, making it square between the three of us, like we're a part of a club or something?"

"Sounds like a plan RG. Now after going through all that, I believe I can now say it is a pleasure to meet you."

"By the way CH, why do they call this place a speakeasy?" asked Michela, glad to be beyond the tensions of the awkward introductions and learning their names on the card wasn't such a good idea.

CH leaned over the bar, placing his finger against his lips, "Shush, speak softly, speak easy, you don't want to make the crowd rowdy with loud noise and make ourselves known to the law, in the event they're passing by since technically, we are breaking the law. Talk lightly. Speakeeeeasy MB."

"I see. That's quite clever," whispered Michela. "I'll make sure I speak in a hushed tone so we don't get carted to the dusty dungeons."

Ronny smiled at the exchange, warming to the bartender. "CH, what cocktails do you recommend to start our evening with a bang?"

"What's your liquor of choice, your favorite cocktail?" asked the bartender.

"Neither of us have had hard liquor or fancy cocktails. We've heard from Jackson, one of the hotel guests, that you serve a fine red wine from Sonoma, a Sebastiani red. But we're not yet in the mood for a dark, red wine. I hear good things of the cocktails made in the San Francisco speakeasies, but have never been to a speakeasy, or tried a cocktail. I've always been a beer guy, the colder the better."

"And I have always been a wine gal, the whiter the better."

"Well, we would be happy to oblige in both, but our beer kegs are dry and the contents of our wine barrels are colored a shade of red, as told you by Jackson Sebastiani, a tad bit on the dark side, but I do have a couple of my specialty cocktails you may have an interest imbibing in," boasted the bartender. "For you RG, we have *Between the Sheets*, a mix of rum, brandy, Cointreau and lemon juice, although the name, a bit forward with insinuation, is appropriate as a prelude to the evening's end and the bliss of very early morning's beginning. And for you, MB, we have the *French 75*, also appropriately named, given your beauty like that of a Parisian woman, your ivory, shaded skin, emitting the fine aroma of a French perfume. Yes, the *French 75* is you, a cocktail with a mix of Gin, Champagne, syrup and lemon juice, sweet and sparkly, a prelude for your activity between the silk sheets, in your room above, a place to share the bliss, of very early morning's beginning," said the bartender, winking at RG, who managed a sly smile, his unreasonable fear of the bartender's intentions dissipating in the invisible waves of alluring dialogue.

"Well then CH, concoct those spirited and seductive drinks and serve us right away," said Michela, genuinely flattered by the smooth talk of the bartender. "What you recommend is what we need tonight and since my Ronny has an interest in savoring the much talked about cocktails, I'm more than willing to comply with his desires, she said, then whispered "...more than willing," brushing Ronny's thigh lightly, with her long, slim fingers.

"We'll begin with the *French 75*, an elegant, sweet, tasty cocktail befitting a lady of Michela's style. First we start with a tumbler full of cracked ice," said Charles Harrison the Third, "then a full shot and a half of London Dry Gin; a liquor with an interesting history, named long ago in England, the *Mother's Ruin*."

"Why such an awful name?" asked Michela.

"I'm not exactly sure, but some say Gin was originally developed as a form of medicine, others say a cheap form of alcohol for the poor to drink to alleviate their miseries. In either case, the effect on women after excessive use and drunkenness resulted in the neglect of their children, or the effects on women's bodies resulting in not being able to produce children, thus the ruin of mother who is and the ruin of a mother, not to be."

"Why'd they name Gin, Gin?" asked Ronny.

"Berries of the Juniper tree when blended with distilled alcohol gives the Gin its flavor, discovered by some Italian monks needing a way to make tasty their method of man induced meditations centuries ago. The story told me is the name Gin originated as a derived word from the foreign names of Juniper, the French word being *genièvre,* or the Dutch word being g*enever,* originally a form of the Latin word, *Juniperus.* Both France and Holland used Gin for both recreational and medicinal purposes. England and of course, we here, in America, use it primarily for recreational purposes."

"That's a long explanation for a simple name."

"Yeah it is, but it's accurate. So, let's mix this drink and turn it from a *Mother's Ruin,* to a *Mother's Maker,* by sweetening it up a bit and diluting the alcohol content, blended as a sipping drink with less of a damaging effect. We need the lady to enjoy the drink, but not to the point of hurting herself with drunkenness, just to the point of amorous behavior of which the effect would be the making of a baby, which is why I've named it, *Mother's Maker.* I just invented the term *Mother's Maker,* by the way, so if you hear it somewhere, you'll know it began right here in Ryde, by Charles Harrison the Third, its inventor."

"That's a cute term, Charles Harrison the Third, or CB, which is what I thought we agreed to call you, but I already have a baby, now a young man actually, so we don't need to be making babies."

"Well, you'll figure it out, since you probably haven't stopped the pleasurable act of making babies, for fear of having babies. Now, we need to mix the somewhat bitter taste of the Gin with the acidic taste of lemon, so let's take this rather large lemon, slice it in two and squeeze both halves of the yellow chap until all the juice runs out and the lemon runs dry. Now, the sweet part, let's take a full shot of this quality syrup shipped from the land of Maine, throw it in with the Gin and lemon and swirl it a bit."

"Syrup in a drink?" questioned Michela, with some doubt. "That doesn't sound very good."

"Now hold on again MB, you're going to like this. All the women do. Let's put on the finishing touches by shaking the Gin, the lemon juice and the syrup, in this here tumbler with the cracked ice," CB's voice, vibrating with the vigorous shaking of the tumbler, "and strain the liquid through this strainer, into the highball glass filled earlier with the cracked ice, keeping the mixture cool."

"Why do they call it…"

"A highball glass?" asked Charles, interrupting Ronny before he finished the question.

"Yeah, a highball glass."

Charles laughed and said, "I really don't know and will not speculate. I could make something up if you'd like."

"No, go on ahead, I assume you're almost finished making your highball," said Ronny with a smirk.

"Yes I am. Now, the finishing touch. We happen to have a fine bottle of Dom Perignon from northeastern France, named after the monk who blended fine wines a few centuries ago, inventing the cork to keep air from invading the bottles, thus preserving the wine." Charles looked to the roof and stated, "Lord, you know it isn't right that we Americans can't serve cocktails legally in our country, but can legally in other countries, where most alcoholic beverages came to be, from the wonderful creations of nature." Charles sighed, shook his head, looking down to the floor, with a feigned sense of dejection. "Never mind, as always, you don't seem to take the time to listen to me." With a spurt of energy Charles continued. "Let's carry on with the finishing touch. The highball glass is three quarters full, so we take this chilled bottle of Champagne, gently pour until the glass is filled to the brim, plop this cherry on top for feminine effect and as they say in France, *voila,* the *French 75!*" Charles gently pushed the glass across the bar top, opening his palm upward, gesturing Michela to drink. She took the glass, raised it to her lips, took a sip, lowered the glass briefly, raised it once again to her lips; enjoying a much longer sip. Her eyes squinted with pleasure, her lips spread with a satisfied smile. "This is really good. I mean, really, really good. You're going to be very busy tonight, keeping me filled with this M*ommy's Maker.*"

"You mean *Mother's Maker,*" corrected Ronny.

"No Ronny, I mean *Mommy's Maker,* the term Mommy is much more endearing."

"Okay CB, it appears you have satisfied Michela, I mean MB, so now what about me. I hope you're as good, *Between the Sheets* as you are with the *French 75*."

"Never heard a bad thing from my lady friends about my actions between the sheets, but knowing what you mean, I'll take a shot at performing the manlier cocktail, *Between the Sheets,* as your personal bartender."

"Hey bartender, we need a couple of drinks," roared a man from the opposite end of the bar.

"Charles looked to the couple sitting with empty glasses raised, waved and said, "Sorry folks, I need to tend to other guests, give me a few moments and I'll be back to spread the sheets for you." Charles walked to the other end of the bar and began speaking to the thirsty couple.

"What do you think of Charles?" asked Michela.

"He's a pretentious chap," Ronny said with a playful, British accent, "but very knowledgeable of his cocktails. He's well rounded for a railway worker. I wonder where he learned his cocktail making skills and historical references, or maybe he's just fooling us with creative explanations."

"He's certainly doing a good job fooling us, because his explanations at least seem credible. Have some faith Ronny, don't be such a doubter. By the way, I do notice you opening up to the people here in Ryde, workers and guests alike," said Michela.

"Yeah, it's been a surprise which is a good thing. The people we've met so far, such as Lydia, a nice helpful young woman with an eye for attire and Jackson, although a little harsh, he's interesting and has conveyed much of their family history and experiences with their wine business and this man, Charles Harrison the Third, is quite the bartender, even if what he's explained of the cocktail business may be contrived, it's certainly entertaining. I'm learning a lot and looking forward to learning more. I have to tell you, the drudgery of building and growing the strapping business was a definite barrier preventing me from experiencing more in life. Far too many years have gone by with intense work and self imposed social isolation, so thank you for convincing me to take a much needed break. You've been good for me, Michela."

"I didn't want you to end up like my father, who sat in his office year after year, endlessly plotting strategies for his clients and what I considered wasted time spent in monotonous trials in the San Francisco courtrooms, where he focused most of his energy after mother died."

"You did a fine job helping him, sacrificing your life goals by earning his trust as his law associate and I'm proud of you for being such a caring, strong and intelligent woman."

"You give me too much credit, giving birth to Jeff at such a young age and Jeff's irresponsible father leaving us, never to return, was a major factor in my change in life goals. Other than his focus on work, dad spent time helping me and Jeff, after mom died. If it wasn't for Jeff's birth at such a young age, I could've followed in dad's footsteps and been more than an associate in the "Borrus and Associate" law firm, I would've been the other Borrus, in the "Borrus and Borrus" firm, but you know the difficulty of women obtaining a formal education, let alone, a law degree in this day and age."

"I can imagine the difficulty. Frankly, I've always had trouble believing a woman could perform the same work as a man, but meeting you and learning of your abilities, you've changed me. I'm impressed. You've learned so much being an associate. You're already a lawyer of sorts behind the scenes, just not formally in practice or title and for that I'm proud, and I believe your father is very proud of you," complimented Ronny.

"Are the two of you ready to get *Between the Sheets*?" interrupted Charles, arriving from the joyful conversation with the thirsty couple at the other end of the bar, continuing his playful insinuation with the cocktail's name.

"I am," said Michela.

"So am I," agreed Ronny.

"Alrighty then, this cocktail will be a little easier to make."

"I'm feeling a little dry and need to keep up with MB, she's already drank half of her *French 75,* so now it's a French 37 and a half, so let's hurry and get *Between the Sheets,* before she gets down to a French 18 and a quarter," pleaded Ronny, playfully.

"Okay then, we'll slip you under the covers as quickly as possible. Let's use the same tumbler used for MB's cocktail. Now, the ingredients for this drink are manlier and the taste not as sweet as the *French 75.* We have your rum from Cuba, a spirit from the Bacardi family, an interesting history of their rum company to be told, but we're in a hurry, so I'll forgo that tale for another time. We'll throw two shots of Bacardi into the tumbler and here we have this excellent brandy from France, which we'll throw one shot of that smooth warm liquid into the tumbler as well, one shot of Cointreau, a fine liquor also from France, all smuggled, of course, through our normal smuggling channels."

"And how are they smuggled?" asked Ronny, again curious of the business of illicit liquor distribution.

"Smuggled in many ways," winked Charles, unwilling to provide the secret information to a curious stranger. "So, moving on, we mix in the tumbler all these manmade, liquor creations from the ingredients found in nature, I might add, throw in this crushed ice from the scoop here," explained Charles, scooping the rapidly, melting ice from the crystal bowl on the back bar counter, "squeeze the juice from this lemon wedge, shake it, strain into the chilled cocktail glass, we'll hold off on the cherry to remove the aura of femininity, by the way, and *voila,* we have *Between the Sheets,* awaiting MB's entry under Ronny's covers, through her soon to be consumed, *French 75.*"

Ronny raised the cocktail glass, the scent of the exotic mix reached him before the taste elevated his senses to a state of mild euphoria. "You did good CH and now we're happily prepped and ready to mingle. We'll be keeping you busy tonight with requests for many refills and hopefully learn more of the French and their mastery of these scintillating beverages."

"And it was certainly a pleasure serving the two of you and I'm more than willing to convey the mastery of the French and their contribution to the creation of pleasures of sensual concoctions, from the fruits provided in nature. Enjoy the evening," said Charles Harrison the Third, grabbing two cocktail glasses by their stems, moving to an impatient couple, two couples down, their arms waving frantically, in dire need of spirited cocktails.

Michela and Ronny turned, viewing the layout of the speakeasy. The elevated stage held stands in orderly rows, armed with the musical weapons of a sparkling brass trumpet, trombone and saxophone, silver clarinet, drum and a short, walnut stained, Steinway, upright piano, all standing at attention waiting for the evening's musical battle. The dance floor spread from the stage to the dining area and on the slick, varnished, wood floor stood men in suits of blacks and whites and women in flapper dresses of greens, purples and reds, hair bobbed tightly in popular style. They all laughed and talked, enjoying the warmth of friendly conversation. Light, jazz melodies floated from the black man gently tapping the Steinway piano keys and from the white woman, caressing the barrel of the clarinet.

"The couple on stage is playing beautifully. The music is light and airy. I'm looking forward to the rest of the band playing a more upbeat tempo."

"Knowing your love of dancing, the instruments on the stage will provide the thrusting and pounding that'll keep you hopping and bopping and hopefully, not dropping on the floor. Until then, let's find a table before all these people standing and talking begin sitting down." Ronny scanned the room, paused, pointing to the open doors. "Over there, the table by the glass doors, leading to the area by the pool, there's a large, standing fan, blowing a steady breeze, shuffling this stifling heat." Ronny reached to Michela's hand, leading her through the maze of small, round tables clothed in white, surrounded by eloquently carved, wooden chairs, the red, seat cushions embroidered in gold. They sat in the chairs with their backs to the glass doors, their view spanning the expanse of the dining area, the dance floor and the black, lacquer bar, crowded with couples. Placed in the center of the table stood a svelte, oblong, amber vase and within the vase, a single, white rose, bloomed proudly.

"I can't handle the heat," complained Ronny, removing his coat, hanging it on the back of the chair. "Let's sit and feel the breeze from the fan." Michela sat, followed by Ronny, who placed his forearms on the table. "We'll need another drink," he said, raising his hand to the waiter. "Young man, we're going to need another round of the *French 75 and* a *Between the Sheets*, bartender Charles will know how to make them."

"Yes sir," said the waiter, "we'll get them for you right away. We have cigarettes as well, would you like a few?"

"No, I don't think so," he said hesitantly, "I quit a few years ago and don't really need to start again." As the waiter turned to walk away, Ronny changed his mind. "Wait a minute, make that two *French 75*s and two *Between the Sheet*s, given the heat in this room, those cocktails are going to disappear quickly and you know, bring me a cigarette. I may want to smoke one, for nostalgia's sake."

The waiter smiled, nodded, turned and walked towards the bar. Michela and Ronny engaged in light conversation, laughing over banal jokes; picking at the steamed, Delta crawdads silently cuddling with one another, in one of the three bowls placed on the table.

"These tiny lobsters are sure tasty."

"They certainly are, but I wonder if we should be eating before the other guests arrive."

"Shouldn't matter, they're here for a reason, to be eaten," said Michela, picking one between her slim fingers, raising her face upward and plopping it down her mouth.

The music slowed, then evaporated in the smoke filled room, the white woman placed the silver clarinet in the stand, speaking into the microphone. "We'll be taking a break during the dinner portion of our event and begin again with the rest of the band after you've all dined, so please enjoy your meal and we'll return with the musicians' playing the brass section on this evening's, journey of jazz." The crowd of couples began to move to the tables from their clusters of drinking and talking, searching for places of comfort. Two couples walked towards Ronny and Michela's table.

"Mind if we sit?" asked the husky man in a black suit and scuffed, black boots of cowboy style, the side of his cheek showing a bump, where a lump of tobacco squatted.

"Not at all," responded Ronny. "This spot is the coolest in the room, which isn't saying much, because it's still hot as hell, but you may as well join us." Ronny stood, as did Michela, welcoming the man and woman standing by his side.

"My name's Booker, Booker B Bosley and this here's my wife, Carla. We're pleased to meet you and thanks for saving the spot." Before they sat, the second couple walked behind Booker B, with the same question.

"Mind if we sit? We'd like to cool down with the man made breeze, since this scorching heat isn't letting up."

"You're just as welcome. Although the fan is working, it isn't cooling as much as we'd like, but please have a seat. We don't own the table," said Ronny, with a polite smile and a slow gesture towards the chairs.

"My name's William Vandenberg and this is my lovely wife, Clarissa."

They shook hands and exchanged pleasantries, settling into their chairs, marking the beginning of their newfound friendships. The waiter returned holding the platter in one hand, the glasses filled with vibrant color, balanced precariously.

"Here we are sir, the two *French 75s* and the two *Between the Sheets,* as you've ordered and the cigarette you've requested." The waiter set the cocktails on the table in front of Ronny and Michela, placing the cigarette next to the cocktail glass, bumping the glass, spilling some of *Between the Sheets* on the white tablecloth, a few drops wetting the cigarette.

"No worries," said Ronny with a short laugh. "It's probably a warning for me not to smoke." He took the cigarette, lightly blew on the moist end to dry it, placing it in his front shirt pocket.

"Boy," said Booker B gruffly. "We're gonna need something to drink to pump us up, whaddya recommend?"

"Why don't you try the Sebastiani Red?" interjected Michela. "We met Jackson, the man who owns a winery in

Sonoma and boasts of the taste and effect on those who try it. We're going to have a bottle after we finish our fancy cocktails."

"Well, I don't know. We normally enjoy wine for dinner with our meat, but I haven't had the pleasure of a fine, red wine for a while, since this Prohibition brou-ha-ha. But hell, why not? Boy, bring us a bottle, in fact bring us three bottles, one for each of us couples, I'm sure we'll take good care of 'em."

"Yes sir, I'll bring them right away and you can address me as Peter, I prefer that more than I do the word, Boy."

"Okay, Boy, I might call you your real name goin' forward, but I don't make no guarantees."

Ronny, irritated by the disrespectful Booker B, wondered what the rest of the evening had in store for him, wondered if he could tolerate sitting through a meal with what appeared to be potentially riddled with impolite conversation. "So what do you do for a living Booker B?" asked Ronny, hoping to entice a more festive dialogue.

Booker B grabbed an empty glass from the table, put it by his side and spat a brown wad of tobacco into the glass, the bulk settling to the bottom. "Well Ronny, I own a farm, a very big, cotton farm, south of Fresno, in the town of Tulare, miles and miles of cotton, as far as the eye can see."

"How did you get to own the land?" asked William Vandenberg, joining the camaraderie of the table.

"Inherited it. My family's from Georgia, the outskirts of Macon, came after the end of the civil war. My grandfather was one of those confederates who left in shame to

California, since he couldn't stomach being a part of a Yankee nation. He didn't consider California a part of the Yankee North, so came out West. He felt more comfortable around them foreigners; the Chinks, Japs, Spics and Flips, leftover from the missions and Gold Rush and wherever the hell they came from. Somehow, he finagled a lot of land near Tulare Lake and planted cotton. Now we use Spics and Okies; the Okie from the dust bowl in Oklahoma, to pick and pack. Cheap labor, but not cheaper than the free niggers he had picking cotton in Georgia."

Ronny's hair bristled on the back of his neck, but restrained from commenting on the racist references spoken by Booker B.

Michela, Carla and Clarissa carried on a conversation, laughing under the loud, brusk voice of Booker B.

Attempting to change subjects, Ronny asked, "So what do you think of the Delta, this is quite an escape from the drudgery of daily living isn't it?"

"I like it, especially the water. Lots of water these Delta people have captured with this ingenious, levee system built by the Chinks at a cheap price, I bet. I'm gonna get a lot of this water funneled to the San Joaquin valley, where I've purchased more land ready to be sown, grown, picked and packed."

"Don't you have your own water in Tulare?" questioned William.

"Not anymore. We did once, but we're draining Tulare Lake dry, needing the water to irrigate the lands we had and to irrigate the lands we've acquired. We need more water for those lands we will acquire in the coming years.

The water utilities serving the growing orchards and homes in the Los Angeles area are stealing water, from the Owens valley and other water sources, leaving little for us in lower Central California. They're even talking about getting water from the Delta, knowing they're gonna need it sometime in the future. We lost the political battles trying to prevent them from gaining water rights, but whaddya gonna do? There's lots of money backing the acquisition of water for Southern California. A lot more money than I have. I couldn't compete."

Ronny turned to Michela, catching her eye, rolling his eyes, conveying his feeling of consternation. He grabbed his cocktail, gulping the drink, leaving the glass empty.

Noticing the empty drink placed on the table, Booker B said with feigned concern, "Slow down there Ronny, you're gonna get too far ahead of us, we don't want you getting sloppy drunk now, do we?"

Michela leaned in front of Ronny sensing his discomfort with Booker B's demeanor, saving him from answering by asking Booker B a question. "I overheard you mentioning you're going to attempt to divert water from the Delta, for your farm's needs in the Central Valley. It must be a really, big farm. How are you going to do that?"

"Well little lady…"

"It's Michela, Booker B."

"Well little lady, it's like this. I've got a political connection in Sacramento, the primary reason I'm here. My wife and I came here to enjoy the event we heard about from the Senator we met with yesterday in Sacramento. As you can see," Booker B pointed to his boots, "I didn't have the proper shoes; so although the Senator was able to lend me this ill fitting suit, he had no shoes of the kind needed for this evening's event that fit my big feet."

"So why did you meet with the Senator?" asked Michela, becoming more interested in what she was beginning to believe to be an unworthy cause, formulated by Booker B.

"To get water rights and allocation of government funds and rights-of-way for a canal to be built from the Delta to my lands in Tulare and Fresno Counties; to pay the Senator to guarantee the appropriation of these rights and funds to build the canal."

"Isn't that something the people need to vote on?" asked William Vandenberg, engaging in the emerging debate.

"Well now, normally the people in California would have to vote on a bill, or a measure, or whatever the hell you call it, but we're doing it back door, which the Senator can do through his connections in the state and federal governments."

"But that isn't honest," interjected Ronny.

"Not only isn't it honest, it isn't legal," added Michela.

Peter, the young waiter, arrived with the three bottles of the Sebastiani Red, announcing with a big smile, "The wine has arrived for you happy couples. I've already pulled the corks and am ready to pour, if you're ready to accommodate."

Carla perked when Peter arrived, eagerly saying, "Please pour me a glass."

Booker B took command adding, "Hell, pour everyone a glass, leave the bottles at the table and we'll drink the rest when we get to it."

Peter began pouring the wine into Carla's glass. "Dinner will be served shortly. We have fresh venison from the California mule deer hunted in the Sierra Nevada foothills and duck shot in the marshes of Yolo County. Included will be pear salad made of lettuce with thin slices of fresh, Delta Bartlett pears, fresh, sautéed, Delta asparagus, baked potatoes with butter from the dairy farms in Petaluma, and for dessert, vanilla bean ice cream. You have the option of coffee, but given the heat of the evening, a cooler cocktail, or maybe, the Sebastiani Red may suffice." The table remained silent while Peter poured the wine into the six wine glasses sitting on the table.

"Booker B, I want to get back to the issue of your goal of draining the water from the Delta, to serve your personal needs in Tulare," stated Michela, firmly. Ronny sat drinking the second glass of *Between the Sheets,* happy to let Michela take the lead on this argument. While lying in bed with her, he had proofread many of the briefs, dissertations and arguments she had written for her father, regarding property cases for the city of San Francisco and shipping rights legislation, for the ports and docks of San Francisco bay. Ronny knew Booker B was going to get a lashing on this issue.

"It's clear what you're doing isn't legal."

"Well little lady..."

"It's Michela, Booker B."

"Well little lady," repeated Booker B, contemptuously ignoring her request. "It don't matter if it's legal, my connections and money's gonna make it legal, or make it work around the law, much like you and me and all of us here sitting at the table are doing, by breaking the law, drinking this wine."

"That's different Booker B. 'We here sitting at the table', are breaking a law that most in this country don't agree with, a law that infringes on our individual personal consumption habits only, not infringing on all of the people, as a whole. You're talking about stealing water to grow your crops and expand your land to grow even more crops, to profit personally. Your effort will cause a significant negative effect on the people in Northern California, specifically those in the Delta. These people need the water for their reservoirs, crops and wildlife, to allow for their own economic expansion, to serve their general well-being."

Booker B shifted uncomfortably in his seat, highly agitated with the assertive nature of Michela's diatribe. "Who are you?" asked Booker B. "What makes you think, little lady, that you can harangue me with your opinions in defense of this useless marsh and swamp region, you people believe is some kind of Garden of Eden? What I'm doing with the water will not just benefit me, but will benefit those who'll indirectly use my products. Cotton will be produced at a lower price than what any other grower can provide. I'm beginning to think another civil war of sorts will start with the Southern Californians fighting with you Northern Californians, to own the water and here I am in the middle, just trying to get my share. I feel like my confederate granddaddy fighting for what is rightfully ours and to boot, fighting with a lady."

"And just like your confederate granddaddy, you're going to slip away from this state like a defeated, confederate, hunting dog, with its tail tucked between its legs," reacted Michela, laughing harshly at the end of her statement.

"And let me tell you Booker B," added Ronny, happy with Michela's argument and proud of her stance, "this little lady isn't so little in spirit. She's like a bulldog protecting her bone and has experience dealing with legal issues of this nature. She's a feisty woman, living in a male dominated society, with the character and grit to overcome that irritating, nineteenth century, obstacle."

Michela squeezed Ronny's knee lightly under the table, appreciative of his kind defense.

A flurry of activity occurred with the waiters and waitresses entering the dining area. Peter and a young waitress steered towards their table, twirled and whirled, with platters in hand, full of venison, duck and the other side dishes mentioned. "Here we are," said Peter, smiling cheerfully. "I hope you're enjoying yourselves talking of happy things during your wait. You can choose your preference of entrée, of duck or deer, pick the sides you'd like and fill the plates in front of you."

Ronny and Michela; Booker B and Carla; and William and Clarissa, all stared down at their plates in silence.

Peter felt the tension, hurriedly placing the platters in the middle of the table, as did the young waitress. "If you'd like anything else, please let me know and we'll accommodate your wishes."

The table remained silent for a few tense moments, Ronny finally saying, "Thank you Peter, I believe we're fine with what you've provided. If we need anything else, we'll let you know."

Clarissa, silent during the cantankerous debate, feeling the need to lift the table's spirits, raised the platter of venison, handing it to Booker B. "Would you like some venison Mr. B, it looks delicious and here everybody, can we share the food they've made for us? And honey, why don't you tell them what you're doing with your exciting business, rather than the talk about the water these water people and this cotton person seem to be fighting over?"

William responded, clearly reluctant to share his background. He was in the speakeasy to have fun, not to discuss business. "No Clarissa, I don't believe anyone would be interested in what I'm doing. We should move on and speak of fun things and enjoy the food in front of us, and the wine waiting to be drunk."

Carla joined Clarissa with her attempt to lighten the mood. "William, we would like to hear of what you're doing in California. We'd all be interested, wouldn't we, Booker?"

Booker B grunted, slapping cuts of venison on his plate, grumpily handing the platter to Ronny. As the table clinked and clanked, from the noise of the platters and dishes being shared, William began his story.

"Clarissa and I are from New York City, where I'm a manager for Pan American Airways, a company run by a gentleman named, Juan Trippe. After a number of mergers with small mail carriers, the airline has grown and controls the routes from Key West to Cuba, Mexico and the

Caribbean, delivering mail and small cargo on behalf of the government and we're planning to launch even more routes throughout South America." William, unsure if anyone was listening, ceased speaking, cut into his duck and began eating.

After taking a drink of the Sebastiani Red and chomping on a chunk of venison, Booker B pointed his fork at William, "Go on Will, continue, what you're saying is interesting, more interesting than land, cotton and water, which appears to be subjects that ruffle the feathers of some at this table."

"Yeah William, we'd like to know why you're here out west, since most of your business is in the Caribbean and the lower Americas. The planes today can't fly from the east coast to the west coast without airports, they don't have enough fuel to make it all this way," added Ronny.

William placed the fork on his plate and began disclosing Pan Am's plans. "Your point about planes today unable to fly long distances is correct. We don't yet plan on offering service from the east coast to the west coast. Our plans are transoceanic. To fly across oceans, we deploy a strategy called, 'island hopping', a strategy proven with flights from Florida through the Caribbean islands and on to Mexico. Planes will eventually be designed to fly over land, long distances, but we're looking to provide services over water, to locations people and mail need to go. I'm researching the feasibility of establishing a commercial airport, somewhere in the San Francisco bay area. Maybe even in the bay itself."

"But there's already an airport in San Francisco, Mills Airport and you can't have an airplane in the bay anyway, airports need land," offered Michela, interjecting herself in the discussion, her edge slowly smoothing from the acerbic confrontation with Booker B.

"Pan Am has been working with a couple of airplane manufacturers testing newly designed flying boats, that takeoff and land on water," explained William.

"Why the hell do we need a flying boat?" questioned Booker B, with his usual, unpleasant demeanor.

"People don't think they need a flying boat, since there is no perceived need, but we're going to create the need, provide a service, offering the service to fill that perceived need and make it a real need. You know that saying, 'Perception is Reality'. That's our plan, to turn that statement from what our clients don't perceive into a perception that is truly a reality. Our plans are to fly from the California coast to Asia, landing near islands in harbors and coral reef lagoons, throughout the Pacific that are setup with fueling stations, stocked with fuel transported by ships."

"Still doesn't answer the question of why you need a plane that flies and floats," argued Booker B.

"My guess is the islands from here to Asia aren't large enough for a traditional landing strip and the funds to build airports wouldn't be cost effective enough for Pan Am to make a profit," said Ronny, interested in the logistics of yet another business, the business of flying.

"You're right Ronny. Along with Pan Am's strategy of opening transportation, not just for mail, but for larger cargo and for people on business who desire to explore interesting places like Hawaii and those in the Far East, like Shanghai, Singapore, Hong Kong and Macao. Our plans are to provide rapid transportation, for businesses on behalf of companies in the United States, and for people on business and wealthy tourists. It takes far too long to travel across the ocean on a ship."

"Those are some pretty damn high and mighty goals there William, this flying across the ocean business," said Booker B, with continued doubt.

"Juan is a high and mighty leader and I feel good about putting my money on him and his 'damn high and mighty' venture. We are going to succeed," pronounced William, emphatically.

"Not meaning to be argumentative, but I reluctantly agree with Booker B," said Michela, turning to Booker B with a crooked smile of concession. "You'll need to secure the land somewhere along the bay in San Francisco for your originating airport, find and plot the islands from here to Asia, setup some kind of airport to receive the planes, even if they land on the water, setup the islands with some form of refueling structure, build and test the planes and secure all the rights, accommodating all the laws governing the business; not to mention identifying providers of fuel and negotiations with the international governments to allow the use of their land for the service."

William sat silent for a few moments with a look of surprise and with a smile said, "That's our long term plan and yes, all the things you've noted will need to be dealt with. We're planning to operate the service in about five years. You're a bright woman, Michela, maybe you'd consider working with Pan Am as our San Francisco representative. We also plan to raise money, to do all of those things you've mentioned and more."

Michela sat blushing, flattered by William's recognition of her ability to think through the logistics of the flying plane business and by the verbal job consideration. She quietly said, "Thank you William. I'm not doubtful of Pan Am's ability to make this work, just commenting on the huge amount of work, the 'damn high and mighty goals', as Booker B puts it. We can talk about the employment idea later. I'm always open to new experiences."

The air of the table no longer heavy with the weight of conflict, lightened in the thick heat, the couples spoke of their more pleasurable dreams and goals of personal fulfillment. For Ronny, the dream of exploring the far reaching coast and the warm, bioluminescent, blue-green glowing waters of the Sea of Cortez; for Michela, the dream of exploring the rugged coast and smashing, white waves of Northern California and the joy of the quaint community of Mendocino, emitting the pleasant scent of pine; for Booker B, the consistent dream of cotton and water and making money; for his wife Carla, the dream of seeing Booker B's dreams of making money made true; for William Vandenberg, the dream of exploring the exotic islands of the Pacific; for Clarissa Vandenberg the dream of the carefree cafes, cigarettes and Absinthe, consumed on the banks of the Parisian, River Seine; all dreams extending beyond the boundaries of their existence. The conversations finally glided smooth across the table, through the warmth of Sebastiani Red.

The band arrived slowly on stage, the black man softly massaged the keys of the piano. The white woman's slim fingers softly sung the notes of the clarinet. Guests at the tables began moving about, smoking cigarettes, sipping cocktails, dancing loosely to the gentle music. The tall handsome mustache man, seen earlier at the threshold where he and Michela's eyes met, began dancing with a woman after asking her partner for the right and pleasure. The mustache man, smooth with movements, showed a grace and elegance, displaying skill and talent. The dance ended, then began again with the brass section of the band, increasing the tempo with the upbeat thrusting and thumping the crowd had waited for. The mustache man approached another woman, once again asking permission and began dancing to the rapidly, pounding tune.

Ronny leaned towards Michela, whispering in her ear, "That young man is certainly bold." Ronny watched the antics of mustache man, uncertain of whether he approved of mustache man's method of dancing with the women partners of other men.

Michela, who also had been watching mustache man, commented, "I see no harm in what he's doing. He appears to politely ask the men for permission to dance with their partners and the women seem to enjoy dancing with such a skilled dancer. Why don't we join the couples on the dance floor?"

Tired from the day and evening's events, and the hyper social interaction he wasn't accustomed to, and reluctant to dance fearing the embarrassment of his awkward dance movements, Ronny said, "Not now Michela, let's wait until I feel the music and rid myself of the burdens of the cocktails and Sebastiani Red clouding my thoughts."

Michela patted Ronny's hand resting on the table. "When you're ready, Ronny." Watching the dancers quietly, Michela sat; her knees and head gently moving to the beat. After two songs, the mustache man headed towards their table, addressing Ronny politely, "Excuse me sir, may I have the honor of dancing with your lovely wife?"

Michela turned to Ronny, her face filled with eagerness and silent pleading. Ronny knew Michela would enjoy her time dancing with the mustache man, relieving his pressure of having to dance. "I see no reason not to allow my girlfriend, Michela, to dance with you, although she doesn't need my permission. She's not my wife. We've both watched you this evening and find your style of dancing to be, shall we say, enticing. Have fun. Michela, you dance to this song. I'll take a break by the door and catch a breeze."

Michela walked away, moved to the floor and began dancing slowly with mustache man, holding her loosely around the waist. Ronny leaned against the glass door, craving the cigarette brought from his pocket, a craving not had since he'd quit the habit when Ricky was born. He remembered that day, anxiously sitting with Lori in the waiting room, holding Lori's tiny hand, patiently listening to her questions of the impending birth.

"Is mommy Okay?"

The drum began,
a slow rolling beat, lightly pounding,
Michela's head, hips and shoulders, gently moving.

"What will we name it?"
Michela sideways, 'stache man stepping.

 "Can we take it home today?"
The beating drum, somewhat quickening.

"Can we play with it?"
The drum rapidly peaked, lightly pounding.

Ronny's eyes, on Michela moving,
     cigarette from pocket, slowly pulling,
     past happy memories, mildly struggling.

"I shot your cat eye marble with my steely!"

Alto clarinet, drum's sonorous beating,
tenor saxophone, long low rumbling.

"I'm Padded Man";
   soft white pillows,
      'bound 'round Ricky;
         loosely binding.

Michela moved sultrily, slowly twirling,
low drone saxophone, melodiously joining.

"The stairs don't hurt," Ricky laughing,
    rolling down steps, slowly bumping.

    Auburn hair, shoulder's flowing,
    trumpet and saxophone, proudly bursting,
    moving beat, rapidly pounding.

Ronny;
    Sebastiani Red, slowly drinking,
        clouded mind, warmly thinking.

    Band's loud song, smoothly thrusting,
    'gainst 'stache man's chest, strongly bouncing,
    band's bumpy rhythm, strongly pulling.

"Tell us the story of alien brother Smorkel,"
    "of alien sister GmorshGmorsh,"
    "how they were stuck on earth,"
    "how they 'scape from earth."

Ronny's cigarette between,
    fingers rolling,
        looking to Michela wondrously gazing.

    Jazz piano's sound, graceful erupting,
    smooth skinned arms, upward flying,
    long slim legs, outward jumping.

Purple bay fireworks, colors sparkling.
    Tina;

"I love you Ronny," shoulder snuggling.

Trumpet's noise, three bursts blasting,
Michela's teal pearl, lightly bouncing.

Ronny sighs,
    continues drinking,
        liquid grape,
            in mind still swarming.

The music flows, melodies rolling,
    trumpet bursts, instant thumping,
    saxophone bursts, long low droning,
    trombone blasts, proudly echoing,
    clarinet tunes, sweetly flowing,
    steady flowing drum, piano beating.

    Then;
      Suddenly;
        trumpet,
        saxophone,
        trombone,
        clarinet,
   silent falling.

The drum beat slowed; quiet thumping,
    saxophone restarts; long tune dragging,
    both smooth melodies; mildly singing,
    Michela across the floor; slowly moving.

Then,

> *saxophone,*
>> *drum,*
>>> *slowly falling.*

Then,

> *The brief lull boomed;*
>> *trumpet's blasting,*
>>> *dance floor's frantic erupting,*
>>> *Auburn hair smoothly flashing,*
>>> *beats of the drum loudly thundering,*
>>> *clarinet thrusts sharply screaming*
>>> *tears from Ronny slowly forming.*

> *Then,*
>> *harmonious bursts, instant stopping,*
>> *beats of the drum, slowly quieting,*
>> *dance floor slows, gentle pacing*
>> *Ronny's tears, gradual flowing.*

>> *Then,*
>> *Again,*
>>> *The trumpet thrust a loud long note,*
>>> *the saxophone strung a high pitched tune,*
>>> *the drum pounded a quickening beat,*
>>> *one final thrust,*
>>> *one final time,*
>>>> *the band fell silent.*

The instant calm smoothed Ronny's spiralling thoughts; he gazed at Michela, admiring her beauty; her long auburn hair adorning her shoulders; her blue eyes sparkling; her skin shining ivory smooth; her indigo dress shifting; shades of blue, violet, gray.

"Was it right for me to turn from my family?" he mumbled, feeling discomfort from his wife's last words when stepping out their door that misty San Francisco evening, remembering that moment, one year ago that day, their daughter Lori pulling his shirt. Sadly. Softly. Silently. Imploring him to stay.

"If you leave us Ronny, It'll tear a hole in your soul."

Shifting his teary gaze from Michela, he now knew. Ronny walked to the Ryde water tower, leaned against the black steel trestle, lit the cigarette and took a deep puff while gazing over the rows of corn at the stars in the moonlit darkness.

The Dream

Wong Chow saw them again. Smiling and waving from the railing of the steamboat, they were as he remembered them. Sister, brother, father and mother dressed in clean white clothing. This time the river was different. In place of the surrounding lands of Big River, the banks and lands were of the Pearl River in China. Large, blue mountains displaced the lavender sky; wispy, thin, white clouds stood motionless above the peaks. But the dock on the Pearl and the dock at Courtland were one. Chinese junks and California Delta steamboats floated up and down river. Pear crates with colored labels, English words and Chinese script were stacked along the pier waiting to be loaded. Men and women in western clothing and Chinese clothing strolled along the riverbank. It ended the same way. The steamboat passed the dock and continued upriver, his family smiling and waving. Upon awakening, Wong Chow yearned for the ending when the steamboat docked and his family embraced him. "I am getting closer to home," Wong Chow murmured. After forty years away from the Pearl, his dream was changing, his homeland blending with the familiar fixtures of Big River.

SATURDAY NIGHT

Tony flicked the burning cigarette over the bridge rail
watching the glowing ember sail and fall to the green river
below. Behind, the lights on the smokestacks and
buildings from the factories of Antioch and Pittsburg
defined the shore of the Sacramento River; piercing the
lightly darkening, August sky with yellow, blue and white.
He opened the car door and sat in the driver's seat. The
drawbridge lowered into place. The deep hum of rubber on
steel rumbled as Tony slowly drove across, where
farmlands of the Delta revealed tules, weeds and crops on
each side of the road. Steering the Buick on the flatland
beyond the bridge and to the levee, Tony steered right and
upward; blue-green water reached the levee's brim on the
river side of the road, leading a winding path along the
farmlands. The river's glassy shell lay bordered by the
levee's banks; its surface shimmered like sparkling
diamonds from the sun's bright rays; flashing crystal
lights, in a seemingly timeless array. After miles of silence,
Paul, from the passenger seat exclaimed, "Isn't the river
great? We're lucky it's so close. There's plenty to see, boats

and bridges and ducks, and hey, look, up ahead, by the side of the road, a rabbit."

Tony looked to the scruffy, brown rabbit standing upright on its haunches, arms and paws raised, the rabbit's eyes looking towards the car. "Yeah, I see him. He's ready to dart across the road, not sure what he's waiting for but he better not wait too long. They say rabbits tend to tempt fate, to dart in front of trucks and cars as in a game, a race teasing the driver. I don't think he'll be the victor in a race with me. He sure has a lot more to lose than I do."

"I've never heard that about rabbits," wondered Paul. "It doesn't make sense that an animal would be so daring."

"They say their brains are smaller than ours. Rabbits don't think like we do."

"Who are they?"

"They are the people who know about them rabbits," answered Tony, jokingly.

The car rumbled to where the rabbit stood, when ten feet away the rabbit hopped; darting past the front of the Buick, reaching the land side of the levee.

"What did I tell you," said Tony, slapping his hand against the steering wheel. "That bonehead rabbit did it. He took a chance and ran right in front. I could've turned him into a flat, rabbit pancake."

Paul turned and looked back, the rabbit stood on his haunches, looked toward the rear of the car, his head angled upward with pride. "Yeah. I guess their brains are bigger than you think. Ol' Jack rabbit appears to be taunting you. Gotta hand it to him. That was a ballsy move." The Buick slowed to Three Mile Bridge, the bridge drawn across the slow currents of Three Mile Slough, two large fishing boats approached to pass under.

"Crap," said Tony. "It's gonna take a long time to get to where we need to go." He stopped the Buick, opened and slammed the door and stood leaning against the front fender. "How do people here deal with the bridges always drawing? Gotta be damn frustrating."

Paul stepped from the Buick on the passenger side. "Relax. We'll get there, take a deep breath, waiting is good for you. People here are low-key because of their focus on farming. Their days are long and their movements slow. A few moments waiting creates little stress. Unlike us, they don't have to deal with the complexity and noise living in larger towns," said Paul.

"You relax. You know what I need," said Tony, looking towards Mt. Diablo.

"I know what you want, not what you need. Enjoy the beauty of the river, the scent, the warm breeze. It's worth the wait. Why are you staring at the mountain?" questioned Paul, with interest.

Tony stood silent for a moment, looked to the mountain, took a pack of cigarettes from his back pocket, pulled one and lit the end. He looked down to his shoes, took a deep puff and with head cocked at an angle turned to his brother. "I see a big tit pointing upward, a woman lying on her back, the biggest, damn breast in the whole damn valley reaching to the heavens." Tony paused and took another puff from his cigarette. "There is a native legend in these parts of Queen Latita." Tony paused again, continuing, "Yeah that's it, Latita, the mountain is her tit, the rain water flowing, like the milk of Queen Mother Latita, from the peak like a giant nipple nourishing the lands below, including the lands where we're standing right here in the Delta. I shit you not. And what do you see brother?"

Paul burst into laughter at the description. "I don't see a tit, although I understand how you perceive that image from this bridge. However, from Pittsburg, the mountain actually shows two peaks, one slightly larger than the other, sort of uneven, sometimes like a woman's breasts they say. With regard to the breast milk flowing, that's a creative story but I don't buy it. I see something more pure, a monument, a large, peaked mountain standing prominently along the horizon, green hills at its forefront spread with a yellow carpet of flowers, tall, brown grasses waving in the breeze, trees dotting the landscape with brown and green, the scene covered in a translucent haze, the sky covered haphazardly with wispy, shapeless clouds, confused by its appearance."

Tony looked up at the mountain and after a brief moment sighed, shook his head back and forth sideways, and said, "Wow, now that's some flowery language. I don't know what the last part of what you said means, that translucent part, but the phrase sounds like some kind of poetry. Paul, you really gotta get laid. Might help you think better. Might change your mood a bit. You seem a bit deep today. In fact, since Dad and Mike died, you've been acting strangely."

"Come on," said Paul, testily. "It's only been a year since they disappeared. You may be able to shake it off but

I can't. It's been difficult losing a father and older brother. Maybe you can handle it better than I, but I've been more introspective, which isn't a bad thing."

"I haven't shaken it off. I miss them too. I just handle it differently. The less I talk about it, the less I hurt. I think about them every day. I just don't show my emotions like you do. I often wonder what happened to them. Do you think they'll ever find them where they were lost in the waters along the Monterey coast? They found the parts of the boat, but no bodies. They just can't disappear. We know they're dead. Will their bodies ever turn up?"

"Those are a lot of questions, Tony. It's highly unlikely they'll find them, it's been too long. That's what's so sad. We can't bury them with a proper church burial. Dad and Mike, more than likely, became fish food, which is ironic, since they've provided for our family selling the fish they caught to the canneries, for the canneries to sell as food to other families. It's a revenge by the fish soldiers winning a small battle in the war with the family soldiers, like Dad and Mike, who slaughtered them in droves," said Paul.

"I don't see Dad and Mike as soldiers, they're just trying to make a living, but the idea of the remnants of their bodies decaying in a mass of pulp at the bottom of the ocean is not appealing, and although I'm religious," said Tony, "you don't need a church burial to honor those in your family that have died. You can honor them and bury 'em in your mind."

"You're right about not requiring a church burial, but your admission of being religious burdens me. I'm beginning to have doubts of the existence of God," said

Paul. "If God existed, God wouldn't have allowed Dad and Mike to die. God hasn't proven to be a good God as professed by the church and in the bible. In fact, there are stories and passages in the Bible that indicate at times he is an evil God, filled with threats of punishment and death, for not following his rules."

"The rules in the Bible are God's words. It's God's will. You can't go against the will of God," stated Tony.

"God's will and God's words? The words in the Bible are the words of man interpreted supposedly as words told to someone by God. The Bible consists of many stories written by many different men and maybe even women, some stories patched together, some not included written by others, many stories of which were borrowed from tales and myths of other cultures, other times. So you believe they're God's actual words?" questioned Paul. "Let's say they're God's words that communicate the messages of God's will, then why would God will the death of Dad and Mike, both good men, never harming anyone? The God's will excuse is the same excuse given by religious people who can't explain difficult things occurring in life, negative things that can't be explained or attributed to any reason, but can be explained as the will of God. That explanation doesn't cut it for me," said Paul, clearly agitated by the thought of Tony believing in what Paul believed to be a myth.

"But believing makes me feel good," said Tony, Paul's non beliefs swirling uncomfortably in his head. "And what you're saying confuses me."

The drawbridge lowered the steel portion of the bridge

road, the giant chains extending from the twin towers clanked noisily until the road settled in place. Paul and Tony entered the Buick and drove across the slough. The Buick rambled on for a few miles, the engine clunking, interrupting the quiet of the river, once again approaching a drawbridge, once again raised for passing boats, a solitary sign pointing to the town of Rio Vista in the direction crossing the bridge.

"It's a good thing we aren't going that way, another bridge drawn, three in a row, must be a record. We'll continue straight along the road on this side hugging the river and get to Locke eventually. I didn't think it would take this long," said Tony, impatiently.

Tony flicked his burning cigarette through the window, the glowing tip bounced on the road behind, bursting in a red, orange and yellow spray of embers. Immediately grabbing another cigarette from the pack, he lit it from a match pulled from behind his ear, took a deep puff, exhaling a cloud of smoke, which Paul aggressively swept away with his hands, attempting to protect himself from the acrid scent.

"You're smoking too much. It isn't good for you."

Tony stared straight ahead, ignoring Paul's complaint.

"Have you ever read a book from the outside in?" said Paul, abruptly changing the subject.

"What the hell do you mean by that?" asked Tony, with bewilderment.

"Well, I have done it once, a novel called, *"Ulysses"*, written by an Irish author named *Joyce*, about people in Ireland. I read the inside chapters, then the ending chapters, then the beginning chapters. It was tough figuring the story. It forced me to ask questions of the characters' identities in the middle chapters, then their fate in the ending chapters and finally their introduction in the beginning chapters."

"That's the craziest damn thing I ever heard. How can you figure out the story reading that way," questioned Tony.

"You can't. The chapters are mixed up and find themselves in places they shouldn't be, confused like the seed of a flower blown on a rotting log floating in the river, to grow and bloom, yet not in its natural setting. The challenge for the blooming flower is to get off the log."

"What bullshit. You need to visit Father Gabriel to drive that crap from your mind," exclaimed Tony, becoming more agitated with Paul's frivolous demeanor. "And by the way, I have read a book the way you described, sort of. I read parts of the bible, the last chapter, *Revelation,* first; because I heard it was disturbing, the first chapter, *Genesis,* second; because I heard it was fascinating, and attempted to read a couple chapters in between by picking the chapter names I thought sounded important, named something like Filisteses and Eclastisisis, I can't really remember. I couldn't get through the Bible with all the "thou's" and "thy's" and "thee's" and "begats", and the strange names of people I couldn't keep track of, it was kinda complicated."

"It's *Philistines* and *Ecclesiastes,* Bible Boy. Get it right. So, you believe in God, even though you don't understand the Bible, the word of God, that God created the world in six days, took a break on the seventh, magically created man from dust, created dust from who knows what, and then God created woman from the rib of man, and that naughty woman chomped a bite from a piece of fruit, opening the earth to sin and bad behavior; that God created all you see here, the river, the land, the clouds and that crazy rabbit back there. It's hard to believe such a wild story," said Paul.

"You gotta believe in something. Give me another explanation," demanded Tony.

"I have no other explanation, but there has to be one other than the tall tale of a mighty and all knowing God."

"Why are we talking about this stuff," said Tony, clearly exasperated. "I just wanna get to Locke to relieve some tension."

"You know Anthony, somewhere in the Bible, it is said that what you want to do is against the will of God, the word of God. Having sex with a woman you aren't married to is a sin with the result being you not entering the kingdom of God," said Paul, making known to Tony the contrast between his religious beliefs and his firmly entrenched goal of getting laid.

"That's what priests are for. Sins can be fixed. It's easy, all I gotta do is sit in the Saint Peter Martyr church confessional box. Father Gabriel hidden behind the wall with the small opening for him to hear my confession, say a prayer and receive his forgiveness. Then I can move on."

"Move on to sin again," sighed Paul.

Tony looked at Paul, frowned, saying nothing.

They sat silently, the Buick rolled ahead winding

around the bend of the river. Paul looked to the land side of the levee. Tony hunched over the steering wheel staring intently at the road ahead. On the side of the road behind a worn, wooden, picket fence stood a giant, wild turkey with a tail spread wide, like a fan from the Orient; the feathers colored in auburn, white, grey and black, alternating vertically, his chest puffed like a proud gladiator, his neck flush with red, adorning his egotistical chin.

"If I were a turkey, I'd want to look like him. He's a stately looking bird. I wonder why he's out here all alone. He too, like the rabbit, seems to be staring. I wonder what he's thinking?" questioned Paul.

"He's thinking why the hell are these jerks staring at me? I'll stare back. That's what he's thinking. His stare is full of scorn, like a warrior ready to do battle," said Tony.

The Buick passed the turkey slowly, the turkey turned, his tail flared wider, his stare penetrated deep into Tony's eyes, following the Buick until the Buick disappeared around a bend of River Road.

Paul and Tony sat silent for a short while, Paul breaking the silence with a light and hopeful tone. "We could hang out on the river bank and grab a couple of beers from Al the Wop's and just talk. The guys at the cannery say they serve beer and wine Saturday nights, and other illegal drinks."

"Just talk? You sound like the butcher's daughter, Anna Macaluso. At nights when I take her to the cannery docks when no one's working, I always try to get her to go all the way, to let loose. After kissing and feeling the parts of her that excite me, she pushes me away and says, "Tony, why don't we just talk?" Just talk. Now that don't work for me. I've waited way too long to lose my virginity. I'm not gonna wait until I'm an old fart like you. I'm not gonna wait until I'm eighteen, that's a whole 'nother year. Now's the perfect time. The night is warm, the moon makes the river glow, the sound is mellow and the scent is fresh. How's that for flowery talk? It's the way you're talking about the river tonight, all flowery like, so this would be a perfect evening for you, getting it done in this setting. I don't understand why you're not up for this. Are you saving yourself for Maria?"

"Maria wouldn't be too proud of me doing this with another woman. I sure wouldn't want her doing this with another man."

"She wouldn't know. I'm not gonna tell her. I'm not gonna tell nobody, except maybe Hank Aliotti and Joey Cardinale."

Paul snickered. "If you tell those two guys, the whole town of Pittsburg will know. They're not very good at keeping secrets. Even if it were kept secret, I'd know. I'd feel bad when I saw Maria. The lie on my face would betray me. It's easy for you, you don't have a girlfriend."

"Damn glad I don't have one. Girls are too much trouble with all the manners you need to show just to get a kiss. This is easy. You pay some money, you get what you need, then do somethin' like go fishing."

"Romantic. It's no way to have a relationship, no way to start a family."

"You're only eighteen. Why'd you want to start a family? You're still young. Sow an oat or two."

"Eighteen is not so young, little brother. You even said I'm an old fart. It doesn't matter. I'm not ready to start a family. By the way, what does *sow an oat* mean?" questioned Paul.

"I dunno. I hear the guys at the cannery say it when they talk about doing a woman. I think the oat is the woman. Not sure what sow means, but when they say they're going out to *sow their oats,* I think they mean, to find some ladies. And do 'em."

The Buick slowed on the downgrade heading into the town of Isleton. Tony veered onto a street to the right, passing by shops and wooden homes, a few painted brightly in red, green and orange hues.

"Those colored homes are where some Chinese live," said Paul.

"I thought they lived in Locke."

"They live there too. Some rich Chinaman arranged a deal with the landowner, a guy named George. The land extends to the river below the levee, on the landside. The Chinaman worked with other Chinese and built a store, a school, a church and houses for the Chinamen workers."

"Why'd they name the town Locke? That's not very Chinesy," questioned Tony, playfully.

"It wasn't always named Locke. At first, it was named Lockeport, not very Chinesy as you say, but the town was originally named that name out of respect for George, the landowner, whose last name is Locke, and added the word "port" at the end, because it's next to the river and used by the Southern Pacific railroad, to warehouse the produce harvested from the farms in the Delta. Once the crates are warehoused, a riverboat sweeps by, picks them up and unloads at the docks in Oakland and San Francisco. The suffix "port" was dropped, because it was assumed to be easier for the Chinese to speak a one syllable word rather than a two syllable word, although I'm not really sure. Interesting though, the Chinese still spoke it as a two syllable word, by pronouncing the 'e' at the end of the word Locke, as a long 'e', not a silent 'e', ending up sounding like '*eeeee*'; somewhat like a screeching tire. At least that's what someone told me. I'm guessing with some semblance of accuracy based on what I've heard. So Tony, Locke isn't just a big whorehouse for guys like you to wander through and satisfy your needs," emphasized Paul. "It actually serves a purpose, a town to house and support Chinese workers."

"How'd the Chinaman guy get rich?" asked Tony, ignoring Paul's derogatory comment.

"Gambling houses. They built a gambling house and a bar. The Chinamen in the town like to gamble with small, funny looking, colored blocks like dominoes and card games and lotteries. Other strange games too."

"I'm beginning to like these Chinamen. They're like us Italians. They like gambling like we do. They like drinking like we do. They like ladies like we do. How do you know about all this stuff, Paul?"

"Mac. Mac Kelly. He's the old Irishman living in the cabin on the south side of Nortonville road. He's the guy that told me about how Locke was named. He's often visited this area. He worked the coal mines in the low lying hills at the foot of Mt. Diablo. When the coal gave out, he decided to stay and not leave like the other Irish, Welsh and Scottish workers. Now he works on the land gathering acorns and roots for food and hunts small game and bird. When he was younger, he'd take trips here in the Delta. Now he's too old and doesn't have the energy or the desire. He knows a little history of the Chinese in the Delta and the building of the levees. Mac did some gambling of his own, didn't win anything, but became friends with some of the Chinese. He knows the Chinaman who built and runs the gambling house," explained Paul.

"I thought that old guy was a hermit. I'd see him wandering in town, walking from the hills. How'd you get to know him?"

"I'd walk through the area near the coal mines to think, to get away from the stink of the fish in the cannery and the hooligans roaming the docks. I met him while he was gathering acorns lying among the leaves and under the oaks in the foothills. He has lots of stories. He's a really good guy," said Paul.

"I didn't know that about you. Hmm....Paul the wanderer, kinda like Marco Polo. You sure get around. I didn't know that about you."

The Buick slowed to a stop along a walkway next to a diner. White men stood leaning against the walls of the small buildings. Chinese men sat on chairs, their voices like lutes competing with the white men standing, playing banjos. Tony erupted from the driver's seat, "I have to piss," he said, walking briskly to an alley between a bait shop and a hardware store to relieve himself. Paul stepped from the passenger seat and leaned against the fender of the Buick. He looked to the sky, recognizing the big dipper, its stars peeked dimly through the darkening summer night. He noticed three men across the street, a Chinaman and two white men laughing and talking.

"Excuse me. How far to Locke?" questioned Paul, politely.

"Why. You lookeeng for some *mei mei*?" asked the Chinaman.

"If I think what I believe you mean by the words, *mei mei*, the answer is yes, sort of. I'm not looking for some *mei mei*, but my brother is," laughed Paul. "He can't stop talking about getting some *mei mei*, as you put it. Says he needs to satisfy his needs."

"His need good thing. Need men populate world with *mei mei*. Need boy baby grow, work levee, work field."

Tony overheard the conversation while approaching the group, zipped his trousers, adding to the conversation, "Then we'd need more girl babies to grow up to be *mei mei*, to satisfy the needs of the boy babies."

"Cook, clean, makes clothe," laughed the Chinaman, rapidly rolling the conversation along, with the two white men, laughing loudly.

Tony and Paul stepped into the car, waving to the Chinaman and the two white men. Paul turned to Tony, his demeanor emitting a tinge of contempt. "That was a slam against women, speaking of them like they're nothing more than a roll in the hay and a slave to the needs of man."

"Damn Paul. Lighten up. I thought you thought those quips were funny, but now you're acting so freaken' serious. Sit back and enjoy the nature thing you're talking about so much this Saturday night. Let's enjoy the time bantering with the boys and the thoughts of what's up ahead at Miss Janey's place." Tony started the Buick and drove from Main Street back upon River Road.

"Did you notice the street sign on the corner, the name Main Street? It certainly is the main street since there are no other streets. It was appropriately named," said Paul, switching his behavior, emulating the persona of Jekyll and Hyde.

"Maybe they should've named it Only Street."

"That wouldn't have worked. If they added another street then it wouldn't be the only street. They'd have to change the name back to Main Street," countered Paul.

"Then they should've named the street, First Street, since it's the first street in town. Then they could name the next street, Second Street, when they added another street and then Third Street and so on."

"I suppose that would've worked through infinity, they'd never run out of street names, since they'd never run out of numbers."

"Brilliant Galileo. You should go to college," teased Tony, happy Paul was finally engaging in some light banter.

"I am," said Paul, to the surprise of Tony, who immediately feared Paul's relapse into his Hyde like demeanor. "I'm going to be a lawyer, a prosecutor."

"What the...a prosecutor? Why the hell do you want to be a prosecutor?"

"Well, at first I wanted to be a fisherman, like Dad, but after he and Mike bought the farm and ventured to your heaven, it forced me to reexamine that goal. Besides, working with the fish at the cannery these past two years, I concluded it's a smelly, dirty business that isn't particularly enjoyable."

"You didn't answer the question. You said what you didn't want to be, you didn't explain the reason for your decision to become a prosecutor."

"I need to leave Pittsburg. I feel locked in. There's little reason for me to stay. San Francisco would be a good place to practice law. It's close to Pittsburg, so I can travel to visit you, Mom and sisters' Rose and Andrea, once a week. We could have dinners on Sundays, like before, as a family, with mom cooking the good pasta, sauces, fresh bread and the occasional abalone you and I could dive for near Bodega bay, like we used to with Dad and Mike. I plan on earning a degree at the college in Berkeley and finish law school at Hastings in San Francisco. I hear a bridge will be built linking Oakland to San Francisco, so I can live in San Francisco and buy a jalopy and visit. It'd be a long drive through Richmond and along the river, but once I'd reach Antioch, I'd be able to drive across the new bridge connecting Antioch to the Delta. It'd be easier than traveling by steamboat," explained Paul.

"You're gonna need to work on this prosecutor thing 'cause you're not focused, prosecutors need to be focused. You're still not answering my question. You've explained how you're gonna do it, not why. Plus, you're gonna need a lot of money to be a prosecutor."

"Why am I going to do it? I'll tell you why," reacted Paul, offended by Tony's criticism. "I'm going to be a prosecutor to put away those low-level Mafia hoodlums in Pittsburg and Monterey and other riff-raff. Dad was always complaining about how the Mafia's dirty, business deals and sometimes, violent ramifications hurt others, decent people that couldn't fight back. Dad had a lot of integrity, but not the legal knowledge or authoritative position to fight back in a non-violent manner. He wasn't a violent man and wouldn't use violence to solve the inequities he observed. What Dad couldn't do, I want to do, through non-violent means, through efficient execution of the law," said Paul, with strong emphasis.

"Those are some pretty lofty goals."

"Next year, you're a high school graduate. What are you going to do when you grow-up?" asked Paul.

"I'm already grown-up. In a year, I'll be even more grown-up. Unlike you, College Boy, I like working with my hands, not my brain. Thinking too much makes my head hurt. I like the smell of the fish at the cannery and I don't mind working the canning machines. The sad thing is, I don't think the cannery will be in business much longer. They say Booth will be shutting down soon, focusing on packing sardines in Monterey. Local fisherman say there are fewer fish in the Sacramento River. We've noticed it, fewer fish in, fewer cans out. We Italians and those Greeks are overfishing. Even Dad was having trouble catching what he needed to pay the bills. That's why he started fishing with Mike, off the coast of Monterey, with nets in search of sardines. I would've liked to have tried fishing, but I've become more reluctant. I'm afraid what happened to Dad and Mike might happen to me. Maybe I'll take a shot at construction. There's a new company in town building houses on the land beyond the Santa Fe railroad tracks. The owner is an Italian, like us, from Sicily. He drives a big, beat up, yellow truck, up and down Railroad Avenue, hauling lumber from the docks with his two sons. It's a small company, but growing because of all the people needing homes working for the new industrial companies along the river."

"If he's a Sicilian he may not fit in with some of the Italians in Pittsburg. There are prejudices. Sicilians and Italians may not like each other," explained Paul.

"Why wouldn't they like each other? Italians and Sicilians are both from Italy."

"Same country. Different regions. Sicilians suffered like many colonized peoples who once resided as independent regions. The people of Sicily were subjugated by the Greeks and subsequently, the Italians. Where there were once political and geographical boundaries that separated Italy from Sicily, they no longer exist. Physically they're still separate, since Sicily is an Island off the coast of Italy, but other differences do exist. There is a slight difference in appearance, differences in the food they eat, cultural influences that vary and even slight language differences. The most significant difference between Italians and Sicilians is Cosa Nostra; Mafia. All Sicilians are categorized and stereotyped as belonging to that disruptive and violent organization. It isn't fair, but the prejudice exists. So all of those differences and animosities have carried over with the original immigrants into our country and like most peoples in this world, often create the 'us' versus 'them' divisions," answered Paul.

"To dislike someone because of the differences you mention just doesn't make sense and the Mafia connection really makes no sense. All Sicilians aren't Mafia. I couldn't tell the difference between a Sicilian and a Chinaman. Well, maybe that's a stretch, but you know what I mean. Those other things are no reason to dislike people. I'm pretty sure I'm gonna like the Chinese I'll meet in Locke. I liked the Chinaman back there in Isleton. He spoke a little funny and looked different, but he seemed like a nice guy. And I know I'm gonna like the China ladies in Locke, but obviously for different reasons."

"We're different. Mom and Dad taught us well. No one in our family hold any prejudices against any other race or variation in people. We've our share of different people in Pittsburg. Our family seems to get along with them fine. I worry about you working for a Sicilian. You know how some of the Italians are in our town, they dislike people, not like them, for the slightest of reasons," reasoned Paul.

"I can handle the pressure. Dad always taught us to not back down. Remember how he stood up to the Rossini family after they accused the Negro brothers, Eric and Jerry, of stealing Tommy Rossini's fishing nets from their boat, *Piave*. Dad knew that bad boy, Joe Ferrante, a cousin of the Rossini's, was the guilty one. He verbally railed on Joe, until Joe admitted stealing the fishing nets. Dad wouldn't let those Negro boys get punished for something they didn't do."

"Yeah, Dad handled that well. Don't get me wrong Tony. I know you would succeed working in construction. And I know you can handle yourself. I guess I'm worried about the reaction of others and the potential negative perception and impact on you and our family. Pittsburg does seem to be growing. I hear the chemical and steel companies on the river are expanding and other manufacturing plants are planning to build. It's a good place for a man who enjoys working with his hands. And don't berate yourself stating your head hurts when you think too hard. Thinking hard is the only way to make your head exercise, to allow your brain to work better."

"Thanks for the compliment. Let's get back to this lawyer business. I know you've been the smarter of the boys and girls in our family, but where are you going to go? How are you going to pay for tuition and make things work?" asked Tony.

"I'll figure it out. We Ripolis are from good, family stock. I'm no smarter than you or the other members of our family. I read and think more frequently than the rest of you. We're all smart, hard workers and have the propensity to succeed. I've saved enough money working at the cannery to afford one semester at the university in Berkeley. I can study and work odd jobs for families in the area or part time jobs at small businesses and pay my way through the other semesters. Once I finish in Berkeley, I'll apply at Hastings Law School in San Francisco and hopefully be accepted."

"When are you going to have time for fun? Every man needs to have fun."

"Studying is fun. Reading and writing are fun. Physical fun or pleasures such as the ones you envision for yourself will come later. It may sound strange, but I have fun learning and creating things using words and stories, creating written works, like molding a statue from clay, when read can be viewed as a form of intellectual art. I write stories unbeknownst to you, the words written are words from within, words devised from the feelings and emotions of one's being, not words that conform to the strict edicts of grammar and structure, but words that emanate from the soul, not unlike the visual expression of a painter, a painter who paints on a canvas what the painter sees and feels, what the painter interprets in colors and shapes, not exact, but with variations, some subtle, some abstract, an image to be appreciated by others, a personal image from the painter's soul, or in the case of a writer, the writer's soul. I plan on using the passion for writing and creativity to effectively work through the logic and methods of proving a criminal is guilty or innocent of a crime they are charged with. In other words, the writing and thinking are brain food for expanding the possibilities practicing those methods."

"Sounds like a song with all those words you used, most I don't understand, but they do sound purty when you string 'em together, 'specially the ones in the beginning with the clay, painting and soul stuff. I don't know Paul. Being a lawyer and the writing you talk about sounds a little deep and boring, but hey, if it gives you pleasure then go for it. If you feel strongly about it, I'll throw some money your way when I can." Tony touched Paul's shoulder. "I want you to succeed in your goals. You and I are so different. We're all a lot like Dad. He had brains like you and manual skills like me, a personality like Mike and tenderness like Rose and Andrea, all good traits in one man. He was good and we're all lucky to have had him as our Dad. We five kids are all chips off the ol' block, as they say."

"Only four chips now with Mike no longer with us," said Paul sadly.

"And the block isn't here anymore either," added Tony.

"By the way, who would *they* be that made the *chips off the ol' block* statement?" questioned Paul.

"Hell. I don't know. Go with it."

Tony pulled another cigarette from the pack and lit it. Paul looked at Tony and frowned.

"Don't start, Paul. It's clear you have a book reading and writing habit. I have my smokes," he said, taking a deep puff. The Buick continued along the winding path, the green water gently flowed guided by the levee's banks, the sun casting its rays around the levee's bends. In the shallows, stood a tall, white swan with a long, arched neck, head turned, eyes targeting the slow moving Buick.

"Why is that damn bird looking at us? There's some kind of conspiracy going on here," said Tony, flicking his burning cigarette out the Buick's window at the swan. "First, the cocky rabbit, then, the arrogant turkey warrior, and now, this swan staring at us and the drawbridges up, slowing us down, all attempts to distract and prevent us from getting to Locke."

"Maybe it's God's will," answered Paul, sarcastically.

"Don't throw that at me. God wouldn't be involved with something as minor as our trip through the Delta."

"But God could know you're about to sin and is trying to

prevent you from doing so, to save your soul. God knows all. It is God's plan."

Tony shook his head in frustration, irritated with Paul's negative demeanor and blasphemous attitude.

They drove through a tall strand of eucalyptus trees towering over the road on the river side and the land side, the musty smell of the leaves flowed through the car windows, the dusky sun peaked through the branches and leaves in a canopy casting a mosaic of light, shadow and shade on the road. The warmth of the day disappeared with the cool of the shade briefly and again the warmth of the day reappeared after the Buick exited the eucalyptus tunnel. Approaching a bend, beyond stood a bridge, where they rolled to a stop in front of the lowered crossing arm, turned off the motor, stepping from the Buick. They stood staring at the office positioned on the side of the bridge.

"Well, at least the bridge isn't drawn, the road across this bridge turns sideways, to let that fishing boat pass," said Tony.

"Same effect. We can't cross."

"Good point, but I think this is the last bridge. Look at the guy in the bridge office through the window. He's got a book open, a bottle sitting on the table and a tin mug. The bottle looks half empty."

"The bottle resembles the bottles I've seen at Mac's cabin. Mac says the bottles are made from the sand they mine in a rocky ravine near Somersville, the town where the coal was mined, until coal became too expensive to mine and the coal they did mine was of a bad quality. Some men still mine coal, but not as part of any company.

Anyway, apparently, the sand is shipped to a factory in Oakland. Mac called the sand Silica. In the factory they heat the sand at a high temperature, until it turns to liquid. Then it's poured into a mold in the shape of a bottle. When the liquid dries, it turns to glass and from the mold comes a bottle. Mac's bottles were filled with bootleg liquor, called Jackass whiskey, distilled in a rocky ravine somewhere between the towns of Somersville and Nortonville, the other coal mining town."

"Did you get a swig of that Jackass whiskey at Mac's cabin?"

"Yeah. I almost puked. The experience was like swallowing the rotten stem of a thorny, rose bush."

"Do you think the man controlling the bridge is tight? Can't be too safe crossing. We don't know if he's gonna get the bridge back the way it's supposed to be," laughed Tony, pulling a cigarette from the pack in his back pocket and lighting it.

"It can't be too hard. All he's doing is pulling and pushing a couple of levers. It must be relaxing for him to sit, reading a book and drinking whiskey, while waiting for boats to pass." The man in the bridge office turned and noticed Paul and Tony leaning against the Buick's grill with arms crossed, Tony's cigarette hanging from his lips. Their eyes met. The man acknowledged their gaze, smiled, waved and gestured with his arm towards the bridge entry, pushing the lever, raising the crossing arm allowing passage. Tony and Paul waved back, returned to the Buick, started the engine and drove across the short, bridge road over Georgiana Slough.

"Guess he wasn't too tight. We got across," said Tony.

They turned at the sign with an arrow pointing left, the letters, *Walnut Grove,* in faded white, painted on the weathered, wood plank. Finding themselves again on River Road, the Buick drove slowly past a man sitting on a bench, staring at a white and red buoy in the middle of the river.

"Look at that man. What's he doing just sitting there, staring, mesmerized and motionless? He's dressed to the nines in his double breasted, button down suit, a thin, gold tie with a brown, derby hat, a red rose on his lap, doing nothing, nothing at all. Maybe he's part of the conspiracy," said Tony, sticking with his theory.

"It is eerie, the palms of his hands set down on his knees, his back, straight like an arrow, his head perched high on his neck, like that white swan a ways back standing in the shallows under the trees on the levee's banks. And that rose just lying there, he's meditating or something," acknowledged Paul.

The man turned slowly, deliberately staring at Tony as they drove slowly past, Tony bewildered, wondering of the man's purpose.

"Let's drive along this road to the right and back up again to see some of the sites in this wayward town," said Tony, quietly conceding to Paul's lack of urgency getting to their destination. He veered the Buick down the path leading to the buildings below River Road; his curiosity aroused having encountered yet another odd occurrence on the long road trip through the Delta.

The Buick drove down the road, the setting sun cast

dark shadows along the street and walkways. In the middle of the road stood a grayish-white, horned goat, hitched to a post in front of a building, baying loudly; the goat staring deeply into Tony's eyes. "I gotta bad feeling. That goat is staring, like all the other varmints and the odd man on the bench, staring. I swear there's something weird going on. Like something bad is gonna happen, something like the devil warning us, threatening us. Let's get the hell outta here," said Tony, pressing the gas pedal to the floor, speeding past the goat, down the street and up to the road onto the levee.

Driving in silence, during the few moments prior to entering the main street below the levee's banks, they pulled into the town of Locke and parked on the side of the road, a few buildings from Al the Wop's.

"Are you coming?" asked Tony.

"Nah, you go on ahead. I'll walk up to the river bank and hang there. I've got some thinking to do. By the way, you mentioned your fear of the swan, the turkey, the man with the rose and the horned devil goat, staring during our journey, maybe warning us. I believe they were warning you, warning you to prevent you from doing your sinful deed. You may want to think about that. Maybe it's your God warning you, speaking through the swan, the turkey, the devil goat and the man on the bench, maybe even Ol' Jack rabbit, like God spoke through Jesus, or maybe it's you warning you. Either way, face the warning brother and do what you need to do."

Tony opened the door to Al the Wop's, the energy from within burst into the street like a heavy gust of wind swooping through the branches and rustling the leaves of a giant oak. He walked over the threshold, stepping delicately with trepidation, uncertain of what lay ahead. His confidence drained as a result of the road trip, the waiting at the bridges, the odd occurrences of the birds and animals, the confusing conversation with Paul. Tony's uncertainty gingerly crawled through his mind like a spider in its web. Looking down, Tony stepped towards an empty stool, near the corner of the bar. People engaged in talk and laughter, men and women stood in the corners and near the bar with one another. Chinese women dressed in pink, purple and green, their short heels clicked, as the women shifted uncomfortably on the uneven, wooden floor, lightly brushing with slim fingers, the chests of the men.

Tony sat on the lone stool between two men, one to his left, brushing the straight, black hair of a slim, flat faced Chinese girl, one to the right, in boisterous conversation, with a farm worker, dressed in blue overalls and brown boots. Attempting to get the attention of the bartender, Tony yelled above the raucous noise of the bustling crowd. "Hey bartender, what 'cha got to drink?"

The bartender walked towards Tony, leaning and placing his forearm on the bar top. "What 'cha want?"

"How 'bout a beer?"

"You ain't old enough for no beer kid. You ain't yet legal."

"You ain't legal neither," retorted Tony. "You shouldn't be serving nobody, 'cause the law grants you no right to serve no alcohol."

The bartender paused, peered at Tony, evaluating the

red haired, freckled face and Tony's eyes exhibiting anxiety and determination.

"You're right kid," said the bartender, sympathetically. "I'll give ya' a pass since yer' up front nature shows strong character. You're a smartass, but I respect what ya' say. But, jus' so ya' know, the law here have no say on Saturday nights. They give us a break. Saturday night is the night when the law got no jurisdiction."

The bartender turned to the shelves lining the back of the wall, pulled a rusty mug from the middle row, stuffed a dirty, green towel into the mug and wiped the inside before filling it from the barrel below. He brought the mug from under the bar, slamming it on the bar top in front of Tony. "Here ya' go kid. This one's on me," said the bartender, turning to another man, screaming for attention.

Tony stared at the mug; the suds flowed down its sides forming a puddle around the base. He grabbed the mug, lifted it to his lips and gulped three times, setting it half empty to its puddle on the bar.

"Hey young man, I heard bartender Joe mention we're drinking here without fear of the law. We're safe here from the law, because the owner of this property designated the land as his own little country, negotiated with the local law men to leave us be on these Saturday nights. Needless to say, gratitude is expressed with a couple of jugs of beer and bottles of wine. The laws of Prohibition are skirted only two nights a week, but it helps the people in this area who enjoy drinking, smoking and conversation, after a good hard week's work."

Tony turned to the man, surveying his face, the rough,

sun-burned skin, dark-brown, curly hair, bushy mustache and a smile exhibiting a sense of warm joviality. Tony immediately connected Paul's description of the man's personality, characteristics talked about during their trip along River Road, to this town of Locke.

"I take it you're the guy my brother Paul told me about, George, George Locke. He told me a story about your happy, little community. Too bad, Paul isn't man enough to enjoy it," complained Tony.

"No, I'm not George. I know George though, he's a good man. People say we look alike, but I don't think so. I hope Paul's story didn't put him in a bad light. My name's Tim, Tim Hansen. I farm the land bordering George's property. George and I helped these Chinese build this community for them and for the locals, like me. It seems you are a little upset with your brother, accusing him of not being a man. Let me guess your situation. You're here to enjoy the things you believe a man should have the right to enjoy, like drinking, smoking and being with a woman, and paying for it. Paul is home with no desire to engage in your sinful activities and has no desire to violate the laws of Prohibition. A *goody two shoes,* so to speak."

"Nah. It ain't exactly like that. He came here with me like a good brother and is sitting on the levee's bank waiting for me to finish my adventure. He's thinking, getting all infatuated with nature. And yeah, I came here to drink, smoke and get laid and I'm the religious one. He isn't. He laid a bunch of crap on me during our drive from Pittsburg, about his disbelief in God and how I should question my belief and frankly, although I believe in God,

I'm gonna do the things God says one shouldn't do and he doesn't believe in God and he's not gonna do the things God says he shouldn't do. I'm not sure I'm making sense, but in short I believe in God and I'm gonna commit sins against the will of God and Paul doesn't believe in God and isn't gonna commit sins against the will of God, 'cause to him there is no God and therefore, no sin. So he isn't religious and doesn't commit sins and I'm religious and I'm gonna commit sins. So who then is the religious one and why if he isn't religious, does he reject a God who rejects the same bad behavior as Paul? Shouldn't he be the one who believes in God?"

"Based on what you've said it appears your River Road trip has baffled you somewhat. It certainly baffles me the way you've explained it. Paul seems to be finding himself in a different way than you. I know it sounds *touch feely,* but one doesn't need to believe in God to do the things Paul feels are right, or not do the things Paul thinks are wrong. That's Paul's choice, an innate decision based on his physical being. Tony, you don't need to feel guilt based on what Paul thinks you should, or shouldn't do, nor should Paul question your comfort in your belief in God."

"He is forcing me to think through things I've never thought about before. I'm not feeling too good right now after the anticipation and excitement of coming to this place to get laid. This Saturday night was supposed to be fun."

"I know your frustrations and Paul's as well. I don't meet many men like Paul on my visits here on Saturday nights. Most men who come to Locke, like you, are committed to their behavior and don't back out. Men need a place to release their pent-up energy, so George and the Chinese merchants provide that place. Gambling, drinking and prostitution are methods men use to do that. They aren't sins by the Chinese definition, nor should they be considered sins by our definition. One should be free to practice those *vices,* as we term them under the laws here in America. Unfortunately, our laws are set according to moral values influenced by churches and other groups with opinions and a vested interest in imposing edicts, based on the interpretation of their sacred books. It is said a moral, structured and orderly society must be governed with laws that corral individuals in specific behaviors for the good of all. The laws imposed to ban gambling, drinking and prostitution are examples of governments influenced by a minority, imposing their will and sanctimonious beliefs upon we people in this great country, and those laws will not survive over time. People don't want to be told what to do, when they're going to do it anyway. Locke is George's private property paid for with his family's own money. He's leased a few acres to these Chinese folk after their homes and shops mysteriously burned to the ground in Walnut Grove. We heard some churchies over in Rio Vista got their undies in a bundle over the Chinese living in a white man's town and influencing the white man with the sins of the Chinese. America, our fair and equal opportunity country, passed a law disallowing Chinese from owning land of their own. It isn't fair. Their money is as green as ours. Major prejudices exist in this country and in the California Central Valley evidenced by the fire in Walnut Grove. Some things aren't so good in our great country. But this is George's little America. He worked around the country's laws, but for the most part still within the law. Our country's laws are sometimes unfair due to biases of individuals and groups. Leasing the land provides a needed and fair end result, a spot for the Chinese to build their community, within the law. The Chinese are good people; they work hard, are congenial and have an interesting culture. They need a place to congregate and practice the ways of their original home in China, while learning the ways of us Americans. Selfishly, we need the cheap labor to tend our crops and harvest. The Chinese have contributed much to the acquisition of miles of Delta soil, with the construction of the levees over the past decades. The Chinese have built a community, a little Chinese American community, within a big American country. We farmers of the Delta owe it to them. Locke has its own one sentence unwritten law, *live free and don't make trouble.*"

"So let's see if I get it. You use a lot of big words, like Paul, but I think I understand some of what you say. George provides his own land to these Chinamen and makes them pay some sort of rent. Allows them to setup businesses that serve them, then care for them by providing the opportunity to practice their own customs and by doing that provide for the needs of men like me, which go against the laws of our country. But the whole arrangement sounds like some form of Communism, a dictatorship of sorts. Is George a Communist like those Russians?"

Tim laughed heartily. "No. The money earned from leasing the property is for George to spend, how he wants and for what he wants and the money the Chinese businesses earn is for them to spend, how they want and for what they want, not for the government to take and produce what they believe people need, like that crazy communist country believes. Capitalism is our country's economy, which certainly has flaws and our country's government is democracy, which in theory creates laws wanted by the majority of the people, but that system is also flawed, because the majority of the people aren't always represented in the manner they'd like. Often laws are passed without true consensus of the majority of the people. Our country overall has flaws, but it's a good country."

"You said you come here every Saturday night. Is that why you're here tonight, to release your pent-up energy, like us?" questioned Tony.

Tim leaned back from his bar stool. "I'm here for the camaraderie. I've known George for a long time and know of his intentions and philosophy; at least I think I know. I have a lovely wife, Katherine. She likes being called Kate and two great children, a daughter named Beth, Elisabeth formally, but she's perky so Beth is more fitting. Beth and I spend time grafting pear trees in the orchards, experimenting with different types of pears. She's becoming quite the agriculturist. My son's name is Robert, he's a little stiff. I call him Rob, to try and loosen him up with a casual rendition of his name. He's a good kid. Rob and I go fishing every Sunday, on the river at Steamboat Slough. I think he enjoys our weekly trips, although I'm not sure. Bottom line, I'm happy, I have what I need in life, what I want. I come here every Saturday night, to enjoy this once a week activity, observing the pleasure of the people of Locke and conversation with those passing through. It allows me to keep in touch with the world outside of the Delta, learning from visitors like you. I don't mean to go on and on, but I tend to get talking about my family in too much detail. By the way, what's your name?"

"The name's Tony and go ahead, keep on talking. I'm learning something and I don't mind hearing about your family."

"Look Tony, I understand how you feel. I was there once, with the same frame of mind, but learned over time a man must choose to remain free, or settle down. Some men are able to settle down more easily than others. Take Paul for instance, the way you explain his behavior, he's a thinker. Always reading, observing and interpreting the physical nature of things, getting pleasure from the outcome of his thoughts as he perceives the reasons for their being. It appears he's causing you some irritation on this Saturday night. Now take you, you're a doer, hankering to get your whistle wet, the carnal fervor bubbling within your insides, can't wait to release the pressure and get what you need. Each of your thoughts are nudging you both down different paths in your lives. This ride along River Road has allowed you both to vent, to make your thoughts known to each other. The river has that effect on many; a place for pondering. A place where one can touch nature and be a part of it. Each of you has made your own individual decisions based on your response to life experiences to date and your biological instincts. Almost every man has those sexual needs as strong as yours, some stronger than others. Take Caesar for instance?"

"Who the hell is Caesar?" interrupted Tony.

"Caesar's my stallion living in our corral next to the farmhouse."

"But he's not a man, Caesar is a horse."

"Stick with me on this Tony and listen to what I have to say. It's pertinent. Caesar shares the corral with three mares. Two of the mares are average looking as far as female horses go, but one in particular, Blondie, is an especially beautiful horse. She has a dark, shiny, chestnut-brown coat, the fur of a real, live animal, unlike the fabricated or dead fur worn by those fancy ladies in the cities, and she has a golden blonde mane and tail, a striking, color contrast that attracts attention. Her thighs are strong and firm and her head rides high above her slender, muscular neck and she carries herself with an air of royalty. If she were human, she'd be a princess. If I were a horse, I'd want to be Caesar, but let's not go there. The other two mares, Bertha and Gertie, are stodgy, their names belie their appearance and sloth-like movements tend to make one ignore them. If they were human, they'd be chunky housemaids. Now, getting back to Caesar, coming from the fields after checking on the workers plowing, picking or packing, I notice Caesar, on occasion, hanging around Blondie, a neighing and a snorting and causing a ruckus, clearly showing an energetic interest and affection towards Blondie as a partner and sexual mate. He gallops around her in circles nudging the sides of her neck, a neighing and a grunting, tail a wagging, intent on mounting her and satisfying his needs, which I catch him doing often. Caesar doesn't limit his urges and acts to only Blondie. Blondie rebuffs Caesar on occasion, though most of the time, she lets him do his thing, since she clearly enjoys their pleasurable exchange. When Blondie rebuffs Caesar due to some horse headache or mood change, he mounts either Gertie or Bertha unimaginatively and gets what he needs. Once the need is satisfied, he tends to go back and hang around Blondie, while behaving in a demure manner. My point being, Caesar is like a man, a man horse, with urges required to satisfy his needs and although favors Blondie, uses Gertie and Bertha when Blondie is unwilling. Caesar is a horse who knows what he needs, resulting from his natural and biological urges, but has his favored mare, Blondie, and appears to show guilt and remorse when he deviates from Blondie."

"But do the urges stop? I have a feeling I'm gonna like what I'm about to do, like Caesar and will wanna do it more. How did you do it? How did you control your urges? You said you were like me when you were my age and here you are, an old guy, married with children, talking to a young guy, in a bar filled with guys like me and Chinamen and Chinawomen, noise bouncing off the walls, liquor and smoke being enjoyed by all; the sinful things the church says a man and especially a woman shouldn't do."

"First of all, the reason I tell you the story of Caesar and his tidy, little, mini, mare harem arrangement, is to explain having the urges you have are natural, they aren't really sins in nature. They are sins judged as immoral and bad behavior, as defined by church and religion, regardless of the deity that church or religion believe in, and the rules developed by those of that church or religion define. The urges that exist are natural instincts that mankind has attempted to make rules, to control, so as not to conflict with other instincts of mankind, such as the sense of ownership and jealousy. I don't see any of the mares exhibiting territorial or jealous emotions, so my point with Caesar as an example, is the natural world appears to treat sex as a duty, to procreate with some instances of pleasure, as a result of the instincts to procreate. That it's okay. I still have urges, but I control them. We are part of that natural world as well. However, we humans appear to be different than some in the animal world, we experience territorial instincts and emotions of jealousy, when either men or women hop in the haystacks with any man or woman they choose. That is the dilemma and the reason to either commit to be a wanderer, or commit to one partner and stick with that partner. Second of all, I'm not an old guy. I'm only forty. Young, old, middle aged, are labels that package a person in segments, within a society. When you get to be my age, you'll still feel young like a teenager, such as yourself, but life experiences hopefully make a man older in his thoughts. I attended an agricultural college of sorts, in Davis near Sacramento. I didn't receive a traditional college degree, since our great state, California, didn't offer students of such a perceived limited discipline an accredited degree. Nonetheless, I learned a lot specific to my family business and while in Davis, met my wife at a soda shop in the town. I fell in love with that women, after experiencing other women in the town of Davis and Sacramento and knew she was the one for me. I had satisfied my needs prior to meeting Kate and only occasionally, when I saw a pretty woman with nice gams and honkers, did I ever think of getting a need taken care of, separate from my wife. It takes discipline. Man was built by nature to procreate, that biological urge never completely leaves a man or a woman, I think. I can only speak as a man and understand to be content when a man decides to have a family, he needs to control it."

Tony lifted his beer, turning the mug bottoms up, gulping the cold liquid gold, ordering another. "Hey bartender," Tony yelled, lifting his voice above the loud laughs and talk of the bar patrons, "gimme' another." Tony turned to Tim, lowering his face downward, with a signal of defeat. "You're like Paul, telling me things, but not giving me answers. He doesn't believe in God and he can't tell me what to believe. You're telling me of man's faults that aren't really faults, identifying mine by what you observe my thinking to be and telling me generally how to control the urges most men have, of which I'm guilty of having. But what you're suggesting might not work for me."

"A man has to find his own answers on how to control his specific urges and other personal matters. The God thing, I'm not going to touch it. The concept of an all knowing God can't be proved by anyone in our lifetime, or possibly ever. The question of a God's existence is a many centuries old question I choose to sit the fence on, to not ruffle feathers in this community. Many different cultures and peoples have their own God or Gods and their own interpretation of their God's edicts and mandated behaviors. Who's to know which cultures or beliefs are right, if any? Those who claim that God doesn't exist are punished socially and called that name with the evil stigma, atheist. Paul will have to fight the God battle on his own, risking being ostracized and deemed a social outcast. He's lucky though, often in the past, non-believers were tortured or killed for their lack of belief in God, or unwillingness to verbally commit to God. So I'll deflect the God issue, since it's a heavy one, like a giant anchor we'll drop in the river, chainless from our Godless boat, setting us free for the purpose of our discussion. In many instances, man doesn't realize the God anchor can weigh him down. Let's get back to the reality of life, this important and ubiquitous urge issue, we know exists. With Kate, I felt a sense of guilt when I thought of other women, but was able to set the guilt aside by focusing on the good things I had with my wife and kids, Rob and Beth. I'd spend time playing board games, roughhousing in the outdoors, reading and sometimes, just talking."

"There's that just talk phrase I'm hearing over and over again," interrupted Tony, with a deep sigh.

"I also engage in hobbies," continued Tim, "fishing, hunting and chess which I play with Ed Felton, a few miles down the road in Courtland. A man needs to find diversions."

"But what if those things don't work?" asked Tony. "What if I'm not satisfied with my wife, my kids and chess games with Ed Felton? What if I need many women over time to satisfy my urges?"

"Then you need many women over time to satisfy your urges. Don't get married. You should go with it as long as you understand the potential consequences of your actions. There is nothing wrong with behaving in the manner you describe to satisfy your urges, as long as you don't hurt anyone. Create your unwritten laws governing Tony and stick to those laws. If you don't follow the main rule of your laws of not hurting anyone and violate it by satisfying your urges with other women while married, you'll cause trouble. You'll cause trouble with your wife, your kids, your family, her family and others. Doing it while married will cast dark, hurtful shadows over the people you love and others you may not envision. But you'd be amazed how having a good wife and children change your thinking, diverting attention from the urges you may have. For me, the urges have pretty much disappeared over time."

"Is that why women don't have the same urges as men?" asked Tony.

"I can't speak for women, I'm not one. Women have their own urges. Men don't have a monopoly on pleasurable fulfillment from sexual acts. I've known a number of women who behaved like men, but they tend to be more discreet. Take Maria..."

"Is Maria another horse?" interrupted Tony.

"No," chuckled Tim. "Maria is a woman I met in Sacramento at *Sam's*. She waits tables and when I visit Sacramento now and then, I'd stop by *Sam's* for a burger.

Maria and I got to know each other over time, since she waited on me often and we became comfortable with each other. We got to talking about life and somehow began a discussion on the sexual habits of men and women. Don't ask me how we got there, but I learned she was a feisty woman with a sexual appetite equal to that of Caesar. I learned by talking, not by doing her, although she was physically someone worth doing and although I had the urge, I was able to suppress it. Anyway, I learned she is from a poor family, living a few miles upriver and was disowned, after being accused of staining the family name by catting around with many men. She was always mumbling something about the Vasquez curse, which infected her with the desires and pleasures of sex, whose symptom was an unquenchable need to become fulfilled. Society is less forgiving of women's sexual habits than those of men. Why, I don't know. Having experienced and observed my wife Kate's pregnancies, I learned when a woman has a baby, that little critter squeezes from and pops out of her, a living thing with a head, arms, hands and legs moving, all covered in muck. From that point on, she tends to focus her attentions and pleasures to that child. The pain and resulting pleasure must be quite a sensual experience," explained Tim.

"Like the feeling you get taking a big crap and the pain experienced," said Tony, "and then the disbelief and wonder of seeing arms and legs growing from the muck of its being and relief and pleasure, when it's finally pushed out."

Tim smiled a very wide smile. "I suppose that's an

analogy you could use to relate to the experience, a little warped, but you understand the point. The questions you have asked of me, your observations of Paul as explained prove you are inquisitive and have profound thoughts in a crude way. You'll figure it out through experience, but you have to experience life, whether by choice or by chance. You'll make mistakes as you grow to be an old man like me, although I'm not really old, I've had time to experience more in my lifetime than you and have learned not to make the same mistakes twice. If you're comfortable with your religion and belief in God and if believing makes you feel good, go with it, stick with that belief."

Tony looked into Tim's eyes, sensing a genuine sincerity, similar to the feeling he experienced when talking with his dad. Tony liked this guy and felt a need was fulfilled by Tim, in this modern day town of both Edenesque and Sodomesque tendencies. "You know a lot. I actually understand some of what you say," said Tony, his head hurting from the tumultuous feelings and torrent of information, spewed from the mind and mouth of this man.

"Remember Tony, you don't need a college degree and believe in God to learn the lessons of life. All you need is to pay attention to your thoughts and recognize the behavior of those around you, and the results of those behaviors, and rely upon your natural instincts of what's right and wrong to drive the direction you take. Now get on up and get what you think you need."

Tony stood from the bar stool. "Thanks for the advice. You've been helpful. I've enjoyed our talk."

"It was great meeting you. You've been my weekly

diversion on this Saturday night. A good diversion, I might add." Tim extended his hand, Tony extended his. Both firmly grasping and shaking them.

Tony turned and walked through the doorway, closing the door behind. The quiet and darkness of the street muffled the murmur from inside the bar. Tony stood on the walkway, breathing the river deep into his lungs. The thoughts of the evening blended with the dark scent of the river, the street silent, free of movement and sound. His memory drifted back where he and Paul's trip began, their wait at the Antioch drawbridge and the discussion of his intense desire of getting laid, the short ride from the bridge to the edge of the river on River Road, the water glistening in the setting sun, the stop at Three Mile Slough drawbridge, the fishing boats passing under, the distraction of Paul's question of the description of Mount Diablo, the anticipation and tension of waiting, the promise of reward at the end of their journey, Paul's recognition and verbal acknowledgement of their father's and brother's deaths and the blasphemous admission of Paul's non-belief, the promise of a fun evening conflicting with Paul's gloomy demeanor, the ride through the town of Isleton and encounter with a Chinaman and the two white men, and succeeding comedic banter, and, once again, Paul's negative reaction and accusatory remark about Tony and the men's disrespectful attitude towards women, the discussion with Paul and Tony's discovery of Mac, and of Paul's desire to become a lawyer, the eventual softening of Tony's urges and admission of his own future work prospects, the ride atop the winding levee road to the third bridge, once again blocked and their wait in front of the crossing bar at Georgiana Slough Bridge, with the bridge road turning sideways, the man in the bridge office controlling the bridge road and speculation of the Jackass Whiskey in the bottle, the odd occurrences of the crazy rabbit, the turkey, the swan, the goat and the well-dressed man with the red rose on the bench, all intimidating Tony with stares of scorn and mockery, the story of Caesar, the horny horse, and his harem of the beauty, Blondie, and the homely, Bertha and Gertie, poor Maria banned from her family for violating the religious rules of chastity, all incidents and thoughts culminating in the weakening desire of getting laid, after many miles of driving River Road with Paul, and then there was Tim, good ol' Tim, man of the Delta, like a modern day Jesus, the enlightening experiences conveyed and knowledge Tony gained conversing with Tim, the substance of that conversation, he had hoped to have with his dad. Tony shook his head in an attempt to shake the balls of thought bouncing haphazardly within the walls of his skull, his brain constantly exercising with the weight of heavy thinking. Tony's shoulders slumped, his urge withered like a lone, water lily stranded in the heat of the mid-day sun, during a river Delta low tide.

"This Saturday night sure ain't turning out the way I thought it would," whispered Tony, emotionally exhausted from the evening's events. "I suppose that's not a bad thing." Tony walked to the red light under the balcony of the corner, wooden, two story building, the universal beacon of the playpen designating Miss Janey's place.

From the phonograph inside, the thumping, jazz music vibrated dully through the door as he reached for the handle. Tony stopped short of touching it, lowered his arm, walked past the door, through a dark alley and up the splintered, wooden stairs to River Road. He crossed to the bank of the levee, noticing Paul, barely visible in the darkness, sitting on a thick, broken, eucalyptus trunk skipping rocks across the river's surface. Tony's steps crunched the gravel on the shoulder of River Road, interrupting the quiet of the river.

Paul turned and asked, "Did you get your needs taken care of little brother?"

"Yeah. I got my needs taken care of," answered Tony with a tired smile, picking up a flat stone, flinging it sideways, the stone skipping three times; its thump sounding on the rocks bracing the banks, on the far side of Big River.

Steamboat Explosion

The explosion cracked and smoke rose above the wharf, ahead of the flames. The steamboat split and caved inwards. Raoul steered his fishing boat towards the wharf viewing the carnage. Debris spread hundreds of yards from the wharf. Pieces of vegetable crates and green bits of asparagus floated among shattered remnants of the hull. Bodies scattered throughout the debris. Chinamen ran up and down the wharf yelling and screaming. Raoul spotted a man bobbing upwards with large, round eyes wide open. He seemed to smile as the boat drew closer. Raoul began pulling the Chinaman into the boat and the Chinaman was nothing below the waist.

DELTA MOON

She gently touched the steamboat's rail, gazing at the Delta Moon, full and bright, its light drowning the stars in luminous white and she recalled yesterday's moon, a celestial sentinel, guarding the area of the city of angels where she had fallen, her pure, white wings seared from the heat of hell's flaming abyss. Jenny giggled at her imagined angel's wings, wings of pure white, the color of goodness and knew it wasn't so, for the whiteness of yesterday's moon didn't prevent her dark deed, a deed necessary to preserve her integrity as a woman, her goodness, her beauty and her talent. She giggled again, thinking, "What is the real color of goodness anyway? It certainly isn't white."

*   *   *   *

Two days prior, in the early evening, Jenny stood at the big shot producer's house; he'd recently wed to Lauren, the blonde, buxom movie star; now Jenny's ex-husband, divorced with his claim of her insanity. Admittedly she felt a bit off soon after their matrimonial bond. She was fixed now. Back to reclaim her rights to her man, to show her changes, her skills as an actress, her beauty and clarity of thinking. Her blue cotton dress tightly fitted around her body, still firm in the fortieth year of her life. "I may not be as young as his new wife now, but I'm still vibrant and beautiful," Jenny whispered to herself.

Martin greeted her at the door, hugging her warmly. "Hello Jenny, you look well and healthy, please come in," he said guardedly.

Jenny silently crossed the threshold of the door to a large entryway tiled with a warm, brown and red Persian motif, stepped into the living area covered with varnished wood flooring, and floor to ceiling windows running the full length of the room, the windows opening to a wondrous expanse of ravines with small trees and chaparral. The color of the land, dry. The color of the weather, blue. "You seem to be doing well, Martin. You appear to be happy with your young and famous wife, your successful career; your warm and welcoming home," said Jenny, her voice, tinged with bitterness. "Having me committed to the sanatorium and initiating our divorce, seems to have freed you to move on to better things."

*   *   *   *

Jenny recalled the sanatorium in upstate New York, the huge white building with large white doors and large windows, its rooms spacious, sparsely furnished with white dressers, white beds, white tables, white bedding, white towels and white linen, hiding the evils behind a clean and clinical façade. Jenny was accompanied by Martin when admitted and he promised to care for her until she regained emotional strength. "I'll wait for you until you're better. I have enough to absorb my time in the theaters on Broadway. I'll visit you often. I love you," said Martin, as Jenny walked down the hall between two, male orderlies in white pants and white shirts. Turning her head over her shoulder towards Martin, she nodded gently, airily, expecting to be with Martin, soon. Ten years would pass until she would be freed to return.

*   *   *   *

Martin, ignoring her sarcastic comment, smiled and steered her to the waiting couch. "You must be exhausted travelling from the east to Hollywood, please sit, rest. Would you like something to drink, water or soda or…"

"Something stronger would be best, a glass of scotch or Champagne, anything with a kick," interrupted Jenny, curtly.

He walked into the next room, returning with a bottle and two, tall glasses. Martin poured the Champagne into each glass, carefully filling them to the brim, bubbles racing to the top like small helium balloons rising to the sky.

"To your health," toasted Martin.

"To your new wife, and her success."

Both raised their glasses, touching the edges against the rims, the high pitched chime penetrated the quiet of the room. Jenny sipped the Champagne, sat back, crossing her legs. "Where is your wife, the glamorous movie star? I saw her in a movie where she plays a promiscuous woman. Did she entice you with sex and marry you to get those roles in the movies? Is that her strategy for success? My God Martin, Lauren's twenty years younger than you. A baby when you were experiencing your lust as a young man. Aren't you ashamed? She can't be attracted by your good looks. You aren't exactly Clark Gable, with your balding head, slim frame and pointed nose," said Jenny, angrily targeting his physical insecurities. "Is she successful because of her beauty, her sexual demeanor and her connections with you as a producer? She really can't act, she isn't talented at all."

Pummelled by the flurry of questions, Martin sighed and moved to the couch, placing his hand gently on her knee. "Jenny, Lauren's at her mother's house for the weekend. She was sent so I could be with you and talk this evening. I wanted to reacquaint with you as friends. I love her. Lauren's a good woman. I had mixed feelings about seeing you today, knowing you might be resentful, given your perception of me abandoning you. But I didn't abandon you. I paid generously for your stay at the hospital, provided money in trust for your new start in life once you were able, for clothes, an apartment in New York, a large sum for furnishings and a chance for a new beginning. I waited for three long years, sending letters weekly, your responses vague and dreary, reports from the staff of your irrational behavior and degrading mental condition, with no signs of improving. Your responses became less frequent, so I wrote letters less often. Then your responses stopped. I couldn't wait for your recovery, believing it wouldn't happen, so I moved to Hollywood, to begin a life of my own, to work in the movie industry, where opportunities exist, where fresh ideas and people come, where dreams are fulfilled. I didn't intend to fall in love again, but I did and I'm not sorry for it. I'm sorry we couldn't make things work and I lost you, or rather you lost yourself, but I am still very fond of you and want to remain friends."

"Friends? You want to remain friends? Now how is that going to work?"

"I don't know," answered Martin, lowering his head.

"Look," said Jenny, sitting upright, pushing Martin's hand off her knee, speaking aggressively. "I struggled at the hospital. Things were happening that I couldn't control. The men orderlies in their bright, white smocks and bright, white pants molested me. I reported them, but their superiors laughed at my accusations, accusing me of lying and being a crazy woman. The reports of my irrational behavior were fabricated, to appear I wasn't improving, that I was in fact, crazy. I don't believe I was. Everyone at that white hospital misled me, with the perceived cleanliness and fairness of the color white. At first they welcomed me, but in the end, betrayed me."

Martin sat back in his chair. "I don't believe you're telling the truth."

"Are you calling me a liar?" roared Jenny.

"Not a liar. Still emotionally disturbed and out of touch with reality."

"Then you are calling me, crazy, Martin, which is worse than being called a liar."

"Not crazy. Emotionally disturbed is a softer and more appropriate term," explained Martin, with a puzzled look. "I recall your claims of abuse and your obsession with the color white, of white representing evil. My first visit at the sanatorium was one of surprise, as you sat in the chair, ranting on and on about your room being white, bland and uncomfortable. I thought this startling, since your sense of reality seemed to have shifted to a negative perception of things that were white. White is not evil. White is bright, represents purity and innocence. White is a good color."

"All things were white," emphasized Jenny. "White, sterile, clinical and evil."

"What made white evil?" questioned Martin, calmly.

"White represented evil in many forms. In your first visit I was overwhelmed with the world's whiteness, my world which was all white," stated Jenny.

"My second visit in the winter during the big snow, you sat in your armchair staring through the window, mumbling of the whiteness of the snow, its coldness, rambling about how it prevented you from enjoying the outdoors, how its evil limited you as a woman, limited you from achieving your goals, the simple goal of sitting in the outdoors, enjoying the warmth of the sun, a sun prevented from shining."

"Well, it did those things and still does," said Jenny.

"My third visit, you didn't seem to be getting better. Your condemnation of the color white, due to your complaints of the full, white moon, wounding you every month, blood staining your clothing, a natural biological incident experienced by most women in your age group," explained Martin.

"Those incidents especially affected me, since the presence of the full moon and its pull upon me was embarrassing. There is a connection."

"Jenny, you simply didn't take the necessary precautions like other women did and still do. The fact of your ignoring the easy prevention of the embarrassment was proof of your fragile emotional and mental incapacity. I can't believe you can't or won't understand that."

"White is evil," said Jenny, citing her original accusation against the cursed color.

"Jenny, you frustrate me. You can't justify your position. Your statement has no merit. One can argue that white isn't even a color, but is a state that's the absence of color. White symbolizes purity, good, honesty. Objects and white animals are revered by mankind."

"White is clinical," reiterated Jenny, speaking in a raised voice.

"White represents more than clinical. Clinical can be categorized as clean, which in some ways can be construed as clinical. But clinical isn't evil."

"If you agree white is clean, then you can agree white is

sterile and sterile is evil," Jenny again, raising her voice, highly agitated.

"Jenny, you are maddening and your argument runs in circles without any valid comparisons, other than general meaningless statements. Throughout the culture of mankind, white has been used as positive symbols," reasoned Martin, attempting to retain his composure against the anger building within. "The Romans, Greeks and Christians all wore garments of white, held celebrations with symbols of white, such as the white dress of brides and the white gowns of priests, all representing purity. American Indians gave belts of white shells as a pledge of honor and there are many more examples of white in various cultures, representing good, not evil."

Jenny sat silent for a few moments abandoning the debate of the color white and its symbolism. "Martin, you're like all the others, against me, attempts to justify all my supposed problems with skewed logic and comparisons to what you all consider normal. Look at me. I'm pretty. I'm shaped nicely. I've acted in a number of Broadway plays. I don't have large boobs, like your new wife the queen," she said, sarcastically, "but I'm more talented than she and more mature. I'm the woman you need in your life."

"Jenny, you are pretty. You have a nice shape with the right curves, but your boobs are not big. They are adequate. Not that it matters. And you can't act, you don't have talent, you've played bit parts on the stage and frankly, aren't yet, emotionally well. At your age you should be thinking of finding serenity and a normal life and not the stress and pressure of the movie industry, where you will fail."

"My boobs are adequate?" yelled Jenny, angrily, thrusting her breasts forward. "What are you saying? At my age? I don't have talent? I should settle and live the rest of my life in some sort of solitude? What kind of advice is that? How cruel can you be? I love you, Martin. I need you. Why don't you understand?" yelled Jenny, frantically.

"I loved you once Jenny and I love you now. But it's a different kind of love, a love of friendship. As I've said before, I still want to be friends."

Jenny calmed from her frenetic state, levelling her voice. "My dear Martin, a friendship exists when one person can freely call on another at any time, under any circumstance. Are you going to feel comfortable with me calling, visiting you here at this dream house, in this dream town, taking strolls along the beach, dining in the quaint cafes? Will Lauren be comfortable with that type of friendship? Will you? I know the answers to those questions, so don't mislead me with this let's just be friends talk. You know it can't happen."

"You're right. It wouldn't work."

"I want to swim," stated Jenny, rising from the couch, rushing quickly towards the open door leading to the pool. "It must be nice to have a pool at your home under the stars and the bright, evil, white moon, to bask in the warm air and refresh in the cool, clear water." Jenny walked through the open, glass, double doors, past the gardener pruning the bright, red bougainvillea along the pool's edge.

Martin anxiously followed and spoke to the man pruning the bougainvillea. "Gerard, you may leave to the keeper's bungalow, Jenny and I would like some privacy."

"Yes sir, I'll be available if you need me." Gerard nodded, wiped his pruning shears with the white rag hanging from his back pocket, turned and sauntered down the path leading to the small bungalow under two palm trees, at the edge of the ravine furrowing towards the coast.

Martin turned towards Jenny, who disrobed, her blue dress flung towards the side of the pool, her shoes thrown at the bougainvillea, one dropping on the pool walkway, the other in the green vines, leaves and red flowers. Jenny dove into the water, disappearing under the splash and wake. Martin leaned back on the wicker chair, watching Jenny breaststroke towards the opposite end of the pool. The weather warm, the air still, a sense of motionlessness weighed upon his home. Jenny looked beautiful in the crystal waters, like a mermaid, the wake rippling slowly and gently behind her, her pearl-white skin, blending with the pearl-white moon rising over the horizon. Looking at Jenny and believing her mind was still awash in confusion, thought of their time together, the years of fun and laughter, the intimacy on the beach, in the woods, on the vacant stages of the various Broadway plays. A pang of sadness and guilt began to overwhelm Martin. "What happened to her?" he asked himself. "Why did her mind degrade in the manner it had? Was I wrong to move on? Had I not been patient enough?" He watched her turn, swimming back and forth to each end of the pool, skimming the water gracefully with each gentle stroke. "Was Jenny right with her comments of Lauren using me for advancement in the movie industry? Had I exercised enough patience and not waited long enough for her to heal? I do have an odd pointed nose, slight body without muscle and scraggly hair on my rapidly balding head. Am I so enamored with her beauty and filled with so much pride having Lauren, the famous movie star, as my wife?"

Jenny stopped in the middle of the pool, lifted her head, smiled an eerie yet loving smile, and then resumed her slow, water ballet. Swimming back and forth for a long while, she intermittently stopped in the middle of the pool, performing underwater somersaults, continuing her slow, methodical water dance. Draining the last of the Champagne from the bottle, Martin watched silently, mesmerized by Jenny's graceful movement. Jenny stopped, laid her arms on the edge of the pool, her legs moving restfully in the water, her lips smiling a wide, eerie smile.

"Martin, you mentioned all white things are good. I've been pondering the legitimacy of that statement and, contrary to your opinion, concluded all things white aren't good. Snow is white and may look beautiful when viewed from a distance, but is dangerous when one is exposed to its cold, deadly grip. Polar bears and white lions may be beautiful and admirable, but are menacing animals to be feared in the wild. Albinos, although not dangerous, are disgusting to look at, making white sinister. The Ku Klux Klan, are attired in white robes and are dangerous to those people not of their color, which is white."

At the end of Jenny's statement, Martin leaned forward, feeling the negative effects of the Champagne, lost his temper and yelled, "Damn it Jenny, why are you so damned stubborn? The examples you've cited are elements and animals in nature that serve a positive purpose within the environment where they thrive. They're not negative symbols. They're living things and natural occurrences and are not specifically good or bad. Snow is snow. Snow is neither good nor bad. The bear and lions you refer to are neither good nor bad, and aren't negative symbols. Your arguments hold no water. Regarding albinos, what can I say; they're also a natural occurrence, an aberration, not a negative symbol. Your reference to them as sinister is frankly, offensive. The only part of your argument with validity is the white, robe, wearing, Ku Klux Klan symbolism, whose evil is far outweighed by the symbols of white that represent good."

"So you agree white is evil."

"God damn it, you don't get it. Sometimes I think you are so dense I wonder how I ever loved you," and in the middle of the statement, Martin threw the empty Champagne bottle across the pool in frustration, the bottle bouncing off the trunk of a palm tree, landing at its base.

Jenny shocked and deeply hurt at Martin's reaction, rose from the water and slowly walked with her head lowered through the patio door and into Martin's bathroom. Standing in front of the mirror, her face stared back, fraught with tension and disappointment. Staring into the mirror, tears flowed from her eyes, sobbing softly. Gripping her hands around each end of the porcelain sink, she breathed deeply. Turning and walking towards Martin's bedroom, she noticed the dresser and opened the right, top drawer, remembering Martin had hid the revolver in their Manhattan apartment long ago under his shirts. Lifting the

garments, Jenny felt for the gun, smirking at Martin's
predictability. She grabbed the smooth, polished, wooden
handle with one hand and stroked the cool, silver, steel
barrel with the other. She remembered the gun lesson
Martin taught her, the safety mechanism, the check for
bullets and the click when clasped back under the barrel.
"What a wonderful feeling, not unlike the feeling of holding
a man's manhood," she thought, giggling. "So this is what
it feels to hold such power, a man can point his gun barrel
at any target and shoot for the pleasure of shooting, similar
to the power felt by a man when making love to a woman
and the pleasure felt when the man bullet leaves the man
barrel. There is a feeling of power and control holding a
gun, a power that feels good." Walking slowly down the hall
to the living area and out the open, double doors to the
patio by the pool, she approached Martin, where he sat
gazing at the large, white moon, the moment silent,
interrupted by the occasional chorus of crickets in the
surrounding bushes and trees. Sensing a slight rustling,
Martin turned his head and stood. Jenny walked towards
him. He recognized the shiny revolver in Jenny's right
hand. Her arm hung downward, clutching the wooden
handle. She looked bewildered. Face flush. Lips set in a
wry, thin, evil smile. Her red, teary eyes, squinted in a
direct stare. Martin nervously backed towards the pool,
reached his arm outwards, palm opened upward, pleading,
"Jenny, please give me the gun." She walked forward with
focused intent, he stepped back. Jenny raised her arm,
pointing the revolver at Martin. Martin shakily said, "No
Jenny." The shot fired sending Martin backwards into the

pool, his blood leaving a wispy, thin, red trail flowing like a feather in the wind, the moonlight reflecting the water, a fluid painting of white on a canvas of blue with a bright red accent. The shot boomed like a cannon, echoing through the shallow canyons. Zorro the cat jumped high from Gerard's lap. Gerard threw the newspaper on the floor and ran towards the pool. Jenny stood with gun in hand at the pool's edge, glaring at Martin floating in the water.

"Oh no lady, look what you've done," shouted Gerard. Gerard jumped into the pool and swam to Martin, holding Martin's head upright while swimming back to the steps leading from the bottom of the pool to the corner surface. Gerard checked Martin's wound and knew Martin was dead. Dragging Martin up the pool stairs, Gerard laid him on his back and walked towards Jenny. "Give me the gun, put on your dress and sit here on the chair," ordered Gerard, pointing to the chair and grabbing the gun from Jenny's outstretched hand. "I need to make a call. I'll be right back." Jenny slumped into Martin's wicker chair and bowed her head, silently complying with Gerard's demand. Gerard walked to the inside of the open doorway and dialed a number on the phone resting on the tall, pine wood table. Jenny listened, missed the beginning of the mumbled conversation, but hearing the ending clearly.

"Yes sir. I am sure he's dead. He's not breathing. She got him in the chest. Blood all over." Gerard stood silent for a few moments with phone to ear anxiously listening, occasionally turning and glancing towards Jenny. "Yes sir. I won't call the police until you arrive." Gerard paused. "And yes, I'll make sure she stays."

The screech of the tires announced the arrival of the black, luxury Duesenberg. The Ford followed behind. The driver and passenger jumped from the Duesenberg. A man walked in front dressed in a black suit, white shirt and black tie. The driver of the Ford calmly stepped from the car. The three men walked through the front door. The man in the black suit walked briskly to the chair where Jenny sat, Gerard standing over her. She stared across the pool in a daze. "Does anyone know what happened? Did anyone hear the shot?" asked the man, gruffly.

"Me, and the lady know what happened. Like I said on the phone, she shot him dead," replied Gerard.

The man in the black suit glanced at Jenny and walked to Martin lying motionless on the side of the pool. "What a shame. Martin had so much right in his life, a promising career with our firm, a beautiful wife, a lovely home and success in our exciting movie industry. Movies were made for both he and Lauren. He turned and looked at Jenny, "I knew you were visiting. Martin often spoke well of you and felt sadness due to your condition and breakup. I knew the divorce affected you based on Martin's comments to me, but I never knew your visit would put him in danger. Why did you kill him?"

Jenny sat silently, offering no response.

"How do you want to handle this?" asked one of the two men, trailing the man in the black suit.

The man in the black suit reacted swiftly. "We have to clean up this mess, make up a story. We can't have this hit the papers with the truth. The truth would damage our movie company and tarnish Martin and Lauren's reputation. Martin's reputation mainly, due to the publics' lack of knowledge of Martin's previous relationship with this crazed woman. Lauren will survive and possibly garnish sympathy from the public. She wasn't aware of this previous, dysfunctional relationship. We need to make this unfortunate event appear to be a suicide; less scandalous for Lauren then a crazed ex-wife murdering her ex-husband. Hell, nobody knew Martin was married before. I'll write the suicide note with Martin's reasoning being the pressure felt with his work responsibilities and difficulty as the husband of a famous movie star, the effects of jealousy and physical insecurities; the usual inferiority complex syndrome bullshit. It'll be useful in this case. Gather the glasses and Champagne bottle, get rid of them and any trace of Jenny's presence. Wipe the gun. Throw it in the water. Gerard, the story is simple. You heard the shot and ran to the pool, observing Martin in the water. You dove in and brought him to the side of the pool and realized he was dead. Got it?"

Gerard nodded.

The man in the black suit, having taken control of the situation, turned once again to Jenny, speaking softly. "Jenny, you don't know me, but I've heard of you as I've said before. Martin spoke highly of you even with the ailment you've experienced, expressing sadness of your condition. You've done a bad thing shooting Martin. I don't know why you shot him, but we need to get you far from here to protect you. Can you tell me where you are staying?"

Jenny looked up at the man with an expression of

confusion, once again, smiling a thin lipped, wry smile, slowly looking away, apparently in shock.

The man asked her again. "Can you tell me where you are staying? Why won't you speak to me?"

Jenny remained silent.

The man in the black suit walked to the man in the brown suit, pulled his wallet from his trousers and placed a wad of bills in his hand. "Henry, take this money and drive Jenny to United Airport in Burbank. I have a colleague in the airline business with a number of new Boeing planes that fly long distances. I'll call him to make a plane ready for a flight to Mills Airport in San Francisco. He owes me. You accompany her to ensure she gets settled as far away as possible, in as short a time as possible. Check her in at the Plaza Hotel. Purchase from the concierge, a one way ticket to Sacramento on the Delta King or Queen or whatever the hell royalty name the boat has. Leave the ticket in the room with an envelope full of the money given you and write a note to Jenny explaining the ticket. Provide instructions to purchase clothes and other necessities for her trip and beyond. Shops along Market Street are there willing to assist her. Once she arrives in Sacramento, she'll be on her own. Hopefully, she'll have enough sense to remember not to disclose where she's been, or best case in her crazed, lethargic state, will forget." The man in the black suit ordered loudly to everyone, but no one in particular, "Let's get this done."

Henry and the driver of the Duesenberg gathered Jenny's bag and one shoe, not finding the other. "We can't find her other shoe," said Henry.

"Forget the damn shoe. You need to go quickly. She can buy new shoes." The man in the black suit walked into the house and within minutes returned with the suicide note in hand, placing it on the small table under the abalone shell ashtray. Henry and the driver of the Duesenberg raised Jenny from the chair, held her arms and walked slowly to the Ford. The man in the black suit rushed to the Ford and held the door open. Both men eased Jenny into the back seat. Henry entered the Ford, started the engine, switched on the headlights and slowly drove along the winding road.

"Gerard. Make the call," ordered the man in the black suit. He and the driver entered the Duesenberg and drove away. Through the Duesenberg's window, the man in the black suit gazed at the Ford's taillights fading in the distance, slowly shaking his head back and forth.

"What a shame. What a damn shame."

*   *   *   *

Her eyes opened slowly, the scene before her, the back of a brown, leather seat. She felt a rumbling vibration, the constant hum of an engine, the slight scent of oil, the chill of the window on her cheek contrasting with the warmth of the plane's interior. She turned her head, noticing a man sitting next to her, calmly looking forward. Feeling Jenny's movement, the man turned, smiling warmly.

"Hello Jenny. I'm Thomas," said Henry, the lie of his name hiding his identity. "Do you know where you are?"

"No," she replied meekly.

"Do you remember where you were and who I am?"

Jenny paused for a minute attempting to remember her circumstance. "No," she murmured.

"You're in an airplane flying to San Francisco from Los Angeles. I've been asked to escort you to ensure your safe arrival," explained Henry.

Jenny looked at Henry carefully, the long face, short slick black hair, dark brown slacks, white shirt and hazel green eyes; vaguely recalling a similarity to someone she'd seen recently. "I sort of remember you but I'm not really sure. I don't recognize your voice but you're somewhat familiar. I really don't know. I'm in an airplane? I've never been in an airplane before," she said, giddily. "I've been on trains, but not airplanes." Turning and looking through the window, she admired the carpet of bright stars splaying the dark and the bright, white moon, scanning the landscape below.

"She doesn't remember. This may work." Henry looked deeply into Jenny's tired eyes, explaining in a steady even voice. "You were visiting a friend, who abruptly left you due to a personal emergency and he asked me to accompany you to San Francisco. He arranged this plane to get you there quickly. The plane is from an airline owned by a colleague of his, who agreed to have you flown in comfort."

"But why San Francisco?" asked Jenny.

"Your friend thought San Francisco is where you're staying, but didn't know specifically where," responded Henry, looking away, again hiding the lie in his eyes.

"Okay," said Jenny, still confused, thinking, "I don't

remember getting into the plane. I don't remember where I was. I don't remember the friend Thomas is referring to. I don't even remember this man talking to me right now." Henry gently padded Jenny's knee and softly said, "You rest. The memories will return after a good sleep."

Jenny again turned toward the window, viewing the moon and stars, the moonlight casting shadows on the rocky coastline, the white foam of the ocean waves rolling in a rhythm along the beaches. Viewed from the sky, the land was beautiful in the dim darkness under the pale light of the moon, benevolently providing a path along the coast. The hum of the engine and the gentle swaying of the plane riding the current of air, hypnotized Jenny into a light sleep.

Landing on the runway with a thump, the plane rolled to the empty airport terminal. The engine stopped, revealing the silence and solitude of the night. Henry lightly shook Jenny. "Wake up. We're here. It's time we get you settled. The pilot recommends the Plaza Hotel downtown." Leading her down the steps from the plane to the runway, they walked towards a Packard waiting, the driver holding the door open.

"To the Plaza Hotel," ordered Henry.

"Yes sir," replied the driver, stepping in, starting the engine and driving away.

"Why are we going to the Plaza Hotel?" asked Jenny.

"We didn't know where you were staying, so we thought once you'd slept a while then after you've awakened, we'd decide where to take you. I'll check into a separate room. We can figure this out in the morning over breakfast."

The ride to the Plaza Hotel was relatively short. The San Francisco ocean fog clouded the Packard's windows, hiding the view of the watery bay. Jenny and Henry checked into separate rooms on the top floor and dropped on their beds with Jenny falling into a deep, long, sleep.

Jenny woke in the morning to the sound of the streetcars clanging down Market Street. She yawned and stretched, removed the blankets and stepped out of her bed. Walking to the window where the sun brightened the white lace curtains, with both arms outstretched, Jenny grabbed each of the curtains, snapping them apart. The sun's rays abruptly penetrated through the window. "What a beautiful day," she thought, her wide smile beaming through the window to the street below. Unclasping and opening the window, she inhaled deeply, absorbing the clear, cool, crisp air of San Francisco bay. Turning and viewing the room, the bed lie eloquent with brass frame and fluffed, white pillows. Next to the bed on a small, mahogany table, a bright, crimson rose in full bloom stood upright in a crystal vase, a thick envelope leaned against it. Reaching for the envelope, she opened and pulled out the note, the ticket and a wad of money. The note read:

Dear Jenny,

When you read this note, hopefully you'll be well rested. I've left you money to assist with the purchase of items you may need. You should consider patronizing a boutique and shoe store at Market and 7th Street. You'll require some clothes and shoes since only one from your pair was found.

Enclosed is a ticket for the steamboat, Delta King, a ride through the river Delta and your journey's end, Sacramento. I hope you enjoyed the plane ride. I did. It was a first for me as well.

Best Regards, Thomas

Jenny placed the note on the table, flipping through the thick packet of money. "There's a lot of money here. I could buy a whole wardrobe, shoes and nice jewelry and still have plenty left over." She placed the money on the table and touched the ticket, admiring the steamboat's picture, reading the information:

Delta King
First Class Passage
San Francisco to Sacramento
One Way
Dinner Included

"I suppose Thomas had to run. I'm disappointed. I really liked him. Why am I going to Sacramento? Oh well, I've never rode a steamboat before. It'll be fun." She walked to the powder room. A tub lay nestled in the corner. Turning the white, faucet handles, she adjusted the water until warm and slid into the tub, head submerged, face poised upward, staring at the ceiling. After washing her hair, she spread soap slowly over her body, rinsing and resting in the warm water. When the bath cooled, she stepped from the tub and towelled, leaving a deep feeling of relaxation, refreshed and ready to purchase the clothes and shoes needed for her journey. Placing the rumpled dress over her shoulders, she walked through the door, down the stairs and through the lobby of the hotel. The vibrancy of San Francisco hit her as if awakening in the center of an amusement park, people walking and talking, streetcars rumbling down Market Street, police whistles blowing and the street vendors crying out their wares. She smiled and walked across the street, noticing an ornate façade fronting a small building, a sign stating, *Market Street Boutique,* in classic gold and bronze lettering. "I should be able to find something to wear there," thought Jenny. She walked through the brass and glass revolving doors enjoying the aroma of the new fabric. The neat, clean clothing contrasted with her crumpled, worn dress sagging from her shoulders; her feet placed bare on the thick, maroon colored carpet. A balding man dressed in a suit and tie approached Jenny, his thick, brown mustache twitched downward in a facial gesture of disapproval.

"Good morning Madam. You seem out of place, you are lacking shoes and you, may I say, have seen better days."

Jenny looked down at her feet, wiggling her toes.

"Well…," she giggled, and then paused, looking at the man. "What is your name Sir?" she questioned, bruskly.

"My name is Samuel Wilkinson. I am the proprietor of this establishment."

"That is a very nice name, Mr. Samuel Wilkinson. I have no shoes because I lost one. I left the one I hadn't lost in the room at the Plaza Hotel. I didn't want to look like a one shoed Cinderella, a rather garish image, so I thought I'd present the image of a barefoot, country girl instead," said Jenny, a smirk forming wrinkles at the corners of her mouth. "So, clearly Mr. Samuel Wilkinson, I need some shoes, three pairs to be exact and some dresses and a suitcase to carry my new clothing. I'm boarding the Delta King this evening on a journey to Sacramento, in first class passage, so I want to look nice."

"Do you have money Madam?" asked Samuel, looking doubtingly and becoming aggravated by her obviously, pompous and false claim.

"Of course, silly man," said Jenny, pulling the wad of bills from her small purse. "I have lots and lots of money," she goaded, brushing the bills against Samuel's face.

Samuel's eyes flashed wide, forcing the lines in his forehead to be shaped in waves. His face brightened, his mustache twitched upward in a facial gesture of approval. "I am confident we can find you fine apparel and shoes for your pretty, little feet and, of course, jewelry to match. Come to the dress rack and let us begin." Reaching Jenny's hand and gently squeezing her small fingers, he led her to the rack of dresses in the front of three, standing, walnut-framed mirrors. Jenny jerked her hand from Samuel, sweeping the line of dresses, touching and appreciating the linen, cotton and silk, the feel of the fabric titillating her senses.

"You may choose as many as you would like. Try them and admire your image in the mirrors, which I must say is a fine image, an image of beauty and elegance. If it pleases you, I can offer my opinion on your appearance in each one," suggested Samuel, expressing himself in an excessively, enthusiastic manner.

"Mr. Samuel Wilkinson, your opinion is not necessary," said Jenny, arrogantly. "I know what I want and what makes me feel good. Just don't show me anything white," she said, creating an unknown discomfort with her expression of the term white.

"Yes Madam. May I be so bold as to gain your permission to address you with your first name, whatever that may be?" asked Samuel.

Jenny looked at Samuel, scanning him from his balding head to his shiny, black shoes, stating curtly, "You may not be so bold, Mr. Samuel Wilkinson. I prefer Madam." She pulled a green, cotton dress from the rack and walked into the dressing room, returning to view her image in the mirrors. The green cotton fabric molded her curves and after trying on many dresses and posing with self-admiration, she selected four dresses, the common green, cotton dress with a high hem line; of Italian make, an elegant lavender and crème colored silk, sleeveless flapper dress, flowing to her shin on one leg, above the knee on the other; of Parisian make and two, light-brown, linen dresses; of New York City make. Jenny strode to the section of the boutique where women's shoes were displayed. She sat on the chair and raised her foot, wiggling her toes, recalling the day her mother commented, "Honey, your feet are long and skinny like a rabbit. You could probably ski in the snow without skis." Jenny giggled and wondered what mother would think of slipping her tootsy skis into the fancy shoes about to be purchased. After trying on and finding the right size, three pairs were selected; a pair of mint-green slippers with silk, velvet-gold trim; a pair of cocoa-leather oxfords and a pair of elegant heels, studded with sparkling, artificial diamonds.

Samuel waited in the front of the store with two suitcases. Jenny approached the counter. "These are the two we have available. Do either of these suitcases appeal to you?"

"The one on the left will do."

Samuel began packing the clothing in the suitcase with the first two pairs of shoes, saving the third pair for last. Picking one shoe from the third pair, holding it, admiring its beauty, he said, "This is a fine shoe Madam, the type worn by the beautiful actress, Lauren Hirsch. I am a great admirer of her work."

Jenny looked at the shoe feeling an odd level of discomfort. "I do believe you're right Mr. Samuel Wilkinson. The actress married to that producer, a man named, what's his name? Let's see, Martin, yes. Martin as I recall." After paying Samuel for her new wardrobe, she excused herself, with suitcase in hand, briskly walked through the door of the boutique. "I remember," she gasped. She ran across the street to the Plaza Hotel, climbed the stairs to her room, opened the door, threw the suitcase aside and jumped onto the bed. "Lauren Hirsch, the actress. My husband's new wife, I remember where I was and why I was there. I killed him," she cried, the cobwebs once clouding her memory, swept away by the sounds of the city. She lay on her back staring at the ceiling. The previous day's events came back to her in fragments of time. Unable to move, paralyzed, her mind stirred with emotions of the shock, the grief, the relief and oddly, the happiness. After lying for hours, she ignored the abrupt knock, the words "housekeeping" seemingly screaming from outside the hotel door. "Go away, not now," she yelled. Lying on the bed, she remained stiff, arms across her chest; hands clasped together; her eyes staring at the crystal chandelier; the chandelier hanging from the center of the room. Searching her emotions, she found the shock, a remembrance of the shooting of husband Martin; she found the grief, a reaction to the death of losing the one she loved; and she found the relief; relief from the realization of finding the memory of the events of the past day. She couldn't find the happiness, but knew the emotion wandered there, somewhere, within the recesses of her mind. The clock on the end table showed six o'clock. Rising from the bed, she fetched the ticket from the table, listing her departure time from the Market Street dock; eight o'clock. Slipping the brown, linen dress over her shoulders, she stepped into the brown, oxford shoes and placed the gold and pearl necklace around her neck. Grabbing her suitcase, she walked the flight of stairs to the lobby and through the hotel doors, waited briefly on the corner of Market and Seventh, then boarded a clanging streetcar heading towards the dock at Market Street's end. The streetcar rode past businesses lining the street. People briskly walked the sidewalks. The streetcar stopped at each intersection, boarding and un-boarding passengers along the way. Oblivious to her surroundings, she sat silently, processing the torrent of memories rushing through her mind like a wild river during a horrendous storm, clearing the debris of useless information. She remembered clearly the events, but couldn't understand why she pulled the trigger and shot her dear, Martin.

"End of the line," the conductor yelled, clanging the bells of the streetcar, awakening Jenny from her stupor.

Stepping from the streetcar, she carried her suitcase to the nearest bench facing the bay and the bright, white Delta King. Sitting from the bench, Jenny viewed people along the waterfront, street vendors stood behind tables selling artifacts; goods from the local Chinese and Japanese districts; bottles of soda, trays of crab, salami and pizza from the Italian district, the hubbub energized the waterfront. Fishing boats drifted on the bay, docked at piers along the waterfront, stretching to the giant bridge being built; creating a gate from the city to the hills fronting the northern coastline. A rocky island stood proudly in the bay's middle, the infamous Alcatraz, where the heathen of the country languished like sardines, tightly packed in a tin can.

"Murderers live there. I should be there too. I'm a murderer, a killer," thought Jenny. Her attention to the lonely buildings perched on the rock was interrupted by a boy passing the bench, the sound disrupting her thoughts. "Suicide in Hollywood! Headline! Headline!"

"Here boy," motioned Jenny, "Give me a copy."

The boy handed the newspaper to Jenny, Jenny handing back two nickels.

"Too much," said the boy, attempting to hand one coin

back.

"It's only money," said Jenny, impatiently shooing the boy, grabbing the paper, reading the headline.

"Lauren Hirsch – Husband - Martin Mayer - Commits Suicide." A picture of the actress displayed an aura of ebullience and beauty.

"Poor Martin, even in death, that wife of his grabbed the spotlight." Reading the account of the published suicide, she detected the lies. Everything became clear, the lies contradicting her memory. She recalled the sequence of events, starting with her arrival at Martin's; the discussion of their divorce and of her obsession with the color white, of her swim in the pool, of Martin's anger towards her, of her feelings of resentment and hurt, of her taking of the gun from the bedroom dresser, of her shot to his chest, of the arrival of the men and the flight with that man, Thomas, a name probably faked in an attempt to hide the truth. "All lies," she said to herself. "They buried it. They buried the truth to protect that harlot." It all came clear to Jenny. She threw the paper in the trash bin near the bench, grabbed the suitcase and walked towards the Delta King. She stepped to the back of the line of passengers who were already boarding. Once across the boarding plank, she handed the ticket to the crew member.

"Good evening Miss. Welcome to the Delta King." He took the ticket from Jenny's hand. "I see you are entitled to first class passage. A fine compartment with many luxuries, I might add. Our attendant will escort you." The snap of his fingers brought the attendant dressed in black pants, white shirt, gold vest and black bowtie. Taking the suitcase from Jenny and motioning towards the lobby, Jenny and the attendant walked up the three, short, stair flights, to the top of the layered decks. Entering the room, the large, horizontal shutters faced the bow, offering a view of the city skyscape.

"Miss...,"

"You may call me Jenny."

"...and you may call me Phillip, Miss Jenny," said the attendant, looking into Jenny's green eyes, noting a bit of sadness.

"You just called me Miss, Phillip."

"I'm sorry," said Phillip, shaking his head. "It slipped. You know, it's difficult ignoring the formality required by our owners and the repetition of our manners on each of our overnight voyages. I'll try hard to address you as Jenny, Jenny," said Phillip, emphasizing the name Jenny while smiling. "As you can see, your compartment is a fine, luxury suite. Here is the sitting area," gestured Phillip, setting the suitcase on the plush, golden carpet. Pointing to the other end of the suite, he said, "Through the opening, behind the curtains, is your sleeping area, with all the comfort required for a restful, overnight trip through the Delta and on to Sacramento. If you're not too tired, it might be to your benefit to lie awake long enough to view the shore under the moonlight and the stars in the sky. August is the time of year when the view from the deck and specifically this room, is a wonderful experience with the beautiful scenery. And since the moon is full, the scenery is more beautiful in the bright moonlight. Through the door, at the end of the suite, is the powder room with all the required toiletries for your personal needs. On the wall next to the bed, is a brass button, when pressed, will summon me or another attendant on duty to tend to your needs. Is there anything you require before I leave?" asked Phillip.

"No thank you, Phillip. I believe I'm okay."

"We are serving dinner in the lounge at nine o'clock. The menu includes our special San Francisco bay crab and steamed clams, Tomales bay oysters, butter braised asparagus, arugula salad with Italian dressing sprinkled with pine nuts, and strawberry sorbet for dessert. We also have coffee from Kona, Hawaii, freshly ground, roasted and brewed."

"I'd like dinner in my room. It'd be a shame not to enjoy such a beautiful setting, especially since I won't be able to enjoy it for long."

"Of course, Jenny, I will ensure your dinner is delivered to your room, by nine o'clock."

Phillip closed the door, leaving Jenny peering out the window, the sun setting beyond the buildings lining the length of Market Street. She gazed at the scene before her, and after a few moments, turned slowly, admiring the room's décor. The elegantly decorated sitting area with two, amply stuffed, crème colored armchairs, rested in front of a small, low-lying, mahogany table with carved fish, dolphins and whales, swimming vertically along the table's legs; carved sea gulls and pelicans flew, wings spread hovering across the table top; a layer of thick, clear glass, covered the aerial scene. Magazines were placed neatly on the glass sitting room table, inviting the occupant to read. Tall mahogany book cases containing leather bound books, rested behind the glass doors. Three titles caught her eye, *The Octopus,* by *Norris*; *Ramona,* by *Helen Hunt Jackson*; and *Two Years Before the Mast,* a *Dana* classic; all books of interest describing life in the coastal state of California, all books Jenny made a mental note to read in the near future, all books started in the sanatorium but never finished. Gold curtains with tassels dangled, fronting the entry of the sleeping area; the bed behind lay with layered crimson, silk covers and large, golden pillows, neatly placed against a mahogany headboard. A wide smile spread across Jenny's face, "My, what an opulent room, so elegant, so exquisite." Feeling the need to be a part of the beautiful setting, she quickly opened the suitcase, pulled her silk, flapper dress and artificially studded, diamond heels from within. Removing the brown dress, she flipped her shoes against the walls across the room. In front of the standing mirror, she admired her shapely body and small, perky breasts while turning lightly, revealing her round hips. Gracefully pulling the sleeveless, silk dress over her shoulders, she sighed deeply, the dress falling gently in place. Sitting on the chair, she carefully placed her feet into her shoes, standing tall once again, turning and admiring the enhancement to her femininity the dress and heels provided. Although no music filled the room, she danced back and forth, feeling the caress of the cool silk, traversing a path between her bed and sitting area, providing visibility to the crew standing at the rail, waiting for the steamboat's release from the dock.

"That woman is a bit overly energetic. She's dancing

with no music, but spunky like an Aussie kangaroo on a
hot, desert plain," observed Tom, the deckhand. "She's
quite the looker."

Philip looked to the suite, viewing Jenny's jerky
movements through the open shutters in the windows.
"She seems to be a nice woman. I escorted her to her suite.
She's pretty, but there's something about her that isn't
right, something in her eyes," said Phillip, his voice
expressing a tone of concern.

"Well, regardless, she seems to be enjoying herself,
although she must be lonely having no partner to share
her dance."

The Delta King's engines revved; the steamboat moved
from the dock, the Delta King began its journey among the
calm waters of San Francisco bay. Jenny slumped into her
chair, exhausted from the endless dancing and prancing in
her suite. She felt the slow, methodical movement of the
steamboat gliding across the bay, the view of East Brother
light station guarded the rocky promontory from the
passing ships, clearly visible in the fogless evening. The
sun began to set; its rays blanketed the shoreline with
vivid color. She stood, opening the door to the suite and
walked to the railing. The breeze from the movement of the
steamboat gently sifted through her hair. The fresh ocean
scent of the bay tickled her senses. The near shore
provided a semblance of security coupled with a sense of
freedom and isolation while plying the calm waters on the
Delta King. Passing through San Pablo bay and on towards
the straits of Carquinez, the sun lay over the low lying
rocks and gap to the Pacific, the dusk, glowing vivid

streaks of purple, scarlet, amber and orange, mingling with the iridescent clouds. "Phillip was right about the beautiful scenery during these August evenings," thought Jenny. "I am really enjoying such a nice feeling." Philip arrived outside her door, pushing a cart with a tray of crystal plates and bowls with the food described to Jenny. He noticed Jenny standing at the rail, the breeze blowing through her dress revealing the soft, smooth skin of her legs and thighs.

"Excuse me, Jenny. Your dinner is ready."

"Thank you Phillip. Please roll the tray inside the room. I'll tend to my meal later. I'm enjoying the bay, the view and the serenity offered, it's such a beautiful setting. You were right about the beauty of the August evening."

"I'm glad you're enjoying yourself. When you're finished with your meal, you may ring me or just set the cart outside your door and I'll come to remove it." He walked back down the corridor to the steps leading to the area below the passenger decks. Jenny continued absorbing the warm, August evening and after a short while returned to her room settling, once again, onto her chair. Reaching for the cart, she picked at the crab, but decided to eat a raw oyster lying under the crab's legs. Realizing she wasn't hungry, she stared at the cart, moved to her bed and slid under the blankets, her silk dress brushing and smoothing her skin. She slept a few hours, her meal remained untouched and when she awakened, the moon's rays peeked through the open slats of the window's shutters. Rising from the bed, she once again approached the railing. Grabbing the steamboat's rails, looking up, the full, white moon dominated the clear, dark sky; the sparkling stars occupied the remnants of the sky not touched by the moon. Interrupting the quiet of the dark morning hours, an intermittent chorus of crickets, sang its clicking song. Muted outlines of water towers, windmills, homes, barns and small shops appeared, revealing themselves sporadically behind the banks of the levees. The sweet scent of the river air floated with the breeze. "I'm in the Delta now," sighed Jenny, with satisfaction. In the distance, moonlight touched a bridge with cement blocks hanging on each end, the steel structure bright gray from the moon's beams. Bushy trees on the river's edge absorbed the moon's rays, the leaves reflecting a shade of grayish-green. The river narrowed, succumbing to the dominance of the Delta islands, contrary to the dominance of the wide waters of San Francisco bay, at journey's beginning. "It's a whole different world out here," thought Jenny, entering a state of deep tranquillity.

*　　*　　*　　*

Jenny felt her slim fingers delicately slide across the varnished, wooden rail on the deck of the Delta King, deep in the heart of the Delta. She felt comfort away from the city of angels, her imagined angel's wings no longer seared, no longer in hell's flaming abyss; healthy again from the soothing massage by the Delta and its moon. "That was quite an adventure," she admitted to the Delta Moon with reluctant admiration, "You are very handsome, although you are very white. Maybe Martin was right. Maybe white isn't always evil. You seem to leave a favorable impression on the things you touch. You did accompany me here to San Francisco from Los Angeles. You did guide me to safety, and here you are again, kindly showing the way to Sacramento during my journey on this lovely steamboat. I especially like the thin, glowing, cloud ring surrounding you this evening. I've never seen that before. Maybe it's you proposing to me. I believe you like me, my bright, white knight in mooning armor," giggled Jenny, yet again. She looked to the dark, calm current flowing past the side of the steamboat. Glancing afar, the river glowed; the bright, white Delta Moon reflected from the surface. The happiness finally came to Jenny, who knew the emotion had been there, somewhere, but lost deep in her mind, and now found. She felt the desire to feel the water's caress. "Why does one feel the need to be nude in water?" she thought, remembering the cool of the pool near the city of angels, sensually caressing her bodily curves. Gazing at the Delta Moon a shooting star streaked. The orange-red tail, diagonally crossed the Delta Moon's face, like a winking eye. "Maybe white isn't evil after all," she whispered, lovingly absorbing the moonlight reflecting from the river surface. The Delta Moon flirted with her; the Delta Moon beckoned her; the Delta Moon spoke to her; the Delta Moon's words floated with the hot, August breeze; the Delta Moon's soft, lyrical voice, steady and trance-like weaved with the hum of the steamboat's engine. She felt the delicate sound of the ripple of the trailing wake; she felt the distant murmur of the passengers' conversations and her own impassioned breathing. The Delta Moon wanted her, its dark spots winked at her and she felt its pull; the white light touched her welcoming lips, caressed her sensitive breasts, romanced her with its want and desire, and she felt its need and her own need to be adored and fulfilled. She removed her shoes and felt the warmth of the wood under her feet. She loosened the silk dress from her shoulders; the dress slipping to the deck around her ankles. Standing nude, her skin glistened like mother-of-pearl, absorbing the Delta Moon's rays, her white angel's wings set to bloom and fly. Climbing the railing, she looked to the Delta Moon attempting flight for the embrace. She jumped from the railing and fell through the night and the river took her. The Delta Moon's cold, dark arms swiftly pushed her to its river lair; accosting her, and as she descended to the river's depths, she looked to the surface, the white light of the beckoning Delta Moon grew faint, and before the light turned to darkness, her thoughts were of the betrayals; the Delta Moon was no different than the others; its white glow lured her proving the Delta Moon evil, and now, the betrayal was complete.

Mountain Idol

"The moon behind Mount Diablo was round and large and white on the last evening of October, 1806. The cool mountain breeze lay heavy with the earthy scent of decaying oak leaves, when five, Spanish soldiers on horses appeared a few hundred yards below the pointed peak. Lieutenant Gabriel Moraga spotted the natives in bushes among a cluster of oaks, the soldiers riding high in their brown, leather saddles. Charging forward, their screams violated the quiet in the tranquil setting. Suddenly, an apparition appeared, flying over the peak, a beast-like man with dark-red skin, bright-red hair, and plumed, feather headdress, assaulted the soldiers with a scream like that of rolling thunder. The horses stopped abruptly, kicked their front legs in the air, and in unison, turned and fled, the Lieutenant and his soldiers defeated."

And this is how the story was told to the little boy, Diego Lara Vasquez, by his father, who was told as a little boy, by his father, who sat drinking wine, on the shaded patio of Rancho Los Medranos, east of Devil Mountain.

PUY

What remained of Rancho Vasquez was not a ranch at all, but a one acre plot of land with wooden structures comfortable and worn with years. On the north side of the river between the towns of Clarksburg and Ryde; the small, square, four room, wooden house sat on the corner of the plot bordered by rows of pear trees. In the opposite corner leaned a rickety, chicken coop, enclosed with rusted wire where ten chickens stood in the shaded parts, pecking at feed and in a water trough. Hidden behind the chicken coop, stood a tall, slim, wooden outhouse, its door unevenly tilted against the frame, the wooden slats, gapped and bent, yellow wasps hovered under the eaves of the roof, its white paint, cracked and crumbled.

Between River Road and the house, in the middle of the plot, stood three trees, one pear, one orange and one fig, and around each tree, a five inch high mound of dirt encircled each trunk. In the hot, summer months, Socorro Vasquez filled the enclosed inner circle with water, where mosquitoes skimmed the watery surface and graceful cats with tiny, pink tongues, lapped from the mini oasis.

Rose bushes surrounded the house in clusters of pink, yellow and white, the sweet fragrance blended with the scent of orange blossoms. A wooden door with two, small steps served as the entrance. Next to the door, a water spout and faucet rose from the ground, the only source of water for drinking, bathing and irrigating. Small windows surrounded the house, each adorned with worn, yet clean pink polka-dot curtains.

The house was built by Fernando Vasquez, a short and proud man, the illegitimate son of Emiliano Vasquez, a California settler, who inherited the small plot of land from his father, a Spanish soldier. Given from a small inheritance given to Fernando after Emiliano's death, and the liquidation of his holdings by Emiliano's lawful wife, Rosa, who originally kept the modest wealth for herself, then fled to Guadalajara, Mexico to live her years in comfort. Weeks later, after succumbing from guilt having confessed to Father Castellanos in the *Catedral de la Asunción de María Santísima* in Guadalajara, she was scolded for abandoning the illegitimate children of Emiliano and told to repent and share her inheritance with his children and the church. "They are all children of the Lord, as are we," reprimanded the priest, "and are deserving of your charity."

During her years in Rancho Los Medranos, Rosa, who could not bear children, endured the indignation of six of Emiliano's children of servants wandering through the house and patios. The servants were of varying ages, some young, some old, some skinny, some fat, none beautiful, but all available to satisfy the frequent urges of Emiliano, at any hour, any day and any night, for his needs were many, blamed on the family curse of lust for women, cited with examples of his ancestors who told tales of the wanton taking of native women. "The illegitimate children should be cared for by their birth mothers," thought Rosa uncaringly, "not rewarded for their unfortunate plight."

After speaking with Father Castellanos in Guadalajara, Rosa reluctantly shared a small portion of her inheritance with currency sealed in white envelopes and wax seals, delivered by messenger on horseback to the children of Emiliano, throughout the lands of the Delta.

Fernando Vasquez loved his father Emiliano and the memories and stories of California bandits, of Spanish wars, of Mexico, of California native legends learned from the Miwok tribes, descendants whom included his mother Kaliska, a Volvon Miwok, a servant, the object of many of his father's affections, affections overheard by Fernando in the room next to his door in their little, two room shack on the fringe of Rancho Los Medranos. Fernando used the money from the inheritance given by Rosa, to buy back a small plot of land from Mr. Bannerman, who purchased Rancho Los Medranos from Rosa. Fernando worked farms and odd jobs, for fifteen months, to purchase scraps of wood, wire and metal for his new land, until the house, outhouse, chicken coop and tool shed were completed. Fernando moved his mother Kaliska to the plot he named Rancho Vasquez; the name proudly retained, although Fernando wasn't a legal member of the Vasquez clan, having no right to the family name. The house was a simple one, with four rooms, a kitchen with a working stove, a living area and two rooms for sleeping. Kaliska was grateful to Fernando and proud of her simple home, upgraded from the shack she and Fernando occupied since Fernando's birth. Fernando met a local girl, Teresita, who charmed him to the point of love, who he married and sprung a family of three children, two girls and a boy. After settling in with his family, Fernando was faithful for only a few years, for he was the unlucky recipient of the Vasquez curse, wandering the levee roads in search of women to satisfy his desires. After a short illness and death of his mother Kaliska, Fernando left Rancho Vasquez, on a steamboat one cold and rainy evening in search of a cure for his curse, among the saloons and hotels in San Francisco. During the fruitless search, Fernando realized the curse had no antidote, after wandering the dark, damp streets and alleys on the bay of Barbary, never returning to his family. Embittered from the lost Fernando, Teresita raised her children and taught the two girls, Socorro and Maria, the Catholic religion and chastity, and taught her son Diego, what she knew of the Miwok spirits, for she did not know what spiritual training would be best. She understood the merits of both, from the teachings of her family's experience with the church in the form of Catholicism, and from the mysticism of the Miwok, as told by the lost Fernando, who entranced her with natural legends of native lore. The teachings of Catholicism and chastity stuck with Socorro, the oldest, who over time understood the reason for her father's abandonment and felt he was damned by God for the sin of fornication outside of marriage. Socorro experienced only one exploration of sin as a teenager with Sal Ferrante, the son of an Italian fisherman, from the town of Pittsburg, who forced her hand on his boyhood, which she quickly pulled away running in shock and revulsion, never to be enticed by such vulgarity for the remainder of her life. Two years later, Sal played his trick on Maria, who rather than revulsion, experienced the feeling of excitement, curiosity and euphoria after going all the way with Sal. The teachings of Catholic chastity did not stick with Maria. She could not overcome her carnal fervor blamed later on the curse, thought an aberration, since it never affected the women in the family; at least it was never admitted. Maria became bored with Sal and bounced from boy to boy, then man to man, as she grew older. When Maria reached the age of twenty, she moved to Sacramento to pursue the experiences that made her feel wanted and alive. Maria worked as a waitress at Sam's Place, a roadside diner, never returning to Rancho Vasquez, for her mother disowned and vowed to never see her for the remainder of her life, which she honored as fervently as her nightly Catholic prayers under the poor, young, dead man with the horned crown, nailed to the wooden cross hanging on the center wall above her bed. Socorro never visited her sister in honor of her mother's wishes, and to keep distance from sin. Diego, however, would travel to Sacramento, twice a year, bearing handpicked pears and oranges, sometimes a live chicken and fresh asparagus, ignoring his mother's wishes. Diego wasn't burdened with the strict edicts of Catholicism. Diego was influenced by the teachings of the native spirits, which were many, for he believed in the natural laws and legends of the Miwok, not the egocentric law of one God, and God's strict edicts and punishments, taught with formality under the cross, and among the statues and stained glass of the Catholic Church.

"Too many damned rules," Diego would say when arguing with his mother and sister Socorro regarding the subject of 'civilized' religion. "Man wasn't made for those rules."

Maria lived happily in Sacramento and became seeded with child now and then by various suitors, dispensing of the nuisances for a modest fee, with a visit to Monsieur Jacque Benoit, a French abortionist, practicing in the musty basement of his J street, Sacramento home. At the age of forty, Maria visited Monsieur Benoit for another procedure, but Monsieur Benoit, unable to, cited the potential for serious damage and potential death for Maria due to the frequency of the procedure, and her advancing age.

"Natural child birth is the only option for you Maria," said Monsieur Benoit, sadly.

Maria accepted the disruptive news and carried the baby through nine months of waiting with belly growing and excitement climbing. Maria gave birth to the child and spoke to him when the baby laid on her chest. "Simon, you are a beautiful boy. I've named you after Simon Bolivar, the only famous person I remember from reading a history book in school. A country was named after him. The book was good, exciting. Simon Bolivar was a brave man, a noble and valiant man. Sharing his name will allow you to start life with a chance of achieving a good reputation, like Mr. Bolivar. So I present you to this world, Mr. Simon

Bolivar Vasquez. Welcome and make yourself proud!" She
loved the boy instantly and marvelled at his clear, green
eyes, light, olive skin and reddish-brown hair, so different
from her appearance with dark, black hair, brown eyes and
brown skin. "Simon," thought Maria, "I don't know if your
father is Giovanni, the grocer who has the same color of
your eyes, or Ian, the bartender with hair of a similar
reddish tinge. I was a naughty woman a few months ago,
but both men were good men, and along with your famous
name, you will be served well." Maria devoted her life to
Simon and ceased partaking in the pleasures of the flesh,
desires replaced by pride and the strength of purpose, of
protecting and nurturing a living thing, a living thing
dependent entirely on her. Diego visited Maria every month
when told of Simon's birth, and brought Simon toys and
carved figures of animals from the dead branches of
sycamore and oak. He enjoyed telling Simon stories of
native legends and bandits, like his father Fernando told
him. Diego was ecstatic with Simon, the new addition to
the Vasquez clan, but mamma Teresita refused to
acknowledge the happy event saying, "Maria's whoring has
produced a bastard from the loins of the devil."

Teresita died on Simon's fifth birthday and was buried
at St. Joseph's Catholic Church in Rio Vista. The funeral
was attended by few, three, elderly lady friends and
Socorro, Diego, Maria and Simon, the grandson Teresita
never met. The priest, after drinking a bottle of the blood of
Jesus, eulogized mamma Teresita and attempting to
remember mamma Teresita's life told him by Socorro,
became confused and told the story of the life of another

recently deceased woman. Socorro, now free from the emotional control of her mother, felt a sense of weightlessness and though saddened, was relieved from the burden of servitude to her mother. Like Diego, she was excited for the opportunity to reunite with Maria and to meet Simon after hearing wonderful stories from Diego of Simon's carefree personality and deep curiosity. Socorro lived her life devoted to her mother, her church and her cats. Upon mamma Teresita's death, Socorro spent her days mothering and caring for her cats and their offspring, until the brood numbered twenty, give or take a few. Diego despised the cats, however, for no reason other than his misplaced feeling that men shouldn't like cats. After the consumption of a jug of homemade wine, Diego would occasionally capture a cat under the auspice of warmth, friendship, and bits of chicken, and once caught, throw the cat in the open hole of the outhouse bench; the cat disappearing into the morass of human stench and filth. Diego wasn't certain of the cat who met its demise, or which saint the cat represented, since Socorro baptized each one in honor of the saints popularized by the Vatican. Each time, after awakening from his drunken stupor, Diego thought of the cat flung in the abyss of waste and was disturbed by the guilt of killing a saint.

"Why did I do such a horrible thing? Did I kill St. Peter, St. Francis, St. Augustine or St Joan, or one of the hundreds of other saints named by the higher-ups in the Catholic Church? Why were only certain people recognized by the church for doing good things? Wasn't doing good things natural? Didn't the average person do good things?

Why weren't they named saints? Our native religions didn't have saints. Didn't need them," thought Diego.

Diego, one year younger than Maria, had evaded the Vasquez curse, although occasionally as a young man, would visit a whorehouse in Locke or Isleton, never enjoying the deed, doing it only after a feeling of male obligation that over the years subsided. Diego's two passions were the worship and search for "Puy", the Miwok spirit of Devil Mountain, and the fermenting of fruit wines made from the fruits of the season, his favorite being pear wine made from the refuse of the damaged pears after harvest. Diego's evasion of the Vasquez curse was considered a good omen in the Vasquez household, but Socorro felt Diego's name affliction was equally as bad. Socorro had once complained to Diego, "Hermano, you are cursed with your fake names you invent to sound more important then you are; you are 'loco' my brother. I fear for you." Diego did appear to have a touch of 'loco', since he kept adding names to his name, to expand his Spanish lineage and to give an air of nobility beyond the family history, a history rooted in the humble occupation of soldiery; from the conquest to the support of the missionaries in their quest to tame the land, to teach the natives 'civilized' behavior, to save their souls from the depths of hell. Conflicted, Diego, although proud to be part Spaniard, closely identified with his native heritage of his grandmother Kaliska's ancestry and idolized, 'Puy', the spirit of Mt. Diablo, the benevolent protector of the Miwok natives and conqueror of the Spanish Army; the mountain named by the Spanish soldiers, after the attempted subjugation of the escaped Miwok tribesmen from Mission San Jose and the Spanish soldiers flight from the verbal wrath of 'Puy'. The mountain's name evolved along with the evolution of those who peopled the area, originally *Supemenenu* as known by the Miwok, and *Cerro Alto de los Bolbones,* as known by the early Spanish explorers, and *Monte De Diablo,* or Devil Mountain, as named by the defeated Spanish soldiers, who insisted the devil, 'Puy', guarded the mountain and the valley.

Unfortunately, Maria died from a serious problem of a female nature. shortly after her mother Teresita died, only two weeks from the awkward funeral conducted by the priest from the Catholic Church in Rio Vista. The solemn funeral conducted in Sacramento was attended by only Simon, Diego and Socorro. Simon and Diego stricken with grief, Socorro ridden with guilt and haunted with regret of time not spent with Maria, vowing to care for Simon for the remainder of his childhood, and happy to have someone to converse with other than the loco and sometimes tedious conversations with Diego.

*   *   *   *

Diego Lara Vasquez Henao Arana Jaen Rodriguez Lopez de la Pollo crouched in the chicken coop, throwing feed at the pecking chickens surrounding him.

"Tia, Tio Diego told me he added another name to his name. I've never asked you before but why does Tio Diego have so many names?" asked Simon, looking at Tio Diego through the open, kitchen door.

"Your Tio invented them, to make him more important than he is," responded Tia Socorro. "He believes we are descendents of a royal family from Spain. Tio Diego is a bit loco. The silly new name, "de la Pollo" means 'of the chicken.' The name his mother and father gave him is Diego Lara Vasquez."

"Maybe we are descendants from Spain. There could be riches in the vault of a bank in Madrid, or Seville, or Barcelona. Our inheritance, we were never notified of, or land with acres of grapevines, or a villa with a patio overlooking the white rocks and light-blue Mediterranean Sea."

"You too may be a little 'loco', Simon. Be careful you don't go down the path of your Tio Diego."

"Tio Diego can be odd at times, but he is a good man, always cheerful and hopeful, he's fun to be around."

"Go out and help your Tio feed the chickens. I have work to do," she barked, while patting the flour tortillas back and forth in her brown, veiny, wrinkled hands. "He is talking to them. They don't talk back. If he talks to you, you talk back."

Simon rose from the green, metal chair in the corner of the kitchen and walked out the door and down the two, short steps to the dusty entryway. "Hey, Tio," he yelled, "Need some help with the chickens?"

Tio Diego stood upright from crouching in sagging, blue overalls, laughing his signature laugh, "Heh heh heh. I could use your help Mijo. I'm getting too fat for this hard work."

"The work isn't hard Tio, you're just getting old."

"Yes, I am Mijo. I remember when I was your age, slim with thick, full hair and much energy. Look at me now, bald and fat from your Tia's cooking and tired from the jug of wine I drink on rare occasions."

Simon laughed, "The occasional wine is more than occasional. It seems to be your drink of choice."

"Heh heh heh, you may be right Mijo, you may be right. Let's sit on the asparagus crates under the fig tree and have a mug of wine now. I am thirsty and need rest."

Walking to the corner of the lot, Diego and Simon shuffled among the dirt and pebbles, to the shade of the fig tree, where flattened dried figs lay, sunburnt, black and wrinkled, peeking from under the browning leaves.

"Mijo," Diego said, pointing to the other end of the lot, "go to the shed and in the old, rusty, red chest are my jug and two mugs. Bring them here and we'll drink." Diego walked to the crates, stacked one upon the other, the crates bolted with remnants of two by fours, added ten years prior to support his well-grown frame. Simon walked to the shed, returning with the dark-green jug in one hand, his finger holding the looped stem, the other hand holding the two mugs looped in each of two fingers. "Sit Mijo, here on the crate next to me and here, take this mug and we'll celebrate my final year searching for Puy." Diego uncorked the jug, filled the mugs, set the jug on the dusty, brown ground and tipped his mug to Simon's for a toast. "To Puy, our protector, may we finally meet," boasted Diego, loudly.

"And to Tio Diego, may he find the spirit he's been searching, and make him rest for the remainder of his days with comfort, knowing Puy exists." Diego and Simon drank the sweet, pear wine with a tongue, swishing swallow. Diego pointed his mug toward the mountain in the southwest. The dark-gray, peaked mountain towered over the undulating, brown hills; the hills bowing in submissive subordination.

"I wish you could go with me to Devil Mountain, but I know you must finish school," said Diego.

"Why don't you go one more year or even better, skip this year and go next year? I can go if you wait another year. I'll be finished at Courtland High, so my October will be freed."

"No Mijo, I'm too old and tired to wait another year. I'll barely have enough in me to make this year. You can go next year on your own or take that girl, Shelly you met a few years ago. She's grown to be a pretty girl."

"She has grown to be a very pretty woman. She's a young woman now, not a girl. It's hard to believe she's changed from the sweet, little girl I'd chase around her Uncle Tim's orchards playing tag. It's amazing how beautiful she's become since last summer."

"You've changed, too, Mijo. You are a handsome, young man and I would bet she has noticed your change."

"We did have a nice time this summer doing things like riding her uncle's horses, Blondie and Caesar, picking pears in the orchard, laying under the stars at night, talking of our futures, sneaking around the Ryde Hotel, peaking in the tall windows at the couples dancing and kissing, and our favorite activity, swimming among the hyacinths in Snodgrass Slough. But Tio, I'm not sure I'll see her next year, after I see her on Thanksgiving break in a few weeks, she's going to college and may forget me," said Simon, with some sadness.

"But she likes you, no?"

"I think so. I did see her and we had a nice swim. We kissed and we were naked in the water. I can tell you Tio, there are parts of her body proving she's a woman. It was difficult saying good-bye not knowing where our relationship would lead."

"Being naked with each other is a good thing, I think. I can't give you advice on how to treat a naked woman. I was never good at it. But she knows where you live and where you work. Her uncle will be farming here for many years to come. You'll see her. So don't worry. Have faith, Mijo."

"I will have faith Tio, although I may be going to college too. I'll work one more year at Chauncey's store after I graduate. When I go to college, we'll be separated, as usual, and possibly during the summers as well, since she may find a new friend. Who knows when we'd see each other."

"Don't worry, Mijo. You're a good boy, a smart boy, a boy with the whole world in front of you, if not with Shelly, with someone else," said Diego, flicking his hand in the air, dispelling Simon's concern.

They both drained their mugs dry and refilled from the green jug while sitting under the cool shade of the leafy, fig tree.

"So when are you leaving Tio and how long will you be gone?" asked Simon.

"I leave tomorrow Mijo, on Sunday. I'll walk over the bridge to Walnut Grove, ride on a riverboat at around nine in the morning, and when I arrive on the docks at Black

Diamond Avenue in Pittsburg, I'll rest and eat. Then, like before, I'll ride the Black Diamond coal train to Nortonville, walk the long walk over the dry, rolling hills to Clayton. That's gonna be a very long day. I'll sleep under the big oak next to the hotel on Main and Center streets. It'll take me another two days to reach the summit; a long climb through the ravines with oaks, grass, weeds and steep rocks, to the new, tall tower with the light that shines in the night put there a few years ago by that oil company, to guide those airplane contraptions in the night. That's where I'll see Puy. Things are changing on Devil Mountain Mijo, things men are building, like that tower built by the oil company that planes fly over, things that may anger Puy. We don't want to anger Puy, do we Simon?"

"No we don't Tio. Angering Puy would be a bad thing."

"Coming back will be faster, because walking downhill will be easier, so all together, I'll be gone about a week."

"That's a long time Tio, aren't you afraid, going to the mountain alone? I heard from some friends who smuggle bootleg wine on the riverboats, that hooligans hang around the Pittsburg docks looking for trouble. You've said yourself things are changing. Maybe the people are changing too, in a bad way."

"No Mijo. I've made this trip for almost fifty years and never had any trouble and won't this year."

"Why don't you bring Grandpa Fernando's old pistol, just in case?"

"That old pistol hasn't been shot for a long time. Since your Grandpa Fernando left and never came back. I don't like guns Mijo. They kill things and I don't want to kill things."

Simon looked at Diego with concern, worrying and wondering of his safety this final year of Diego's journey in search of Puy. Diego had grown older, since many years before, when he arrived in Sacramento on occasion and gave mamma Maria, fruits and vegetables and to him, cheap, colored, plastic toys and animal figures he'd carved from the branches of cottonwood and oaks, his favorite being the awkward-looking woodpecker, no resemblance to a real woodpecker, with the fake beak, round and painted red, eyes of two, apricot pits painted black, glued to its sides. Diego often bore the brunt of kidding made by Simon over the bad form of the woodpecker, how the woodpecker wouldn't peck wood, with the blunted, round beak and eyes blind with black. The woodpecker leaned against Simon's high school, basketball trophy, atop his dresser, in the small bedroom of Rancho Vasquez, as a tribute to Tio Diego. Diego had hair no more. His decades old, sweat-stained and faded, brown Fedora, fit loosely, no longer snuggling on his age-spotted, bald head. Diego's body was much fuller now. His belly hung over the worn weathered belt. His legs creaked with movement. They drank another cup of wine and walked back to the chicken coop, Simon scattering the bits of grain from the burlap bag of feed. Diego leaned against the fence pole, watching and speaking to the chickens. When done, Simon handed the bag to Diego. "We're finished Tio, the chickens look happy. I'm going to check in on Tia and head to Chauncey's store for my pay. It's payday."

"You go Mijo, thank you for helping feed the chickens

and drinking my wine."

Simon walked across the barren, dirt plot and through the door. The light scent of the warming, tortilla dough with the darkened spots filled the small kitchen. Tia Socorro stood over the hot stove rapidly flipping and piling freshly, cooked tortillas, one upon the other, wrapping them in a clean, red towel to maintain their warmth.

"I'm going," said Simon, sternly.

Tia Socorro, startled by the abrupt pronouncement asked, "Where are you going Mijo?"

"Mt. Diablo. I need to be with Tio to make sure he's safe in his last journey."

"No Mijo, you must go to school."

"I can't go to school Tia. I need to protect Tio, like Puy protects Tio."

"Ah Simon. There is no Puy," said Tia, flicking her hand in the air. "You are 'loco', like your Tio."

"I know there is no Puy and I'm not being entirely truthful about worrying for Puy's safety, but there will be Puy this year. Puy will show up. I'll be Puy."

"Oh Mijo, you are muy loco."

"Tio has tirelessly climbed up Devil Mountain for many years, and since this year will be his last, he needs to see Puy, to know he exists."

"You can't be Puy."

"I can be Puy. I'll dress in red cloth around my waist. I'll dab my skin with paint and wear a strip of red cloth around my head, with a long, turkey, tail feather sticking from the edge, just like Tio describes him. I will be Puy," said Simon, with conviction.

"What about the noise Mijo, the noise Diego says Puy makes when he is seen, the rolling, thunder noise."

"I'll use grandpa Fernando's old pistol to make the noise. It won't be rolling thunder, but noise from a bolt of lightning," said Simon, his arm thrusting jaggedly in the air. "But it'll have to do."

"But papa Fernando's old pistol has never been shot, since he left and didn't come back."

"I know, that's what Tio said, but I'll test the pistol, Tia. I'll use the old bullets and walk through the orchards and shoot a pear tree to make sure it works."

"Muy loco Mijo, you make me worry."

Simon walked to Tia Socorro. Her tiny, fragile body leaned against the edge of the stove, one arm resting on her hips. He touched her thin, veiny hand holding it in his, leaned down and kissed the top of her head. "Don't worry Tia, it'll be okay. I'll make it to the top of the mountain before Tio and wait for him before I become Puy. He won't see me. This will be good for him."

"Oh, Mijo, you are stubborn and think you know everything, like your mamma Maria, por Madre. But, I know you are doing this for him. You be careful. I will pray to the Lord for you," she said looking up, pulling her hand from Simon, motioning the sign of the cross over her chest.

Simon grabbed a tortilla from the freshly cooked pile, stuffed it into his mouth, walked briskly to the tree where his Schwinn bike leaned, hopped on the seat and pedalled down the dusty road towards Paintersville Bridge. After crossing the river, mirroring the bridge's image, Simon entered the Chinese section of Courtland, the large sign above, *Chauncey Chew's General Merchandise,* spanned across the road. Simon stopped abruptly, slid his Schwinn sideways, and ran into Chauncey's store.

"Hey Chauncey, where are you?" yelled Simon, rushing down the tobacco and wood scented aisle, stuffed with canned goods, detergent boxes, and other home merchandise. At the end of the aisle, Chauncey, short and leathery, with thin, graying hair, leaned on one knee, unpacking a large box filled with packaged noodles, turned and smiled, "Simon, how are you?"

"I need your help Chauncey. I'm going to need some time off Monday and for a few days after. Will you be alright without me?"

"Of course Simon, you're such a hard worker, it wouldn't be right for me to say no. Why do you need the time off?" asked Chauncey.

"Puy and Diego, they both need me."

"Ah, is your uncle Diego making his yearly October trip to search for that mythical Puy? You know Puy isn't real. Puy is like all those Gods we Chinese invented in China, the God of wind, the God of moon, the God of sun, the God of thunder, the God of lightning, the God of happiness, the God of sadness, the God of prosperity, the God of..."

"I know, I know," interrupted Simon, "people invent Gods and spirits to explain things that can't be explained, like Tio's belief in the God the Spanish and Miwok invented. We both know and everyone in the Delta knows of Diego's obsession with Puy, but this is his last year. He's getting old and won't be able to do this trip next year. I need to pretend to be Puy, to make Diego happy and make him feel all the years of boasting of Puy and the tale he tells is actually true. We all know Puy doesn't exist and think Diego is a little crazy, but Diego has spent his life searching for proof of Puy, and I just want him to know that Puy actually exists. I need to make the trip to Mt. Diablo and be Puy."

"I see Simon. You're going to perform a good deed for your old and tired uncle. But what about school, you'll need to get permission to take off from school?"

"That's what Tia is worried about. I know school is important, but a few days away from school isn't going to hurt me. I'm caught up with my homework, and finished with my book report, and I seem to spend most of my last year in class staring through the windows, at birds dancing in the trees and ducks swimming in the sky. I'll figure out how to deal with it. I'll speak with Mrs. Morris and ask her permission to be absent for a little while."

"You have such an imagination Simon, very creative. I don't see how birds can dance in a tree, or ducks swim in the sky, but you can see such things," said Chauncey, with wonder. "Mrs. Morris is a good teacher, a reasonable woman and you're a good boy Simon. Good luck and let me know if you need anything else for your adventure."

"Well, now that you mention it, I do need a few things. I need some red paint and red cloth to make me look like Puy. I know you have both, so I'd like to purchase those items and a canteen to store water and the canvas, fishing bag on the corner shelf, which I can use to store food. I also need the smoked venison and salted trout stored in the cabinets next to and..."

"Simon, slow down. You do this. Just walk through the store and pick what you need."

"I'll pay for it from the money you're going to give me, it's payday you know."

"I know Simon, but you take what you need and consider it a gift from me as a contribution to the honorable quest of helping your uncle and you being Puy. Maybe proof of Puy will provide the faith needed in our Delta community to bring us together, even though you and I know the truth about you being Puy."

Simon walked to the corner shelf, grabbed the canvas, fishing bag, dropped in the can of paint, red cloth, a canteen, and chunks of salted trout and strips of smoked, peppered venison into the bag. He walked towards the counter at the front of the store, where Chauncey stood waiting with money in hand. Chauncey smiled at Simon. "Here Simon, the money you've earned this week. Be safe and have a fun with your adventure. I've never been to Mt. Diablo, but feel I've been there through the stories Diego tells me of the beauty he sees and feels."

Simon took the money from Chauncey's waiting hand, "Thanks Chauncey. You've been good to me, and I really appreciate the things you've given for my trip. I'll see you in a few days." Simon rushed through the door, raised the red Schwinn and with one arm holding the overstuffed, canvas bag, the other holding the steering bar, pedalled rapidly down the street, where the homes lay comfortably under the sun.

*   *   *   *

Socorro stood and watched Simon pedal his Schwinn hurriedly down River Road in the direction of the bridge. She sighed with worry and heard Diego talking once again to the chickens. "Heh heh heh," he laughed, speaking something muffled that could have been a joke, but didn't appear to interest the chickens. The chickens continued to cluck and peck, oblivious to Diego's attention. Socorro's thoughts went to the fondness for her family, even with the tragedies of the abandonment by their father, the death of their embittered mother, the scandal of the birth of Simon out of wedlock, and the sad passing of sister, Maria. Their life had been hard, but fulfilling. The entry of Simon into their life and the happiness Simon conveyed living with his Tia and Tio, brought joy to the three of them, even with the simplicity their lives held in the Delta. Simon had integrated well with the community, made friends easily, found a job with Chauncey, did well with his studies, was a star high school, basketball player and introduced her and Tio Diego to many of his friends and their families, giving them roots and good standing, even though they lived life poor and without what they thought were simple luxuries common in the Delta. "Mierda," she thought, "we don't even have a toilet." He even met that pretty girl, Shelly, who he appeared to like, but didn't seem to get intimately involved proving he didn't suffer from the Vasquez family curse, like she and Diego didn't suffer. Socorro and Diego, never established intimate relationships and were never driven by the curse, like hermana Maria and papa

Fernando, and the other relatives told through the stories passed on. "Maybe the curse is no more," she thought, with curiosity and comfort. She loved her brother Diego, and her nephew Simon, and knew they all loved each other, making them rich in life. Diego began walking towards the kitchen door, Socorro moved away for fear of being seen staring at Diego and the questions the stare may have arisen. Diego opened the door and stepped into the kitchen, the door gently shutting behind with a dull thump.

"Ah, Socorro, your kitchen smells good as always. What wonderful, tasty food do you have for your little brother this morning?" asked Diego, pulling the chair from under the table, and setting his plump body on the worn, metal seat.

"You are not so little and you're always complimenting me just for my food, *mi pequeno hermano.* I have some fresh tortillas made for you and Simon. Simon's already had one, so there is plenty more for you. Take a few from this pile and I'll fry some eggs you've taken from our chickens. And sit up, don't slouch, it's no good for your back," reprimanded Socorro.

Diego slouched further in his chair to irritate Socorro, and continued his sincere compliments with the motive of getting fed the usual tasty and filling breakfast. "Ah, but your food is so good hermana, you are the reason I'm having much difficulty with my weight." Socorro turned her back to Diego, smiled, giggling quietly at their playfully, contentious conversation. "So you know this is my last year Socorro. My last year searching for Puy."

Socorro stepped from the warm stove and sat on the

metal chair across from Diego. She placed her thin, veiny hand on Diego's chubby hand, looked directly into his cheerful eyes and said with deep sincerity, "I know Diego, and I hope you finally meet Puy. After all these years searching, I know the frustration you must have not seeing him, always wondering of his existence."

"Don't worry hermana," said Diego, placing his other hand over Socorro's. "I'll see Puy this year, and even if I don't, I still know he exists. I feel his spirit every morning when I wake up and look across the land at Devil Mountain above the horizon, and I believe the stories once told by papa Fernando, and told by others as well. He does exist."

*   *   *   *

Simon slid the Schwinn in front of the small green house, placed the canvas fishing bag overflowing with the paint can on the ground, and ran up the steps to the porch, hurriedly knocking firmly on the wooden door. "Mrs. Morris. Mrs. Morris, where are you? I need to ask you something."

A slight rustling was heard as Mrs. Morris walked from the back of the house, through the hall to the door, opening it, smiling and gesturing Simon to enter. "Come in Simon, it's nice to see you this Saturday afternoon. What's so important for you to visit me on a weekend?"

Simon sat on the tan, cushioned arm chair, glancing around the living room; the pretty, red and yellow flowers bloomed in their oval and conical, glass vases, round sun, colored pillows strewn neatly on the paisley, patterned couch, a small canary chirped in its golden, gilded cage. "Where's Mr. Morris?" asked Simon, after settling and calming his rapid breathing.

"He went fishing for sturgeon near the new bridge leading to Antioch with Harvey Ryan. He took Harvey's boat with Harvey yesterday morning and should be back later this afternoon. There are reports of a sturgeon run, and you know John and his fishing. Nothing can keep him from catching the sturgeon when they're running. He says they're more fun to catch then the bass and the eating is much better."

"Harvey's the guy with the fishing boat from Freeport, isn't he? I always wondered why he has two, first names."

"Yes, he's the man with the fishing boat, and I'm not sure why his last name is the same as some men's first names. It might be a good, school project for you to research that curious configuration of names."

"I'll think about that idea Mrs. Morris, although it isn't that important, I was just wondering. I wish I liked fishing like Mr. Morris, but I'm happy to buy the fish. It's a lot easier than having to sit in a boat or on the levee's banks, waiting for a fish to bite. I'd rather be playing basketball at the school with my friends." Simon placed both of his hands on his knees and sat up straight, "Can I ask of you a big favor, Mrs. Morris?"

"Of course, you may ask, Simon. What can I do for you?"

"Well, I need to take a few days off from school, and I know I shouldn't, but its real important Mrs. Morris, real important."

"And what's so important for you to take time away from learning? You know how good school is for you. You're my best student, and I, and the rest of the students like having you in school."

"I know Mrs. Morris, but Tio Diego and it's October..."

"And it's the time of year Diego ventures on his annual trip in search of the Miwok God Puy," interrupted Mrs. Morris, "and I surmise you want to go with him."

"Sort of, I want to go to the top of Mt. Diablo, but not with him. I want to dress as Puy and be Puy, to satisfy Diego, so he will see him in his final trip to Mt. Diablo."

"I don't know Simon. I'm not so sure this is a good idea. It wouldn't be good for you, or your uncle, such an intelligent and ethical, young man to deceive Diego in such a manner."

"But he wouldn't know he's being deceived and I'm not deceiving him for personal gain. You see, Tio would often tell me of his October ritual while sitting near the chicken coop, watching the chickens do what chickens do. Tio for some reason is fascinated with the behavior of the chickens. The story Tio told me is the same every time, when reaching the peak of Mt. Diablo before sunset, he'd light a fire and dress in a robe of red cloth, wrap feathers around his head and drink the last of the wine, while chanting some unknown, Miwok Indian chant devised to bring back the spirit of Puy. Every year he would perform this ritual and every year near midnight, would pass out from his drunken state, never seeing, but always feeling Puy, vowing to return the following year, feeling before his own spirit passed to the native spirit land, one day he would see and meet Puy, which I see now has eluded him in his fifty ninth year, forty years after his first visit to the peak of his Devil Mountain. He needs to see Puy even though he says he'd believe in Puy, even if he'd never saw him. I don't believe Tio. I believe he'd be greatly disappointed if he doesn't see Puy this last time."

"Your Tio Diego is like many of us people, we believe in a God or gods that we don't see. It's something people have to believe in for some reason, atonement to a higher being, whether real or imagined. I believe Diego will believe, regardless of whether he sees proof of Puy, much like I believe in the God I don't see."

"I understand, but I'm adamant about moving forward with what I believe, even if you don't approve."

"Simon, you are a stubborn, young man, stubborn like your mother Maria was, I hear, rest her soul, but you are bright and what you're doing is noble, although I still don't completely agree. But I'll not object to you leaving for a few days and I wish you and Diego luck in your venture."

Simon stood from his chair, moved towards Mrs. Morris, wrapped his arms around her shoulders, and hugged her warmly. "Thank you, Mrs. Morris. I really mean it. It means much to me, that you at least understand my reason for doing this. That it's not for personal gain. It's to make Tio happy." He gently pushed away from Mrs. Morris, passed the canary in the golden, gilded cage and chirped playfully; the canary chirping back. Simon collected the paint can that had fallen from the canvas bag, raised his Schwinn and headed down the street to the outskirts of town where

Ed Felton's farmhouse stood, surrounded by two tractors and a flatbed truck.

Mrs. Morris stood behind the screen door peering at Simon pedalling down the road into the sunlight, her thoughts filled with admiration of the nice, young man Simon had grown to be, from the time they had first met, at Beaver Union Elementary.

* * * *

"Diego, this will be your last year up Mt. Diablo searching for Puy. Why don't you leave the wine home and not drink, other than the water in the canteen? You should stay sober this last time. You always tell me how you pass out at the top of Mt. Diablo. Maybe that's why you haven't seen Puy. You're too drunk," Socorro said, while toweling the clean dishes and stacking them in the open, wooden shelves above the stove. Diego slouched further down the chair, his legs extended across the floor, crossed at the ankles, both hands resting on his belly, breathing comfortably, sighing in an obvious state of contentment.

"I don't know Socorro, I like the wine. It allows me to appreciate the mountain much more and helps me forget how tired I am while walking to the top. I can't do without my wine."

"You need to try. I see you hanging around all these years, working odd jobs at the farms, talking to chickens, talking to Simon and always drinking your wine. Maybe you should try not drinking wine this one last time, so you can see Puy."

Diego twirled his thumbs, his head rose looking to the ceiling. After a few moments of silence he said, "I'll try it this last time. Maybe you're right. Maybe I will appreciate much more of the mountain, and maybe Puy will see me in a different light. Free from the effects of wine. Maybe that's why he hasn't made himself known to me."

"I'll cook a chicken before you leave and pack it with your other things. Having cooked chicken will help you make it up the mountain with a full stomach."

"That sounds good Socorro, but I'll let you kill the chicken. I don't have the heart to kill any of the chickens. I like the chickens."

"You never had any problem killing my cats, *Pendejo*," she said, turning, peering fiercely at Diego.

"You're right, but I only killed them while drunk."

"All the more reason you should stop drinking the wine as much as you do."

Diego rose from the chair. "Heh heh heh, but I still want you to kill the chicken."

Socorro looked at Diego walking away, turned and giggled.

* * * *

Ed Felton sat in the wooden, rocking chair drinking from a glass of fresh lemonade. The pitcher on the small table lay lazy with slices of lemon floating on the surface. Ed's feet rested on the railing of the bright, white open air porch, his wife, Jane, sat on the opposite end crocheting a doily, both gabbing about the weather and local town gossip. "You heard about Denny Loomis and his run in with Tim Hansen. They got in a tiff over Tim's new fence running over Denny's property, had quite an argument the neighbors were saying."

"Yes dear. That Denny has quite a temper."

"Hey Ed," hollered Simon, walking briskly to the porch steps.

"Simon, young man, how ya' doing?

"I'm doing fine, Ed. Hi Mrs. Felton. What are you fiddling with?"

"Just a doily I'm making for the end table in the living room. The one that's under the lamp is old, faded and frayed. It's time for a new one."

"You appear to be doing a fine job Mrs. Felton, a real fine job." Simon placed one leg on the second step of the porch, the first remaining on the ground, placed one arm against his knee, looked to Ed and asked, "I was wondering Ed, if you could give me a ride early Monday morning on your weekly run into Walnut Creek when you pick up the feed for your feed store here in town."

"I certainly could do that Simon. No problem at all, but aren't you supposed to be in school?"

"Yeah, but I got a pass from Mrs. Morris. She doesn't really like the idea, since she believes I should stay in school, but she understands my reasoning regarding my need to help Tio Diego."

"It's that time of year again isn't it?" asked Mrs. Felton.

"Yes it is," said Ed. "Diego was speaking about Puy and his annual journey up Mt. Diablo when I saw him last week near the Imperial Theater in Walnut Grove. We got to talking and as usual, he was very excited about his trip."

"Did you know the Japanese built that theater?" asked Mrs. Felton.

"Yes. The Takeda family," answered Ed, "they sure did a fine job with the construction."

"Don't you ever get tired of Diego talking about Puy, and doesn't the rest of the community get tired as well? My Tia thinks Tio Diego is loco."

"Diego isn't loco, Simon. Diego is very spirited and a little eccentric, but he's a kind man, a man with a fantasy that keeps him filled with hope, a hope that keeps him encouraged with the thought of someday, seeing and meeting Puy."

"Well Ed, that's why I need a ride to Walnut Creek. You see, I'm going to dress up and pretend to be Puy, to fool Diego into thinking he's seen Puy. I'll beat him to the summit from the less steep side of the mountain, south of Walnut Creek, on an old road called the Stage Road in Green Valley, once leading to a hotel of sorts called the Mountain House that burned to the ground at the turn of the century. But the once travelled roads and trails are still there, with smaller trails leading to the summit. I've done some research over the last couple of years asking friends and those passing through, and have tried to convince Tio to take what I found is a shorter route, but he likes doing things his own way, the old way."

"You have an interesting idea Simon and it's very kind of you to want to help Diego, but don't you think you should allow Diego to experience the disappointment of not seeing Puy, and his continued belief in something he can't see, or touch, or hear, but still can feel? You can't support his belief by pretending to be something that may not exist," stated Ed.

"I thought about that Ed, and I noticed you mentioned the phrase, 'may not exist', leading me to believe that there is still a possibility Puy may exist. I've determined there's no difference in pretending to be Puy, no difference then the many priests, preachers, deacons and messengers of the Lord, who say they speak to the Lord, and make others believe what the good Lord tells them. They're pretending too. They're spreading the concept of faith, which is no different than what I would be doing with Diego."

"You have a point Simon. You appear to be logical like your mother Maria was, I hear, rest her soul, but I'm still not sure it's a good idea to validate something that doesn't exist, but I won't argue with Diego's belief in Puy, or your attempt to be Puy, to enable his belief. As you've said, we believe in God, but have no proof either. So, what time would you like to leave on Monday morning? I could even take you as far as Green Valley if you'd like."

"That'd be great. If you could pick me up in front of Rancho Vasquez at around five in the morning, we would arrive in Green Valley with enough time for me to make it to the summit, and be prepared for Diego's arrival Tuesday evening. Could you make room for me on your truck for my bike? I could use it to make my way back to Pittsburg, or Antioch, and hitch a ride on a truck heading back on the Antioch Bridge through the Delta, or on a riverboat."

"Certainly, there's plenty of room for your bike Simon. It shouldn't be a problem."

Simon turned towards Mrs. Felton. "One more thing, Mrs. Felton, do you still have that feather collection with the duck, turkey and heron feathers you showed us students a few years ago at Beaver Union? I'd like to borrow some of the long, colorful, turkey, tail feathers for my Puy headdress."

"I do Simon and I'd be happy to give you the feathers of your choosing. I don't need really need them anymore. They're just gathering dust in the open box under our bed." She rose from her chair, put her unfinished doily on the seat, gesturing Simon through the front, screen door. "Come into the living room and I'll bring them right out."

*   *   *   *

The sun slowly set behind the gray mountain, the mountain melded into the gray-blue sky, the river silent without motion, when Simon pedalled his Schwinn onto Rancho Vasquez, his canvas, fishing bag filled with the canteen, red paint, red cloth and turkey feathers. Simon hid the bag under loose strips of the light gray, tan and white bark, fallen from the tall, eucalyptus tree a few hundred yards from the chicken coop. The chickens' chirping announced Simon's slow walk up the two, short steps into the coffee scented kitchen. Simon felt tired from his journey and visits with Chauncey, Mrs. Morris and Mr. and Mrs. Felton. Tia Socorro and Tio Diego sat at the kitchen table, drinking the hot coffee from blue, tin mugs, talking and laughing, their phrases and babel competing with energetic animation.

"Eh, Mijo, where've you been all day? You're later than usual," said Diego.

"I've been around. Went to Chauncey's to get paid, and ran into Mr. And Mrs. Felton and Mrs. Morris. We talked about the people in town and the weather, you know, little unimportant things."

Socorro looked at Simon with an expression of doubt. Simon responded with the wink of an eye and a guilty smile. He pulled a metal chair from under the table, sat and asked Diego, "So Tio, you're leaving tomorrow. Are you ready?"

"Yes. I'm ready with all my things. I have my blanket, coffee, tin cup, pan, canteen and matches to light a small fire to make my coffee. Your Tia already killed and plucked a chicken, and separated the wings and legs she'll cook for my trip. She even found the wishbone I'll break and use to wish for Puy."

"That's good Tio." Simon impatiently shifted in his chair. "I need to go to Louis's mansion on Grand Island to pick up a bottle of Bordeaux he brought a while ago from France. When I helped plant his new orchids in the mansion's greenhouse last week, he promised to give me a bottle as a gift for Shelly when I see her on Thanksgiving. She'll be visiting her uncle's farm with her family from Lockeford. They're all coming for the festivities."

"Stay now Mijo, enjoy a cup of coffee with your Tia and me, and get the wine later. We'd like to hear more of your day."

"I'd really like to Tio, but I need to go to the mansion

now. I won't have time tomorrow because of my church duties at St. Joseph's and besides, Louis and his wife Audrey are taking their yacht back to San Francisco in the early morning, to deal with some business issues. This depression had caused them some financial problems."

"They have too much money Mijo. Too much money, too many problems," said Tia.

"I guess you're right. They do have a lot of things. We have few things and little money," agreed Simon.

"Simon, you don't need to worry about their problems. Sit with us and visit. We can put some of my pear wine in a bottle for Shelly. She doesn't need fancy, foreign wine. She's a country girl, and my Rancho Vasquez wine is good enough. Stay Simon, it's time for dinner and it's getting dark outside. You must eat the chicken tacos your Tia is preparing," pleaded Diego.

"I can't Tio. I want Shelly to have the Bordeaux, not your pear wine, although I do like your pear wine. It's a Bordeaux Tio, think of it, a wine to be savored, because of its full, earthy taste, 'barnyardy', they say. We'll probably never get another chance to have such a fine wine from so far way. So I need to go. I know it's a long way along River Road, then out to the mansion. I've been there many times running errands for Louis, so I know the way. And it won't be too dark. The moon is almost full so there'll be enough light from the moon to guide me." Satisfied with his excuse and wondering how he'd find Bordeaux, his stomach grumbled from the lies of the day. Simon rose from his chair and walked to the bedroom he shared with Diego. Opening the metal trunk lying at the foot of Diego's bed, he raised the lid, the scent of old things from within floated in the air. Reaching for the Colt revolver from a small box, he grabbed six bullets lying next to the gun, unclasped the barrel, inserting the bullets into their chambers. Simon stepped to his dresser, pulled the small, worn, leather satchel from the bottom drawer, wrapped the Colt under his shirt and walked through the kitchen, smiling and waving at Socorro and Diego. Simon mounted his Schwinn and rode down River Road, turning on the dirt road towards Elk Slough. Nearing the slough's banks, Simon pulled into the grove of pear trees, ten trees deep, dropped his bike, stood and pulled the Colt from the satchel. After releasing the safety and twirling the barrel, he chose a tree, five trees from where he was standing, and with two hands grasping the handle, aimed and pulled the trigger. The thrust of the gun pushed his arms upward and the shot rang true, proving the gun still worked with the shattering of the bark of the unfortunate pear tree.

"She works," smiled Simon. "Good. The noise sounds like short, sharp thunder, not rolling thunder, but it'll have to do." Simon, satisfied, his lying stomach still grumbling, laid under a pear tree in the quiet of the Delta, breathing the cool, crisp, river air while the stars slowly appeared; the growing darkness slowly revealing the star's sparkling lights.

*   *   *   *

The *Coal Runner* chugged along the banks of the calm river, having left in the dark morning hours from the dock at Walnut Grove. Diego sat on the bench, grateful to

Jimmy for agreeing to let him ride to the coal loading dock in Pittsburg. "I really appreciate you giving me a hand Jimmy. I hope I'm not putting you out."

"I appreciate the company, Diego. It gets lonely piloting these long, boat trips through the Delta. I'm assuming you'll be hitching a ride again this year on the old, Black Diamond Railroad, in search of your ghostly friend, Puy. Since I'll be getting some coal for the people in the Delta from the same dock, it's not a problem, not a problem at all."

"I appreciate your company too," agreed Diego.

"It's sad you know. There's only a few remaining miners working after the coal company shut down years ago. I don't know how much longer those left-over miners are gonna keep at it, doing it on their own. I'll have to find some other work in the Delta, since my coal running business will have no coal to run."

"Yeah, I hope they can keep mining, so you can keep working. I'll be riding the rail car this final year and I know this year, I'll see Puy, I just know it. He's real, he's no ghost, Jimmy. I feel it. And you shouldn't worry about not running coal no more. You'll find some work in the Delta. There's lots of folks needing help of some sort." Diego settled in the back of the boat, using the stuffed bag as a pillow, quickly falling asleep under his scratchy, green, wool blanket. Diego slept lightly for a short while, and then awakened from his loud snore, while lying uncomfortably on the rough, wooden deck of the boat's stern. The sharp chill of the morning began the gray mood of the gray day. The *Coal Runner* entered the wider expanse of the river

from the narrow slough merging near the Antioch Bridge.
Lifting his head from under the blanket, Diego viewed the
mountain, looming larger from the vantage point of the
boat, rather than from the vantage point of Rancho
Vasquez, its dark-gray peak and light-gray rolling hills,
blended into the gray, morning clouds hiding the rays from
the morning sun and sky, like a panoramic mural where
the mountain, hills and horizon, melded into indiscernible
shapes.

"Hey Jimmy, where'd the sun hide?" yelled Diego, over
the noise of the engine.

"He ain't hidin'. He's taking the day off. Must've called
his cloud friends and asked them to cover for him," yelled
Jimmy, from the open wheelhouse.

"We're gonna have to do something about that, we can't
have the sun slouching on such an important day."

"What did you say?" yelled Jimmy, "I can't hear you
because of the noise from the engine."

Diego stood and walked closer to Jimmy and yelled, "I
said, we're gonna have to do something about that, we
can't have the sun slouching on such an important day."

"Oh. I don't think there's much we can do. Mr. Sun
picks his own working hours and has no boss to tell him
when to work." Jimmy turned facing the breeze, focusing
on the river route towards the river town of Pittsburg. The
factories lined the shore from the base of the Antioch
Bridge and onward to the Pittsburg docks. "Poor Diego,
such a pleasant but disillusioned man. He sure is
persistent with his hopeless quest."

The *Coal Runner* cut through the river surface, passed

the Fulton shipyard, slowed and slid against the dock, scraping the portside, leaving a streak of black from the tar treated pilings. A thin man with a scruffy, unshaven face, dirty trousers and shirt, stained from the coal filled bins, ran along the dock catching the thrown rope from Jimmy. Diego rose from the dirty deck with stuffed, burlap sack in hand and stepped to the dock tipping his short, brim Fedora. "Thanks for the ride Jimmy, hopefully, if you're here when I return, I can get a ride back to Rancho Vasquez in a few days."

"Sure thing Diego."

* * * *

Butch DiMaggio, Nick Napolitano and Sal "Smiley" Seeno sat on the banks of the river, next to the Booth Cannery, smoking cigarettes and throwing rocks at the white gulls swooping at the refuse from the gutted fish, thrown from the third floor, cannery windows. Butch, the oldest son of the proprietor of *DiMaggio's Meat and Grocery,* had recruited Nick and Smiley to engage in mischievous acts along the Pittsburg waterfront and in the towns of Antioch, Oakley, Byron and Brentwood. Butch, along with Nick, the middle son of an Italian fisherman, and Smiley, the youngest son of a Sicilian builder, were three truants from Pittsburg High School who wreaked havoc through thefts, harassment and bad behaviour, earning the reputation as "*hooligans*". After noticing Diego unload and sit on the cannery loading dock's bench, Butch said, "Now, look at that fat Mexican. Why's he in our town?"

"Yeah, what's he up to?" demanded Nick.

"Let's wander on over," added Smiley, his nickname portraying his semi-permanent smile.

Butch, the leader of the three, took control and stridently walked over the rocks, towards the pier where the dwindling supplies of coal were loaded. The scent of the fish entrails intermingled with the scent of the river foliage, their clothing moistened with the gray morning mist. The teens walked over and surrounded Diego, Butch taking the lead with his speak.

"Hey fat man, what're you up to?" demanded Butch, curtly.

Diego looked from the bench where he sat gnawing on the chicken, smiled cautiously and said, "Not a whole lot. Why don't you just sit and let's talk some?"

"Not gonna happen," stated Butch firmly. "We're just gonna stand here and hassle you, fat man."

Diego thought of Simon's earlier comments regarding the hooligans on the Pittsburg docks, of Diego's safety and began to worry, a feeling he'd never felt before. Butch, Nick and Smiley surrounded Diego with their chests pushed outward in a menacing, threatening posture.

"My name's Diego. I don't know why you're bothering me and call me fat. I don't even know you, and I'm not that fat anyway, just a little chubby. Why don't you just leave me be and after I finish my chicken, I'll be on my way?"

Nick and Smiley stepped back, looking to Butch for a response. Butch pushed forward, "Because you're fat, Mr. Fat Man, that's why. You don't belong here. This is our town and we've never seen you before. You shouldn't be here."

"I've been coming every October and this is my last year. So just leave me be," said Diego. Diego rose from the bench, placing the half-eaten, chicken wing into his bag. Butch pushed Diego back onto the bench. Why do you come every year and why haven't we seen you before?"

"Because you've never been here when I was here."

"That's not a good reason."

"It's a good enough reason. I come here every year and walk to the top of Mount Diablo in search of the Miwok God Puy."

"Who the hell is Puy?" yelled Butch.

"Puy is the God of Devil Mountain. The mountain named Mount Diablo, as known by most in this area. I'm from the Delta and every year I travel looking for Puy. To honor and hopefully meet and thank him for protecting all of us in the Delta, even those like you."

"Sounds like a bunch of crap to me. Have you seen him in any of the years you've come?" responded Nick.

"No, but he's real. He does exist."

"Who is this God Puy and why do you worship him and not the one and only true God, Jesus's dad?" asked Smiley.

Diego quickly countered, "Why do you believe in only your God and not allow others to believe in their own Gods?"

"Because there is only one God to believe in and only his rules apply," snickered Butch, "so help me God."

Feeling intimidated, Diego slowly rose once again and with an attempt to appease the three, stated calmly, "Why don't you travel with me and we'll all see Puy? I know in my bones he's going to honor me in my final year, after I've honored him all these years."

"Look Diego. We have no interest in meeting Puy and since you haven't seen him all these years, what makes you think he's gonna show up this year?" asked Butch, sternly.

"I have faith in Puy."

"Your faith in Puy isn't enough," countered Nick.

"But you have faith in what you believe your God to be. How is my faith in something I haven't been able to prove any different than the faith you have in a God you haven't been able to prove?"

"Because that's what the Bible says," replied Nick.

Diego shook his head with a smirk, "And who wrote the bible?"

"People who know things wrote the bible, the people that have seen and spoke to God," answered Butch.

"Do you mean that Jesus guy who spoke to God?" asked Diego, knowing the answer was no.

"Yeah. Him," said Smiley, meekly with a smile.

Diego knew his belief was unprovable as was the belief of the three, yet still believed the tale of the god, Puy.

"Stop debating this fat man and let him go," demanded Butch.

"But he doesn't believe..."

"I said let him go. We don't have time to waste on this man's bull cockery."

Diego quickly grabbed his bag and began walking to the small coal train a few hundred yards from the loading dock.

"Why'd you let him go?" asked Nick.

"We're gonna follow him to the top of Mt. Diablo. He deserves to be scared, since he doesn't believe in God. We'll get to witness his fear from the gun I'm gonna shoot when he's looking for his god Puy at the summit," explained Butch.

"You're not gonna kill him are you?" asked Smiley, with concern.

"Nah. I don't think so. I'm just gonna scare him. But who knows, we'll see how I feel. He might be worth shootin' to make a point."

* * * *

Happy to be away from the unpleasantness of meeting with the three hooligans, Diego arrived on the Black Diamond Railroad car into the dying town of Nortonville, where sporadic coal miners extracted the last of the usable coal from the deep, dark caves. The small locomotive revealed the growing town of Pittsburg. Each year in the past, stores and small saloons had appeared, the saloons now abandoned from the effects of Prohibition. From the riverfront up through the rolling hills, a smattering of dark-brown, cows and calves, dotted the light-brown skin of the hills, the calves prancing happily behind and around their slow-grazing, tail-swinging, fly-swatting mothers. Diego walked through Rose Hill cemetery and like each journey before, viewed the names of the miners and their families, on tombstones made of marble, tablets made of granite, some made of sandstone. The inscriptions bore names and dates of birth and death. Elaborate epitaphs, some with Welsh family names, Bussey, Jenkins and Buxton. The names brought Diego dignified joy, when inscribed with birth and death dates of presumed long, happy, lives lived. The names brought solemn sorrow, when inscribed with those of a young child who'd never achieved a full life, stricken before having experienced the beauty of living. Diego was moved by the gravesites inscribed Mary Vaughn, eight years of age, Elizabeth Ann Rees, six years of age and Thomas Jenkins, fifty two years of age. The tombstone, "Jenkins and Infant Children", faded from the years of battling sun and wind. Diego felt saddened by some tombstones, with the term, "Infant Children", indicating death at birth, without names, never existing in this world. The tombstone of Rebecca Abraham, its base, bordered in rectangular form with a black, iron fence; the fence elegantly designed with curves and stars, protecting the gravesite. Many years before, a light snow painted the mountain white, from the summit to the hills below during one of Diego's journeys. He'd used the inside, brick, border corner of Rebecca's tombstone for a small fire to keep warm. "I think the year of that cold trip was nineteen eighteen," wondered Diego. "It hasn't snowed in October, or November since." Diego clambered over the rolling hills with the Sunday, October evening, the hills leading to the town of Clayton, the sky cleansed of the earlier gray, wiped clean with the brush of the stars, the air crisp with life. He'd reached the town of Clayton, tired but anxious, anxious from the fear and doubt of not meeting Puy.

Having eaten the chicken during his stop at the gravesite of
Rebecca Abraham, Diego's stomach reminded him he'd
eaten too much, or possibly, worried too much. He waited
in front of Keller's Butcher shop as he'd done each year
past, buying beef wrapped in butcher paper, rather than
hunting animals for food required for his journey. Diego
was no hunter and preferred to keep his spirit pure, to not
kill animals he couldn't consume on his own, to not waste
per the edicts of the Miwok tribe. Diego sat under the
sycamore tree on the lot across from the Clayton Hotel, the
tin coffee mug set upon the pan fuelled by the burning coal
chunks; chunks scrounged from the mines of Nortonville.

*   *   *   *

On Monday, the day after Diego had arrived in Clayton,
Simon pedaled his Schwinn along the weed, strewn road,
leading to the charred, wooden remnants of the Mountain
House Hotel. The beginning of the rocky slope leading
upwards towards the summit, provided a view of sandstone
formations and natural caves, and to the south below,
sweeping views of the brown hillsides and green oaks,
nestled in the creases of the small valleys, where waters
hibernated like brown bears during the hot, summer
months. Simon hid the Schwinn behind a large, greenish,
brown and pink, lichen covered boulder, removed his
canteen from the canvas bag and guzzled the fresh, clear
water, some drops sliding down his sweaty neck. The early
morning ride from Rancho Vasquez to Green Valley was

enjoyable. The gray Sunday, bloomed into a sun drenched, pastel Monday. The light and dark grays of the rock, the light, tan and gold of the valleys, and the blue and white of the sky blossomed from the brush of the rising sun. From Ed Felton's truck, the view from the Antioch Bridge had presented a masterpiece bordered by billowy, white clouds, hanging low in the sky, resting on the distant horizon behind the mountain's peak. Fronting the backdrop, the rocks, valleys, oaks and flora illustrated yet another colourful, centerpiece on one of nature's magnificent easels of time, and now, Simon laid his head upon his canvas bag in the darkness, falling into a deep sleep with a lone coyote singing in the distance.

* * * *

"You're going too fast. Slow down Butch. We can't keep up," yelled Nick, sluggishly climbing a few yards back on the summit trail.

"You're both a couple of laggards. Come on. We don't want to be late meeting that man."

"I don't understand why we're going anyway. He's got no money. He's just going up to be stupid, trying to find this Puy guy. This is a long way to go just to scare him," complained Nick.

"This is important. He's gotta know who's in charge. He's gotta know that you can't not believe in God."

"But it don't matter if he believes in God or not. We're not going to make no money on your little adventure. We could use the time we're spending crawling after this guy to steal something from the stores in Antioch, like we originally planned," complained Nick.

"I'm getting tired," said Smiley, arriving at the top of the steep hill, viewing the next, larger hill encumbering their journey.

"We can't stop now Smiley. We've gotta make it halfway up the mountain before night falls. It's gonna take us till tomorrow to reach the top of Mount Diablo and you know, we gotta get past the old cemetery in Nortonville, because the white witch might come out tonight," jeered Butch.

"Who the hell is the white witch? Is this witch thing like this Puy thing, something made up?" doubted Nick.

"No. The white witch is real. The story told by the guys that walked through dad's store is, she was a real lady that helped the miners' wives deliver their babies. They say she wasn't religious, didn't believe in God and was killed by a horse that fell on her while riding in a buggy."

"Yeah. So. Why would that make her a witch?" asked Nick.

"Because she didn't believe in God. They say she was the wife of the founder of the coal mining town of Nortonville. The founder never was very happy with the buggy driver that drove the buggy the horses were leading. The buggy driver ran off, never to return, so the lady haunts the foothills around Nortonville hoping he'll return."

"Still doesn't explain why she's a witch," added Smiley.

"Well, she apparently didn't make it to heaven, 'cause even though she was a good woman, her non-belief kept her in limbo, so God kept her spirit hanging around the cemetery and surrounding foothills, as punishment. God made her a witch, wouldn't let her into heaven. That's the kind of thing God can do, so she got nothing to do but hang around and find the guy that she feels apparently killed her in hopes of getting to heaven as a reward by God, if she kills that guy in return."

"But why should we be afraid? If she's only gonna kill the guy that killed her, we shouldn't be worried. We didn't drive the buggy," stated Nick.

"They say she's killed a few other guys already. She doesn't seem to remember exactly what the guy looks like, so she haunts and kills any guy she thinks looks like the guy that drove the buggy."

"How long is it gonna take us to get out of range of this crazy witch lady? How will we know when we're safe?" asked Nick.

"They say a lone coyote will yell in the evening, when the white witch is out and about, so we can be prepared if she comes," responded Butch.

"Well. I ain't waiting for that. I'm heading back down to town. This is way too much for me to deal with. See ya," said Nick, turning back around and walking down the trail towards the town of Pittsburg."

"Wimp!" yelled Butch.

*   *   *   *

After acquiring the beef from Mr. Keller and embracing him with sincere gratitude for the many years of help, Diego walked from Clayton up towards Devil Mountain, among the oak and sycamore trees, the trunks and branches grown into cragged forms over the years. The leaves provided shade and cover. The fallen branches crunched underfoot. The sweet, musty scent pierced the crisp air in the late afternoon. Halfway up the mountain, Diego spread his blanket under the great oak, his favorite oak growing large and cragged. From the dry leaves and branches gathered in Nortonville, he started a fire, warming the tortillas and frying the strips of beef in the metal pan. After finishing the meal, he sat on a nearby boulder studded with fossilized shells from the ocean of millions years past, peering down the layers of hills spreading to the flatlands, rivers and levees miles away, the levees separating the brown land, like blue fingers spread from a hand, extending to the mountainous horizon far to the east. "I live there, somewhere," thought Diego, "a place seemingly unimportant, though from this rock makes me important, all things bowing before me, like Puy, the protector of all below." With wings spread wide and tails red, six hawks glided overhead on invisible currents, crossing and forming a hexagon shape while flowing in a constant, fluid pattern, casting a pattern of shadows on the velvety-golden slope. A single dragonfly darted in front of Diego, its translucent, red-tinged wings fluttered rapidly, the dragonfly suspending in flight, its bulbous eyes seemed to stare and speak. In quick succession, two dragonflies veered, one on each side of the centered dragonfly and then, two other dragonflies veered, one to the top, and one to the bottom of the centered dragonfly, all expressing interest in the presence of Diego, all five dragonflies aligned in a seemingly planned formation, a formation delighting Diego. "Hello there dragonflies," greeted Diego. "It's nice of you to visit me, a poor, fortunately sober and tired man sitting on this rock." The dragonflies hovered mid-air, then abruptly, the dragonfly in the middle darted up and away, followed by the one below, then the one on the left side, then the one on the right side, then after briefly remaining suspended, the one above darted forward abruptly, stopping inches from Diego's face, lulled, then darted upward following the line of dragonflies skimming along the red and brown, rocky ridge. Diego sat on the boulder, peering at the Delta lowlands for hours, until darkness showed itself in the comfortable setting. He lowered from the boulder, leaned against its hard smoothness and fell into a deep sleep, with a lone coyote calling in the distance.

* * * *

"I'm getting really tired," whined Smiley, after stopping in the middle of the wide, semi-barren, poppy field, the orange-brown poppies wilting in the setting sunlight."

"Stop your complaining," demanded Butch. "You're whining, like you did when you played on the Pittsburg High School football team."

"I never whined. All the other guys were always teasing me 'cause I didn't play so good in that one game."

"You sure whined enough to have the coach kick you off the team."

"Nuh uh. I got kicked off the team 'cause you're the one

who complained to the coach about me messing up in the big game against the Panthers. I was just sticking up for myself."

"Look Smiley, we gotta get to the ranger station before nightfall. We've almost made it. We can talk more when we get there."

"Okay. But I'm gonna need to rest when we make it. And I know, you're still the one that made me lose my place on the football team, by complaining about me."

After wandering the paths, through the dried creek beds and up the winding trail to the unoccupied ranger station, they entered a worn, wooden tool shed as darkness flowed over the gray, dusty rocks and small oaks surrounding the station and shed.

"This isn't much fun, Butch. Those spiders sure scared me while we were walking through the hills and to this station. You know they might come in the shed here and bite us."

"Those were tarantulas. They are pretty damn big and scary, but they won't hurt you. They look ugly and some people think they're poisonous, but they're not. Let's not worry. Let's just talk some more and get some sleep before we head to the summit tomorrow. I'm all ready with the Winchester rifle I got from my dad's cabinet, and we're gonna have some fun with it."

Smiley laid against the wooden door of the shed, asking again, "You're not gonna kill that man are you?"

"No Smiley. I'm just gonna shoot the Winchester to scare him. I ain't never killed no one and ain't gonna do it now." Butch squatted against the wooden wall, crickets chirped noisily outside the shed. Butch and Smiley talked until the coyote began yelling in the night, warning them of the potential presence of the white witch. Their talking stopped, and they lay worried, until falling into a light, uneasy sleep.

*   *   *   *

Simon woke to the sound of the rooster cock-a-doodle-dooing from the Macedo ranch, in the valley where Ed Felton left him and his Schwinn for his journey to the summit. After quickly eating pieces of dried venison and trout, and leaving the Schwinn behind, he began the climb to the top of the mountain, past the sandstone caves and Manzanita groves. Monarch butterflies danced among the green and white blooming brush. Robins, swallows and warblers, hopped playfully from bush to bush, on light wings singing short, sweet songs. Simon continued to climb the layered rock, reached the summit and placed his canvas bag beside a boulder, on the vista facing south. Simon sat viewing the setting sun above the horizon, falling into a light, comfortable sleep, awaiting the arrival of Tio Diego, on the rocky peak of Devil Mountain.

*   *   *   *

Uncertain of the scratching noise on the aluminum roof above, Butch slowly raised his head to the sunlight peaking through the uneven, cracked walls of the shed.

Smiley lay in the corner snoring, unaware of the noise.

"Crap. Wake up Smiley," yelled Butch. "You gotta getup and find out what's on the roof scratching."

Smiley turned over, facing Butch. "What?"

"I said you gotta go outside and check on what's happening on the roof."

"You go. I wanna sleep some more."

"No. We both gotta go 'cause we're late. We should've gotten up before the sun rose, and when the mountain was quiet, but as you can hear, the mountain is alive and kickin'."

"You go out and check on what's scratching. It's probably just a squirrel or something," complained Smiley.

"Let's both get up and go. At least we know it ain't the white witch, otherwise we'd be dead."

Smiley rose slowly, stretched his arms outward, opened the door, and bathed in the sudden, robust sunlight. Butch followed, turned and looked to the roof where a gray squirrel crouched, nibbling an acorn fallen from the scraggly branched oak nearby. The squirrel abruptly jerked his head towards Butch, ceased nibbling the acorn, and quickly skittered across the roof and down the back wall.

"See. I told you it was just a squirrel. You're just scared to come outside 'cause of the white witch," laughed Smiley.

"I wasn't scared."

"Yes you were." Smiley continued to laugh. "You were scared. Hey, I'm hungry. We gotta get somethin' to eat. We didn't bring anything with us, so what're we gonna do?"

"Let's not worry about eating. We gotta get to the top before fat man, Diego gets there. We'll find something."

"Whaddya mean, don't worry about eating. There's not gonna be nothing at the top to eat, just like there's not nothing here to eat. I'm going back down. Besides, we got lucky not seeing the white witch last night, and I'm not chancing another night."

"Don't be a wimp like Nick."

"I'm no wimp, Butch. Nick's no wimp, neither. You're the wimp, and I'm not gonna waste no more time on your crazy adventure," smiled Smiley, turning and walking back down the trail they'd traveled, past the now lone ranger station.

*   *   *   *

Diego awoke from his deep sleep feeling surprisingly comfortable, unlike the slight discomforts felt during each journey of the many years past. Rather than the gurgling, stomach, and funkiness from the effects of drinking the large, quantities of pear wine, both conditions didn't appear, bearing him a sense of peacefulness. "Socorro was right, I feel much better without the wine," thought Diego. He pulled the cooked chicken legs from the bag, made the coffee from the dried coffee beans, and after finishing his morning meal, began hiking the final leg of his journey to the peak of Devil Mountain.

*   *   *   *

"I ain't no wimp," mumbled Butch to himself. "They're the wimps. I'm the only one brave enough to confront Diego and prove to him there is no Puy." He began the walk up the steep hill, where bushes emitted the strong aroma of something stale, something unknown and unusual, feeding a fear of the unknown of what lay ahead. Passing a large bush, he happened upon a rattlesnake, hovering over the corpse of a gray gopher. Seeing Butch approach, the snake rose upright and arched back, preparing to lunge. Fearing the attack of the snake, Butch raised his Winchester and stepped back rapidly, rushed to the side and up towards the summit. "That was close. I wasn't scared. I didn't shoot though. I should've, but I didn't." He continued the steep climb, past the layers of red, rock and walked towards a dead oak where three, black ravens perched on three, separate, leafless branches. He walked slowly, to not interrupt their seemingly peaceful, yet menacing postures, and once past the dead oak, climbed rapidly towards the granite cliff, stopping and resting. After a short rest, Butch climbed to the east side of the summit, nestled against a rocky slope, laid the Winchester across his chest, closed his eyes and lapsed into a light, restless sleep.

* * * *

Diego reached the summit after the long, walk climbing through the fields of honeysuckle, blackberry, wild grape and blue nightshade, all shrubs, silently entertaining the playful antics of the black and orange monarch, and black and gold swallowtail, butterflies. Climbing near the peak of the summit, a small group of lizards perched on a large, flat rock; basked in the slowing, darkness encompassing the mountain. "Hello, little lizards. Are you waiting for the grand entrance of Puy, this beautiful, October evening? Puy would be impressed with the three of you laying in honor of his presence." Diego unpacked his bag, grabbed the small can of red paint, disrobed and dressed in his old, frayed, red, baggy shorts, tight at the waist, with his belly hanging over the short's waistline. Grabbing a single feather from the bag, and with a red strip of cloth, Diego wrapped the feather around the back of his head. Opening the paint can, he inserted his fingers and spread the red paint across his head and arms and stood, looking to the west. With arms raised, nonsensical utterances emitted from his lips in praise of Puy. He looked to the dark, rocky islands of Farallon, where the sun in the far distance dipped rapidly below the ocean horizon, the colors of the sky in overlapping layers of pastel purple, blue, gray and white.

Butch sat behind a gray boulder, positioned with a view of the Delta in the east, where in the far distance lay a mosaic of tan land, blue rivers and gray jagged mountains, Winchester in hand, ready to fire the shot to scare Diego into believing he'd be accosted.

Simon, clothed skimpily with red cloth, feather headdress and skin covered in red paint, sat behind his gray boulder with a view of the jagged, brown hills and green valleys in the south, Colt in hand, ready to fire the emulated, thundering noise of Puy.

None of the three were aware of the other, until Butch rose and pointed his Winchester at the rock next to Diego. Butch, with only mischief in mind, and Simon, standing with benevolence, looked to one another while Diego continued his spirited, soliloquy. Diego noticed Butch with the Winchester pointed, and the ground began to rumble, a low, loud tone spewing an intimidating intensity; the brush, trees and rock swaying as the tower tilted in the sky. At the bottom of the tower, lavenderish-red smoke rose, lighting the sky, swirling circularly along each of the four, iron trestles rapidly towards the tower's top. The three; Diego the believer, Simon the honorable, and Butch the bad, all looked to the light tower's tip, where the smoke collected into a large, round mass, and with a loud boom, manifested into the form of a man-like figure, legless, torso full, arms raised, head positioned and mouth wide open with long, white teeth, thrusting the noisy threat to the three below.

Shocked, Butch dropped the Winchester, falling backward and rolling down the hill from behind the boulder where he'd waited to threaten Diego. Frightened by the horrendous voice and fire of Puy, Butch stood, then ran down the hillside, cowered with the fear he'd planned for Diego.

Simon, pleasantly surprised by the appearance of Diego's real and no longer mythical idol, watched as Puy quieted his threatening voice, and smiled at Diego with a smile of knowing; Diego smiling back with a nod, acknowledging Puy's magical presence.

Puy turned his head towards Simon, winked with his large, hollow, dark-red eye and continued smiling a wide, sly smile. Simon, unnoticed by Diego, returned Puy's smile, and with a salute, began the slow walk down the trail towards the remnants of the Mountain House Hotel. Passing through the fields of bush, shrubs and rock, his thoughts were of the Miwok God Puy, the mountain idol, finally arriving, presenting himself to Diego on this spirited October evening.

*   *   *   *

The nine chickens cooed in the chicken coop joining the song of the placid river. Tia Socorro and Simon sat on the two green, metal chairs, scooping with warm, hand-rolled, flour tortillas, the chorizo, beans, eggs and melted cheese slathered with hot, chili sauce. Their scooping stopped when the rattling of Jake the Blacksmith's truck sounded along River Road. Blackie, the Labrador, roused in the back of the truck shouting a sharp bark. The rattling grew louder, the noise stopping in front of Rancho Vasquez. Tia and Simon rose from their chairs and walked through the door, the door closing shut on creaking hinges. Tio Diego stepped from the truck. The truck continued, rattling down River Road with Jake's hand waving out the window.

"Heh heh heh, Mijo, heh heh heh, I saw him. Puy is real," exclaimed Diego with animated excitement, his dishevelled, dirty clothing and unshaven, stubbled face, were silently undermined by the clean happiness of Diego's waning, moon-shaped smile. "Come. Let's sit on the asparagus crates under the fig tree and have a mug of wine now." Walking to the corner of the lot, Diego, Socorro and Simon, shuffled among the dirt and pebbles, to the shade of the fig tree, where flattened dried figs lay sunburnt black and wrinkled, peeking from under the browning leaves. "Mijo," said Diego, pointing to the other end of the lot, "go to the shed and in the old, rusty, red chest are my jug and two mugs. You know where it is. Bring the jug and mugs and let's drink like before." Diego and Tia walked to the crates, and Simon walked to the shed, returning with the dark green jug in one hand, his finger holding the looped stem, the other hand holding the two mugs, looped in each of two fingers. "Sit Mijo, on the crate next to me and here, sit Socorro, on my crate, and we'll all celebrate the most recent conquest by Puy." Diego uncorked the jug, filled the mugs, setting the jug on the dusty, brown, ground giving his mug to Socorro. "Hermana Socorro, you drink with Simon and we'll toast to Puy. I have much to tell you," said Diego with joy, beginning his mighty tale, of the mighty conquest, by the mighty Puy, on the mighty peak, of Devil Mountain.

An excerpt follows from the next series of California Delta stories to be available as:

A FAIRER PARADISE II

Set in the 1930's to be published, late 2013.

LEVEE BREAK

Mexican Fiesta

THE GIRL IN THE ORCHARD

Crooked Fingers

PAPER SON

Midnight Man

THE MISSIONARY AND MISS JANEY

Aiko's Wedding

CHINKS, JAPS, SPICS AND FLIPS

River Storm

EPILOGUE

LEVEE BREAK

The marshlands of thousands years past rested
peacefully, presenting a paradise fairer than no other.
Flocks of duck and geese painted the sky in broad strokes
of white, gray and brown. White egrets and white swans,
with thin, long legs and thin, long necks stood, arched in
pose. Elk, deer and bear foraged and hunted, drinking the
waters while lazing throughout the wide, flat valley. Brown-
skinned, black-haired natives in tule reed canoes, weaved
among tall, tule grass, netting shad, bass and salmon, all
living symbiotically within nature's delta. The peaceful
paradise was enjoyed by all, with little interruption, other
than the infrequent whims of nature's storms, quaking
grounds and natural illnesses, befalling the flora and fauna
of the delta marshland paradise. Over time, strong willed
men of "civilized" societies with high-minded ideas of profit,
helped by strong willed men with low-minded ideas of
simple lives, transformed the marshlands into channels of
man-made levees, by and for people venturing from the
new citified nation of the east, and from the Asian
countries across the ocean to the west, and the cool wet
mountains to the north, and the dry brown lands to the
south. And now, the farmlands created from the man-made
transformation, lay helpless, under the violent onslaught of
nature's wrath.

Gary leaned against the nose of the big-wheeled tractor,
surveying his pear orchard and farm house, east of the
town of Isleton. Russ Vieira poked his head from the Ford
pickup parked next to the tractor, the wind and rain

pelting them both.

"How's she behaving?" yelled Russ.

"She's behaving badly. She's angry as a horse with a burr in her bum, pounding on the banks of the levee. If she keeps her anger and keeps beating on the levee's banks, we're gonna get damaged. She's lashing out because of the wind being angry with her; their fight sure isn't gonna do us any good," answered Gary, holding his cap, thrashed by the wind.

"That damn wind. Let's hope they make up. There's not much we can do other than sit here and watch this battle, hoping for the levee to beat back the wind," said Russ, his voice drowning in the wind's, loud thrum.

"Yeah, if the wind beats the river, the river beats the levee and the levee breaks, our crops suffer the wounds, and they got no one to beat on other than our bank account. I can't just stand here and watch my crops and house destroyed by the wind and river after all these years grinding out a living. Let's gather some of the folks from Isleton and the other towns and surrounding farms, and see if we can shore up the weak part of the levee aiming to break, and give us a chance to win."

Gary climbed onto his tractor, pointing down River Road. "You head to Isleton. I'll head on home, grab my truck and drive into Courtland. We'll both spread the word asking for sandbags, haystacks and anything else we can use to stop the river from breaking through. Have those willing to help meet back here as soon as they can."

The rest of the story in "A Fairer Paradise II"

Randall Marcus Gutierrez

NOTES ON TEXT AND CONTENTS

The author acknowledges references to some locations, organizations and fixtures in the stories as fact, some fiction. Examples of organizations of fact include, Al the Wop's, the Ryde Hotel, Chauncey's Chews General Merchandise, Foster's Bar, Beaver Union Elementary School and others. The period of the stories written, describe the organizations at that point in time, whether operational or not. It is believed through research by the author, that all organizations of fact referenced were in operation, although possibly not specifically, in the manner described in the stories.

Locations in the stories are all fact such as Steamboat Slough, Elk Slough, Mt. Diablo, Walnut Grove, Ryde, Courtland, Isleton, Pittsburg, Antioch, Nortonville, Somersville and others, are referenced in the manner depicted in the stories written, as experienced, or researched by the author.

Fixtures in the stories are all fact such as various bridges throughout the Delta, the Ryde Hotel water tower, the steamboats Delta King and Delta Queen and others. The placement or physical characteristics of these fixtures, during the period of the stories written, may not be accurately described. One such example is the Georgiana Slough Bridge, which may not have existed at the time the story depicts its presence.

Characters in the stories are both fact and fiction, some
references of fact include Bing Lee, George Locke,
Chauncey Chew and others, all of which include
conversations and personality implications that are fiction
and do not reflect actual incidents or opinions of those
factual characters. Other characters of some in the stories
are fictitious and constitute intermixed first and last
names of people the author grew up with, or knew of and
do not represent the personalities or opinions of any
specific individual, whether real, or implied, in any of the
stories.

The author also acknowledges the use of two previously
published excerpts that include on the back cover text of
this book, *A Fairer Paradise*, from *John Milton's*, *Paradise
Regained and* an excerpt in the front pages of this book, *A
Fairer Paradise*, a Buddhist quote from the *Dhammapada*.

To summarize, this book, "A Fairer Paradise", is a work of
fiction. Names, characters, locations, fixtures and incidents
are either the product of the author's imagination, or are
used fictitiously. Any resemblance to actual persons, living
or dead, events, or locales is entirely coincidental.

ABOUT THE AUTHOR

Randy Gutierrez is a resident of California, born in 1959, in the town of Pittsburg, on the fringe of the Sacramento River. After decades with thoughts of writing of the California Delta, an area his family and friends frequented, he created a series of stories during almost ten years of sitting in tight quarters, in airplanes and hotel rooms and lounging on the banks of the Sacramento River and surrounding levees; writing in moleskin notebooks, laptops and the unused spaces on pages of no longer needed business documents.

Randy is passionate about many things
and most of all, his two children,
Leslie and Ryan.

For questions regarding this publication or inquiries of the author, use **info@www.grayiguana.com** for communication.

Gray Iguana Publishing Company
www.grayiguana.com

SPECIAL THANKS

Special thanks are extended to my sister, Olivia Rodriguez, her married name; originally, Olivia Gutierrez, at birth, who spent an inordinate amount of time, searching in this book, page by page, paragraph by paragraph, sentence by sentence and word by word; for unnecessary commas and apostrophes, misplaced and misconstrued words and other formatting issues and like an astute interior designer, reconstructed and remodeled those same pages, paragraphs, sentences and words, with the necessary commas and apostrophes and other proper grammar and syntax, into the form you see now. She in turn, I believe, is grateful for being taught by her well respected Hillview Junior High School English teacher and other well learned individuals throughout her life. I've proofed her work and if errors still exist, the blame's on me.

Like a typical sister in a close knit family, Olivia preferred to not be mentioned in this book. But, like a typical brother in a close knit family, I ignored her wishes.

Made in the USA
Charleston, SC
04 June 2013